Ghosts along the Texas Coast

Docia Schultz Williams

Republic of Texas Press
an imprint of
Wordware Publishing, Inc.

Library of Congress Cataloging-in-Publication Data

Williams, Docia Schultz.
   Ghosts along the Texas coast   /   Docia Schultz Williams.
      p.   cm.
   Includes bibliographical references and index.
   ISBN 1-55622-377-3
   1. Ghosts--Texas--Gulf Region   I. Title.
   BF1472.U6W554   1994
   133.1'09764'1--dc20   94-11994
                                            CIP

1506 Capital Avenue
Plano, Texas 75074

ISBN 1-55622-377-3
10 9 8 7 6 5 4 3 2 1
9408

All inquiries for volume purchases of this book should be addressed to
Wordware Publishing, Inc., at the above address. Telephone inquiries may be
made by calling:

(214) 423-0090

Contents

Chapter 1
Ghosts that Dwell in Coastal Towns
and on the Windswept Beaches

Chapter 2
Ghosts of the Lower Rio Grande Valley

Chapter 3
History and Mystery in Far South Texas

Chapter 4
Corpus Christi's Resident Spirits

Chapter 5
The Ghosts of Galveston

Chapter 6
Houston ... a Haunting City

Chapter 7
Ghosts of the Golden Triangle

Chapter 8
Legends Worth Telling Again

Acknowledgements

I am greatly indebted to many people who have assisted me in researching the material for this book. The historians, librarians, newspaper editors, and private individuals who have shared their stories with me have contributed greatly towards bringing *Ghosts Along the Texas Coast* to fruition. I am sure I will forget, and therefore omit, many who were helpful to me, but I would like to especially thank the following individuals who shared their time and their stories with me: Clouis and Marilyn Fisher, Rockport; Sue Casterline, Estes Flats; Julie Caraker, Port Aransas; Charlie Faupel and Susan Purcell of Reeves Thicket Ranch, Victoria; Wilbur Butler, Beaumont; Debbie and Jim Sandifer, Port Neches; Anne Malinowsky Blackwell, Nederland; Diane Cox, Jasper; Pat Chance, Jasper; Brenda Greene Mitchell, Spring; Mrs. Merle E. Eisenhour, Galveston; Eleanor Catlow, Galveston; Paula and Steve Bonillas, Corpus Christi; Colonel Larry Platt, Pleasanton; Mary Lou Polley Featherston, Port Arthur; Father Jim Vanderholt, pastor, St. Joseph's Catholic Church, Port Arthur; Catherine Polk, LaMarque; Nancy Polk, Houston; Mario P. Ceccaci, Jr., Galveston.

Also, the librarians, museum curators, and newspaper staffs who gathered and sent so much helpful material to me, including: Casey Edward Greene, Assistant Archivist, Rosenberg Library, Galveston; Ellen Hanlon, "The Texas Room," Houston Public Library; Yolanda Gonzalez, librarian, Arnulfo L. Oliveira Memorial Library, University of Texas at Brownsville; Bruce Aiken, Brownsville Historical Museum; Newton Warzecha, Museum Director, La Bahia, Goliad; Kevin Young, San Antonio, formerly museum director, La Bahia, Goliad; Derek Neitzel, Resident Graphic Artist and assistant to the curator, USS Lexington Museum, Corpus Christi; Kathleen Hink, former director, Williams House Museum, Galveston; Kevin Ladd, Director, Wallisville Heritage Park.

Many thanks to Sam Nesmith and his wife, Nancy, who as historians and psychics contributed much advice and encouragement.

The following individuals gave me some good leads in tracking down stories, and to them I am most grateful: GiGi Starnes, San Antonio; Dr. Joe Graham, Dept. of Sociology, Texas A&M, Kingsville; Nancy Vernon, Rockport; Faye Duncan, Port Arthur; and Mrs. W.A. Ewert, Riviera. Also Dr. Juan Sauvageau, author of *Stories That Will Not Die* for his encouragement, and Catherine Munson Foster of Angleton, folklorist and author of *Ghosts Along the Brazos* for her help in my research. Also Libby Butler, Raisin; Dorothy Hirsch of Brownsville; Kitten Carter of Houston; Juanita Williams of Jasper; Betty Boriak of Houston.

A great big thank-you to Acquisitions Editor Mary Elizabeth Sue Goldman of Republic of Texas Press, for her constant encouragement.

Lastly, by far the most important contributor towards the completion of this book is my husband, Roy D. Williams, whose constant encouragement and "prodding" kept me on track, as he accompanied me on trips along the coast, interviewing and taking pictures. And when the stories were all done, he spent endless hours at the computer getting the manuscript ready for the publishers. My love and heartfelt thanks, Roy.

Introduction

As a small child, I shivered simultaneously with fear and delight as Halloween stories of goblins and ghosts were told to me. There's a fascination with the unknown, that other dimension wherein dwell the restive spirits of departed souls, that we all have in one degree or another. Perhaps you share with me the belief that there really are such things as "ghosts" or "spirits." Or perhaps you remain skeptical, totally unconvinced that there could be, or are, such things at all.

Because you personally have never experienced the seeing, hearing, or feeling of the presence of a ghost, you may obviously doubt there are such things. Having interviewed many people and corresponded with countless others, I am impressed by the intelligence and honesty displayed by those who have shared their stories with me so that I might bring them to you, my readers. Believe them or not, they deserve your respect and are not to be ridiculed. I for one, do not doubt their stories. Since my first book on the subject of ghosts, *Spirits of San Antonio and South Texas*, which I co-authored with Reneta Byrne was published in December 1991 (Republic of Texas Press, an imprint of Wordware Publishing, Inc.), I have made many radio and television appearances and have given numerous programs and book reviews. It is truly amazing how many people have contacted me after hearing me speak. They must recognize a "kindred spirit." Often I have been told, "I've never told anyone about this before; I was so afraid they would laugh at me." These people realize that I believe that there are such things as "spirits" or "ghosts," and they will have the ear of a sympathetic listener. I have heard some strange, yet believable stories as a consequence, and I have met many interesting people in the process.

Now, I am not a psychic. I have friends and acquaintances who are, and they have been of great help in explaining the "unexplainable" to me. And in consulting with these psychics I have learned that certain times and certain conditions contribute greatly to the sightings of apparitions, or the hearing of "ghostly noises." "Ghosts" or "spirits" seem to be the most common names associated with the unexplained presences that represent the restless souls of now dead human beings. They are, I believe, all around us. Some are kindly, benevolent guardians that protectively watch over someone or over a place they once loved. Others are very disturbed entities, not yet accepting that they are dead. These souls wander impatiently, often frightening us as they appear, disappear, and reappear, over and over again. You see, time means nothing to a ghost!

A common consensus seems to be that these spirits often come back to the place where they actually died, but this is not always the case. Sometimes they just come back to places where they were happy in life with someone they loved. The anniversaries of their deaths seem to call forth some spirits. And then, some ghosts seem to appear with great regularity at just a certain time of day or night. For instance, there might be a regular "6 p.m." ghost, or a "midnight spirit," or a "twilight specter." And, contrary to what one might think, many of them do appear in broad daylight. Some of them look just like a regular human being, while others are transparent, misty, or foggy in appearance. Generally they only appear for an instant and then completely disappear!

A full moon phase often draws out ghosts, and I've been told by psychics that they are generally more likely to appear during hot summer months than during cold weather. (Maybe they "hibernate" in the winter months!)

Some spirits guard hidden treasures or valuables, so the sighting of an apparition might possibly indicate that something of value may be hidden close by. And then, some of them just "hang around" for no particular reason at all!

This book contains stories of ghosts that have appeared in the coastal area of Texas, and it is the result of many months of researching. Most of the stories are well documented. A few are legends, tales that have been told over and over again, sometimes for generations, and which often have several variations. I included a few of these that I felt worthy of repeating once more in the last chapter. Many of the stories appear for the first time in print. The setting for some of them centers around the coastal plains and low-lying marshes and woodlands that constitute the Texas Gulf Coast. The windswept beaches, offshore islands, and mysterious swamps bring forth tales of buried pirate treasure and adventurers such as the legendary buccaneer, Jean Lafitte. There are "big city" stories about Galveston, Corpus Christi, Brownsville, and the great metropolis of Houston. And there are tales centered around the Golden Triangle, which is comprised of Beaumont, Orange, and Port Arthur, and the area surrounding those cities. Historic landmarks, such as the Presidio of La Bahia at Goliad and the Old Lighthouse at Sabine Pass, are included as well.

Some of the stories are sweet and tender. Some of them are frightening. This is because ghosts have personalities just as mortals do. The character traits they had in life seem to follow them to the hereafter, so that kind and loving people probably return as watchful, benevolent spirits bent on protecting their loved ones. Mean-spirited, cruel, selfish and unkind mortals will doubtless return as fearful poltergeists, bent upon bringing horror into the lives of those who see or hear them. And then there are the pitiful, little lost souls who are just sad and unhappy, hanging around because they can't seem to find peace on the "other side."

And therein lies the mystique and the fascination of the entities we call "ghosts". . . .

After reading the stories related in this book, perhaps the skeptics may still say, "Bah! Humbug!" about the tales contained within these covers. Or maybe, just maybe, they might decide that keeping a night-light on in the bedroom isn't such a bad idea after all!

Docia Schultz Williams

THERE ARE GHOSTS.....
Docia Williams

From the sunburnt town of Brownsville,
'Way down near Mexico...
There are ghosts and roaming spirits
Where'ere you chance to go.
They come back to roam the beaches
And the farmers' sun-parched land.
They're in the far flung reaches
Where rolling waves meet sand.
They're known to roam the islands
And the marshlands by the sea.
Their graves cannot contain them,
For their souls roam wild and free.
They're in Galveston and Houston,
Port Arthur has a few;
They're in dark and hidden places,
And in hotel rooms with a view!
Wherever men have worked and lived,
Wherever men have died;
Wherever women laughed or danced,
Wherever they have cried;
They're anywhere and everywhere,
And forever they must roam.
The Texas Coast... their cordial host,
And the ageless land, their home.

The Bolivar Island lighthouse on the Texas Gulf Coast

Dedication

This book is dedicated to my husband, Roy D. Williams, and my daughter and son-in-law, Sarah and Dennis Thaxton, who have been my staunchest supporters, with my love and thanks.

CHAPTER 1

Ghosts that Dwell in Coastal Towns and on the Windswept Beaches

GHOSTS...

From the long and lonely outer reaches
Of swampy lowlands and windswept beaches
    All along the Texas coast;
There are legends, there are stories
Of the tumults, and the glories,
    And of strange and eerie spirits known as ghosts.

Ghostly Guardians of Buried Treasure

Now, Jean Lafitte was a pirate bold,
A pirate bold was he!
He boarded ships and plundered gold
From sea to shining sea.

Now buried on the Texas coast
Just where, we've not a clue;
His gold is guarded by his ghost,
If what we've heard is true!

Tales of buried pirate treasure and the ghostly guardians still standing watch over the ill-gotten booty of the buccaneers who raided
shipping off the Texas coast have been around for many long years. By
now, what is fact and what is fiction is a bit hard to sort out, as there are
so many conflicting tales. However, most all the stories make mention
of that most famous of pirates known to sail the waters off the Texas
shores, the dashing swashbuckler Jean Lafitte.

Although the Encyclopedia Americana lists Lafitte as "American,
Pirate and smuggler," he was actually born in a small village on the
Garonne River in France in the year 1780. Little seems to be known of
his youth. At one time he was known to have been a privateer in the
employ of Cartagena for the purpose of the destruction of British and
Spanish commerce. He soon turned to piracy (where he could be his
own boss!) and around 1809 he turned up in New Orleans, along with
his brother, Pierre, and a stalwart band of followers of the same persua-
sion. Jean opened up a blacksmith shop in New Orleans that may have
been a "front" for his real vocation, which was smuggling slaves into
New Orleans. The hapless blacks were offered at $1 a pound, and
the Lafittes did a big business. At the same time, they supplied New
Orleans' citizenry with contraband goods, which they often sold at

Grand Terre Island in the Barataria Bay. From this locale, it was easy for the pirate band to plunder shipping in the Gulf of Mexico.

Jean was a handsome, dashing figure of a man, and he became a well-known personality in the gambling salons, quadroon ballrooms, at the opera, and at theatrical productions in New Orleans.

The United States government eventually launched a number of expeditions against the Lafittes, but they all failed. A revenue inspector who had been sent to examine their goods was murdered in 1814. Legal proceedings against them in United States courts had to be abandoned because John R. Grymes, the U.S. District Attorney, resigned his office in order to help the pirates! It seems Jean Lafitte's whole career was built more or less on duplicity and double dealing. So successful was he in his various endeavors that he succeeded in transforming himself into a legend while he was still alive!

Now, Pierre was finally captured. During his captivity, Captain Nicholas Lockyer, of the British navy, offered Jean a captain's commission, the sum of $30,000, and pardon for all "past mistakes" if he and his followers would join the British expedition against New Orleans. While pretending to deal with Lockyer, Lafitte informed the American authorities of the British plans. The Louisiana authorities, with the exception of General Jacquez Villere and Governor William C. Claiborne, suspected a plot from the pirate, and they sent an expedition against Lafitte at Barataria. Many of the pirate company were captured, but the Lafitte brothers escaped. Later on, they, and a number of their followers, honorably served under General Andrew Jackson. In fact, Jean Lafitte assisted in the construction of the defenses of Barataria Bay. In command of a detachment of his pirate band, he participated most creditably in the Battle of New Orleans on January 8, 1815. For his services, Lafitte and his men were granted full amnesty by President James Madison in 1815.

Even though the Lafittes were pardoned, they probably felt like their welcome had worn thin in Louisiana, because in 1817 they founded a "pirate commune" called "Campeche" (sometimes spelled "Campeachy") on Galveston Island, which was first called "Galveztown" after Bernardo de Galvez, viceroy of Mexico. Jean Lafitte ruled over Campeche as "president," and in 1819 for a short time he was governor of "Galveston Republic." In the administration of his far-flung piratical empire, Jean made use of the islands off the coast of

Texas. One of his bases was Culebra Island, composed of Matagorda and St. Joseph's, separated only by Cedar Bayou.

For the purpose of protecting commerce against depredations of freebooters and to safeguard the port of Caparo, the Spanish, and after them, the Mexicans, maintained the small fort of "Armzazu" on Live Oak Point. In retaliation, Lafitte maintained a fort of his own on the southwest part of St. Joseph's Island. The village of Aransas (now Aransas Pass) was later laid out near the site of the pirate's fort.

In 1821 the U.S. government, in reprisal of an attack on an American ship by a Lafitte follower, sent Lt. Lawrence Kearny to disrupt the community, although it was Spanish territory at that time. Lafitte is said to have burned Campeche and "disappeared." Actually, after being ousted from Galveston Island, many of the pirates just settled down in the coastal area. The final meeting of the great buccaneer and his men is reputed to have taken place at False Live Oak Point after they had been cornered by British and American navies. Here the booty was divided up and Lafitte supposedly cached most of it at False Live Oak Point in heavy chests, among the oak trees. This done, the pirate and his remaining followers attempted to slip through the American and British blockade. For three days and nights a cannonade was heard by the residents of Cedar Bayou, and Lafitte finally eluded his pursuers.

Later on, it is said that Lafitte conducted most of his activities on the "Spanish Main," which could have been just about anywhere in the Gulf of Mexico or the Caribbean. The famous pirate died of a fever at Losbocas, on the north coast of Yucatan, about fifteen miles from Merida, in 1826. He was forty-six years old. He was buried in the "Campo de Santos" in the little Indian village of Silan.

Now, there are lots of legends concerning Lafitte and his crew. Their latter-day haunts greatly

Historical marker at Galveston

resembled the Barataria waterways they had known in Louisiana. They centered in the marshy Texas coastland below Beaumont and Port Arthur, and around the vast, brackish Sabine Lake, which emptied into the Gulf of Mexico at dark-running Sabine Pass. These secretive waterways and marshes harbor stories of buried treasure and pirate ghosts to this day.

According to a story that appeared in the *Houston Post* many years ago, one of Jean Lafitte's ships was chased across Sabine Lake and made anchor in Port Neches at the mouth of the Neches River. To keep the treasure aboard the ship from falling into the hands of the Spanish pursuers, it was carried ashore and buried in a marsh. Maps purported to show where this treasure was secreted have appeared from time to time, and there has been much digging for it. It is supposed to have never been found. Maybe this is because it was never placed there. Lafitte's treasure simply can't be buried at every place it is said to be!

The late Thomas Penfield wrote a fascinating little book entitled *A Guide to Treasure in Texas*, published by Carson Enterprises, Inc. of Deming, New Mexico. Mr. Penfield really researched the Lafitte treasure locales, and while he didn't find the buried chests, he certainly told some good stories! I'll just bet one reason the treasure has not been discovered is because there are pirate ghosts out there doing a great job of guarding the burial sites!

In his book, *Ghost Stories of Texas*, the late Ed Syres, storyteller extraordinaire, tells us that Henry Yelvington, a notable lorist, discovered the sunken outline of a low-slung schooner. It was the type often used by the Lafittes as a raider. This was in 1921, and the locale was in a lonely stretch of reeds and bayous flanking the narrows of Sabine Pass. From an old coastal dweller whose trapper forebears had settled Texas in 1833, Yelvington learned that the hulk was indeed one of Lafitte's ships. Indians, whose story was told to Yelvington, had seen the ship sunk under pursuing fire. They were unsure whether the crew drowned, or fled. Since we know that Jean Lafitte died in Mexico, we have to assume he was not on this particular ship, or else he managed to escape.

According to Syre's account, "of something else the Indians had been certain. For many years, the waters remained still, the land empty. Then one day, at the lone tree beside the sunken ship, an incredible figure appeared. Running Snake, the Attacapan chieftain, knew this man; he was Jean Lafitte, the chief of boats that had been driven away by the big ships; the man that Indians, far southward, claimed to have seen dead and buried." (This statement probably refers to the inhabitants of the Indian village of Silan in the Yucatan Peninsula.) "And yet, there he stood, all alone; so with his braves, Running Snake approached, and in terrible shock, saw the figure vanish. After that, only from a distance would any Indian watch.

"But watch they did, for the figure returned and stationed himself where the waters hid the long boat. The figure waited in the manner of one who would summon others, and knowledgeable of dark matters, Running Snake's braves were not overly surprised when a strange, shadowy boat slid noiselessly up the narrow waterway.

"From that boat emerged silent men, who, as though directed by their summoner, began to raise chests from the sunken vessel. Mutely they worked, loading their boat and then, with the dead Lafitte standing in their boat, they left as soundlessly as they had come.

"Where did they go? They started towards the big lake (Sabine Lake), then disappeared in a mist. After that, no one came again. Naturally, the braves of Running Snake thereafter avoided the place." Who could blame them?

Now, it's hard to tell whether Jean and Pierre Lafitte and their pirate crew spent more time plying the ocean deep in search of ships to plunder, or whether they spent more time ashore, digging holes in which to bury their ill-gotten goods, if we are to believe all the buried treasure stories that are often told. These stories run the gamut of the Texas coastline, from Cameron County, down near Brownsville, clear up to Jefferson County near the Louisiana border. Why the pirates didn't come back for their treasure is anybody's guess. Maybe they had poor memories, or maybe they partook of too much rum while out burying their loot. I'd buy the theory that the shifting sands on the windswept seashore caused the terrain to change in appearance sufficiently to make the burial spots unrecognizable. And, we must remember, the pirates more than likely buried their chests under cover of darkness as well. It would have been a real chore to find a certain spot among all the almost identical sand dunes and tufts of sea oats and marsh grasses that dot the coastline.

Conversations with psychics, and time spent reading and researching the subject of "ghosts" in general and "pirate ghosts" in particular, have brought out several interesting conclusions. Ghosts, which are the spirits of dead people who can't quite accept they are dead, do come back. In the case of Jean Lafitte and his pirate-followers, they return to guard the treasure they buried so long ago, and never got around to dividing up. But are they there just to protect their treasure? Might be they are there to lead a selected someone to the site of their buried treasure. Maybe this selected person would be someone with whom they could identify, a "kindred spirit" chosen to be the finder. Now, since there aren't any pirates out there robbing the big ocean freighters and tankers and cruise ships today, the Lafitte crew's spirits might have to identify with an airplane hijacker, since they have largely replaced the buccaneer!

For some unknown reason, there has always been a certain amount of romance and mystery attached to pirates. It must have something to do with all that buried gold, because they really were dastardly individuals. Boarding and looting and sinking ships was NOT a wholesome occupation!

Before we can begin to think about the ghostly guardians that protect the pirate treasure, we have to have an idea of where the booty is buried.

Using Thomas Penfield's book *A Guide to Treasure in Texas*, we will come along on a make-believe trip along the Texas coast, county by county, from the southernmost portion, near Brownsville, in Cameron County, where Penfield reported, "unconfirmed is the report that the pirate Jean Lafitte sank an unidentified Spanish galleon off South Padre Island in 1811 with a cargo of $500,000 in gold and silver. One treasure writer speculates this may have been the Santa Maria, and the treasure was valued at around a million dollars." This event took place during the time the Lafittes were still operating from their Barataria headquarters near New Orleans.

Moving on up along the coast, we come to Kenedy County, where it is noted that off the shore of Padre Island there is the wreck of the Spanish galleon *Capitana*. This ship was assigned to defend some smaller Spanish vessels against a band of pirates. In a furious fight, the *Capitana* went down with all hands, and so did the treasure in her hull, said to be over $1,000,000.

Moving eastward up the coast, we hit Kleberg County, where the famous King Ranch is located. There is a peninsula that juts out into Baffin Bay that is known as "Point of Rocks." A Lafitte treasure chest is said to have been buried there and the site marked by a copper spike driven into a crack in a rock.

Penfield reported there are three hills, called "Money Hills," on Mustang and Padre islands. The original Money Hill on Mustang was the highest sand dune, about three miles south of Aransas Pass. Because of the wind, the sand dunes shift a lot, and the highest dune one day might not be that way the next! Therefore, nobody knows where the original "Money Hill" was located. Sometimes it was called "Big Hill" or "Three Mile Hill" because of its location three miles south of Aransas Pass. According to local legend, a pirate ship blew ashore on northern Mustang Island, and the treasure from it was buried under "Money Hill" because it was a good landmark for the pirates to locate. Many coins have been picked up in this area over the years, so the main cache may already have been found.

The northern tip of Padre Island, located in Nueces County, abounds in buried pirate treasure stories. Penfield's guide states, "It is related over and over that Jean Lafitte's men frequented this area while the pirate leader was established on Galveston Island, and for years afterwards. Corpus Christi and the Laguna Madre, then, as now, were havens during the hurricane season. In 1835 the embankments and fortifications of a rendezvous were plainly visible on the north tip of Padre, and along the beaches were many posts yet standing with iron rings affixed to them, which had been used by the small boats that plied between Padre's shores and the larger vessels anchored offshore. There was a secret pass where the pirates could repair their ships, supply them with food and water, and divide their loot among themselves. All of these signs of Lafitte's presence on Padre Island have now disappeared."

When Lafitte was forced to quit Galveston Island, the remnants of his organization drifted on down the coast to the many islands and coastal towns where they were safe from patrols. It was at this time that the legend was born that Lafitte had personally buried a vast fortune under a millstone on the northern tip of Padre Island. A printer from New Orleans named Newell spent a great part of his life, and finally lost it, searching for this elusive treasure. No one ever learned just what information he had that made him so persistent in his search, but it was believed by some that he had befriended one of Lafitte's men while living in New Orleans and was told the secret of Lafitte's treasure in repayment. The markers sought by Newell were a single Spanish dagger (a type of yucca plant) and three silver spikes. He found hundreds of Spanish dagger plants but not a single silver spike. In 1871 Newell's small boat was found drifting in the Gulf, and a few days later his body was washed ashore.

In Calhoun County, where the ghost town and former seaport of Indianola was located, Penfield's treasure guide states: "A number of Texas treasure stories start with Jean Lafitte's inland flight as he was pursued by a U.S. man-of-war. This was soon after he was ordered to leave Galveston Island. One story has it that he sailed into LaVaca Bay and, with the help of two men, buried treasure valued at a million dollars at the mouth of the LaVaca River, across the bay from the town of Port LaVaca. It is said that a long brass rod was driven into the ground directly above the treasure and left emerging to indicate the treasure site.

"One of the pirates who helped to bury this treasure is said to have told of the incident on his deathbed in New Orleans, giving rough directions to the treasure. This story was heard by a man named Hill, who eventually bought the ranch on which the brass rod was believed to be located. One day a man out herding cattle for Hill noticed the rod and pulled it from the ground, not realizing its significance, and he took the rod with him that night. When Hill saw the rod he recognized its meaning at once, but the old cowhand could not retrace his steps to the place where he had found it. Hill is said to have searched for years for the Lafitte hoard, but he never found it.

"Rumors of a pirate ship wrecked at the mouth of the St. Bernard River in Brazoria County have persisted for more than a century. It is said that the ship put into the river about 1816 to escape a hurricane. Before the vessel was destroyed by the storm, the crew took ashore and buried a treasure estimated at ten million dollars. When the storm was over, only one of the pirates remained alive. He is said to have settled down as a fisherman on Matagorda Island, and frequently displayed gold coins. He admitted to having been a member of the ill-fated ship's crew, but insisted that he had not participated in the burial of the treasure, and therefore knew only generally where it was hidden. In support of this story, it is said that Indians living in the area told early settlers of seeing the wreckage of a great ship after a storm had passed.

"The village of Liverpool, located on Chocolate Bayou in eastern Brazoria County, has all but ceased to exist," according to Penfield. He states, "A man named Campbell came here in 1821 and settled on a branch of Chocolate Bayou that eventually became known as Campbell's Bayou. Before long he was joined by another strange character who was known only as Capt. Snyder. It was believed that both men had been involved in piratical ventures with Jean Lafitte, and as neither had any visible means of support but always seemed to have plenty of money, it was rumored that they kept money buried around their places. When Campbell died, Capt. Snyder shortly afterwards disappeared, never to be seen in the area again. It was said that Campbell's widow knew where some of the supposed treasure was buried, but not the main cache."

Now, speaking of treasure believed hidden in Brazoria County, the folklorist and writer Catherine Munson Foster, in her *Ghosts Along the Brazos*, talked about a treasure chest found near old Velasco (now called Surfside). The story was given to Munson by L. Claude Shannon, and by Sybil Andrus, son and granddaughter, respectively, of Mrs. Georgiana Shannon. Mrs. Shannon's unpublished memoirs had included a story as told by an old Negro man named Jeff, whose word everyone in those parts took to be reliable. It seems a couple of men came to Velasco and seemed to be searching for something between San Luis Pass and the Brazos River. The strangers, who were camping, had nothing at all to do with the locals.

They hired Jeff to accompany them to a certain place among the sand dunes one moonlit night, and there set him to digging in the sand. After he had dug a deep hole, his shovel hit a very large chest which was buried there. It was so heavy it took all three men to lift it out with ropes.

When they had brought the chest to the surface, one of the men shouted in triumph, and at just that moment, a huge hand reached up and grabbed the chest, drawing it out of sight. Jeff, who later told of the event, said he was so frightened he ran away! Jeff would never tell where the place was where the chest was buried, but he did swear the story he told was true. When asked to tell more about it, he refused, saying, "It was the devil."

Nobody ever saw the two strangers after the "devil's night," either, and while there were many searchers out looking for the place, no one ever found it.

As might be expected, since Lafitte and his pirate followers lived on Galveston Island for a time, there are many stories of buried treasure connected with that area. Penfield's book cites a number of pirate treasure locations around Galveston. It's said that there may be as much as $27,000,000 in pirate's treasure on Pelican Island, whose 4,000 acres are used largely by industry, including ship repair facilities. The small island is connected with Galveston by a causeway.

Then, Penfield mentions that Dr. James Long of Natchez, Mississippi, who was among the last of the Texas filibusterers, led two expeditions into Texas in 1819 and 1821. For a time, he and 200 followers lived on Bolivar Point at the southern tip of Bolivar Peninsula, opposite Lafitte's fort on Galveston Island. While Lafitte was robbing Spanish ships in the Gulf, Long and his forces seized one of the pirate's small boats which had been left in the harbor at Galveston. Long described this action in a letter he mailed to General E.W. Ripley in Louisiana in 1820. He also mentioned that "some men of Mescatee" (referring to Lafitte's men) knew of $130,000 buried nearby. It is believed that Long had planned to recover this money, but he was killed before he could get around to finding it. It is believed this little known treasure has never been located.

Almost directly across from Galveston, on the mainland side of West Bay, there's a place called Virginia Point. In 1929 a Beaumont newspaper published a "Forty Years Ago" item in which it quoted the *Galveston Civilian* as saying that a hurricane in 1818 had driven several of Jean Lafitte's ships ashore on Virginia Point. The item went on to say that several years later some guns were found at Virginia Point whose muzzles had been stuffed with gold coins, presumably from the wrecked ships. It was said that the finding of the guns had long been kept secret in hopes that more treasure might be located. The story of Lafitte's treasure at Virginia Point persists in legend, but Penfield said there's scarcely a point between New Orleans and Corpus Christi that doesn't have its own legend of buried Lafitte treasure!

Harris County is home to La Porte, in Trinity Bay. Lafitte is said to have sailed a ship into La Porte and taken a treasure chest ashore, where it was buried. Lafitte was accompanied by two trusted lieutenants, who helped carry the chest inland a short distance. Lafitte is said to have returned to his ship alone. Supposedly, the lieutenants were blindfolded as the treasure was buried, but Lafitte saw one lift his blindfold to note the location of the buried chest. In a rage of anger, the pirate chief killed both of the men. They say the treasure chest lies under an old house which was built over it without the owner's knowledge of the treasure's being there.

Another place where Lafitte sometimes anchored his ships was called Seabrook, on Galveston Bay (still in Harris County). It's said the pirate buried treasure near three large trees on the banks of the Lone Oak Bayou. The belief stems from reports that early settlers in the area found strange markings on some of the trees along the Bayou.

Just north of Galveston, we come to Chambers County. The small historic town of Anahuac is situated on Galveston Bay opposite the mouth of the Trinity River. It was well known to Jean Lafitte. About 1900 several doubloons dated 1803 were found on the banks of the bay near Anahuac. For years it has been known to residents that a strange ship, partially submerged in the sands of the inlet, could be seen on clear days. No one thought much about it until 1940, when a man sought permission from the state to salvage the wreck. When denied permission, he explained that this was one of Jean Lafitte's ships, wrecked when the pirate was forced to leave Galveston. It was a secret, he said, that his family had kept for 90 years. He claimed to have proof that this particular vessel had carried the major portion of Lafitte's vast treasure, a sum estimated at more than $12,000,000. It is little wonder nobody paid much attention to the treasure seeker, because all up and down the Texas coast, Lafitte treasure stories are a "dime a dozen," according to Tom Penfield.

An even wilder story concerning Lafitte's treasure ships also comes from Chambers County. According to Penfield's book, when Jean Lafitte was ordered to leave Galveston and his "Campeachy" domain, he is supposed to have loaded up his flagship, the *Pride*, with five bearskins of gold and sailed somewhere into the back reaches of Galveston Bay to bury them. The ship ran aground and developed such a leak that it settled to the muddy bottom of a small lake before the treasure could be removed and buried. Well, in 1833 the hulk of a sunken ship was located in Lake Miller, near the community of Wallisville. It was hidden just below the surface of the murky water in about eight feet of quicksand-like mud. By means of using a long pipe as a probe, a party of treasure seekers was able to determine the outline of the hulk, and the measurements fit those of the *Pride*. A man named John Lafitte showed up and claimed the treasure, if any was found, on the basis he was a "direct descendant" of the famous pirate. However, the search had to be called off because the state-owned lake had not been properly leased, and the searchers were ordered to leave. This section of Lake Miller has now been filled in. The *Pride*, and the treasure, if indeed they exist, are under dry ground today.

Sabine Pass, over in Jefferson County near the Louisiana border, was a thriving village in the days when Lafitte and his pirates roamed the Gulf Coast. Tales of buried treasure abound in this area. According to a story that appeared in the *Houston Post* many years ago, one of Lafitte's ships was chased across Sabine Lake and anchored in Port Neches at the mouth of the Neches River. To prevent the treasure aboard the vessel from falling into the hands of Spanish pursuers, it was carried ashore and buried in a marsh. Maps purported to show where this treasure was secreted have appeared from time to time and there has been much digging for it, according to Penfield in his Texas treasure guide. It is supposed to have never been found, but maybe, just maybe, an article that ran in the *Port Arthur News* on October 28, 1984, will shed some light on this tale. The writer, Denny Angelle, related the story of a man named Marion Meredith. It seems many years ago Meredith told a Houston newspaper reporter about a neighbor of his who had bought a map from an old Mexican woman. It was supposedly a pirate's treasure map. Now Meredith lived over near Port Neches, and the buried loot was supposed to be somewhere near the mouth of the Neches River, not far from his home. Here, pirates led by Jean Lafitte were said to have escaped their pursuers into the shallow waters of Lake Sabine. This one particular ship, bearing a fortune in treasure, was supposedly floated into the headwaters of the Neches where the crew cut the anchor chain, leaving the anchor as a marker. The treasure is supposed to have been buried in the marshy land nearby.

Well, Meredith's neighbor found the rusty old anchor and located the spot where the treasure should be. Naturally, he began to dig! But before he got too deep, something unseen and icy gripped him! The man was seized with such a nameless horror that he fled the place. So terrified was he that he lost his voice entirely, and he is said to have died a few days later, without ever speaking a word to anyone!

Meredith later obtained the map, but he decided he wouldn't undertake the treasure search alone. He enlisted the help of a man known only as "Clawson," a crusty old woodsman with a bit of pioneer salt throbbing in his blood.

The two men set out down the Neches River and, following the map, they soon discovered the ancient, rusty chain. Pointed in a certain direction by the chart, they searched for a tree with a heart cut into its bark, as was noted on the map. Sure enough, they found it with no difficulty.

From the marked tree, Meredith and Clawson paced off a certain distance and soon found themselves high and dry on a small island in the marsh. They found the tools that Meredith's unfortunate neighbor had left behind him, and the hole that he had begun to dig. Meredith grabbed a pickax and eagerly started to dig. It wasn't long before he found a human skeleton, still wearing rotting clothing and boots. Meredith and Clawson put the skeletal remains aside, and Clawson jumped into the hole in order to dig deeper. Suddenly, he leapt from the hole, his eyes wild in a face as white as a sheet. "For God's sake, man, let's get out of here," he told Meredith. Meredith didn't understand, but Clawson begged him to go, saying, "I've just seen hell and all its horrors! We have to leave this place."

The two men fled, leaving their digging tools on the little island.

Several years later, Meredith ran into Clawson in Beaumont. He recalled the day that they had gone digging to Clawson. The man never would reveal to Meredith what he had seen, but he did tell him that "that day" had haunted him every day of his life since then! It truly had to have been a horrifying experience!

Meredith later returned to the spot to retrieve his tools, but taking Clawson at his word, he did not attempt to dig again. Instead, he carefully reburied the skeleton, then hid the map away and never again went near the little island at the mouth of the Neches.

Once, when some young men approached Meredith and asked him to lead them to his "treasure island," he told them, "I'll take you out there, and I'll even watch you boys, but there ain't enough money in Texas to get me to dig that damned hole."

Nobody knows what became of Marion Meredith. It was a long time ago. Maybe he finally learned the secret of just what is guarding that pirate treasure, or maybe he really didn't want to know what that dreadful unknown thing was that his friend Clawson saw and described as the "dark side of hell." He was probably content to just let well enough alone. No doubt the treasure is probably still out there.

There is, without a doubt, a lot of buried or sunken treasure scattered all along the Gulf Coast area of Texas. Maybe someday some of it will be found, since now there are metal detectors and other devices that can aid in such searches. I learned in speaking with Dr. Joe Graham, of the Department of Sociology at Texas A&M in Kingsville, that "ghost lights" are said to shine around an area where treasure is buried, also. He said this belief is especially widespread among the Hispanic population of South Texas.

From time to time somebody finds a doubloon from a wrecked ship. An occasional gold coin will turn up in a sand dune somewhere, proof that there is still some gold out there. Whether or not there are pirate guardian ghosts at all those purported treasure sites, we have no way of knowing. Since we haven't seen any publicity about pirate treasure being discovered, we're reasonably sure that there are a few "sentries" on duty. After all, it was tough work, dragging those treasure chests ashore and digging those deep holes in which to bury them. We can't blame the pirate-specters for not wanting to give up their loot! They must still be out there, patrolling the beaches, guarding their treasure, so that neither you, nor I, nor even the IRS will discover their secret hiding places!

> *The pirates' gold is still around*
> *The legends will not die.*
> *In holes dug deep within the ground,*
> *Their treasure chests still lie.*

The Three-Master

I am indebted to Yolanda Gonzalez, librarian at the Arnulfo L. Oliviera Memorial Library at the University of Texas at Brownsville, for sending me this story. It was told by a fisherman, John Garreau, on Padre Island's levees to a group of fishermen in 1967, in the presence of Peter Gawenda, who wrote it all down. Later the story appeared in *Studies in Brownsville History*, edited by Milo Kearney.

"When the full moon lights up the sky, when the Gulf is choppy, and when shreds of clouds chase each other through the sky, it is possible to become witness of a beautiful but ghostly sight.

"Several times in the past century, fishermen would return from the Gulf with the following story:

Usually at a distance between two to three miles off the coast, straight to the east of the entrance to the former port of Brazos de Santiago (close to today's Port Isabel), a strange object would appear from the direction of the Rio Grande's mouth, moving swiftly towards the open sea. It would seem to be very large and high, and the absence of any noise would make the vision very mysterious. It would move as if pushed or carried through the water. No living soul would be seen. Then, when it would come close, one could clearly recognize a three-master, or French corsair, with every sail set. All the cannon hatches would stand open. The ship would be loaded so heavily that the choppy sea could not influence its course. At one time, the fisherman said, a lieutenant with the U.S. Army from the former Fort Texas saw that spectacle and described the scene to him, saying, "... on it went, glacial white, mountain high, deathly still, a spectral, gliding glory of moonlit space ... it passed, vanished, and made no sign ... "

Whose ship it was, nobody knows. Some people say it carried Jean Lafitte's ghost to the place where he had buried his (never-found) treasures. Other people who saw the ship insisted that it was a Spanish galleon having three masts. It is very possible that it was returning to the area where it was sunk by a storm centuries ago, or that it really did carry some soul's ghost that was not able to find its rest.

El Perro Negro

Another story having to do with pirates and treasure appeared in the collection of stories entitled *Studies in Brownsville History* edited by Milo Kearney. The story, as told by Felipe Lozano in his Brownsville barbershop to his customers, was written down by Peter Gawenda. I am indebted to Yolanda Gonzalez, librarian at the Arnulfo L. Oliveira Library at the University of Texas, Brownsville, for sending it to me:

It is common knowledge that many treasures are still hidden along the coast of the Gulf of Mexico and maybe in some of the riverbanks of the Rio Grande, Nueces, or San Antonio rivers. But nobody knows the exact locations where those treasures were hidden by pirates like Jean Lafitte, by Spanish nobles who had traveled along the coast like Cabeza de Vaca, and others.

Some small valuables have been found and one large treasure has been stumbled upon at several times, but it has not been recovered. And if someone finds it he will try to take it only that one time. This treasure, so it is told, is in a large iron chest, a type of chest that was used by the people in the seventeenth and eighteenth centuries. To find this chest you would have to dig into the riverbank until you come into a grotto. But everyone who has succeeded in finding this large chest has not dared to get close to it. The chest is more than full, and obviously cannot be closed. In fact, gold chains and jewels have fallen out of that chest and cover the surrounding floor.

But the reason why no one dares to get close to the treasure chest is a large black dog that sits on the chest's cover. It looks as if it is ready to jump. It has reddish, glowing eyes, and growls viciously, baring its long yellow fangs. If anyone has dared to bother the dog by throwing a stone or has tried to shoot the dog, immediately that person has been attacked himself.

Usually the growling alone has caused people to just leave everything and run. Whoever dares to stay longer would become hypnotized by the horrible reddish eyes. This would account for the many skeletons that are said to be lying in the grotto.

It is difficult to say who or what that vicious dog is, but Felipe said that it could be a cursed crew-member of the pirate's ship who now has to suffer for his greed.

One strange thing usually happens. If someone returns to the place where he had found the grotto before he had run away in terror, he will find the whole area looks untouched, as if someone has covered up and camouflaged the hole. No matter how much the individual will dig a second time, it will be useless.

House Plays Host To Live-in Ghost

When Clouis and Marilyn Fisher moved into their "new" Victorian home in 1979, little did they know the charming old house was already occupied! The Fishers first saw the house while they were driving around Rockport, a quiet little town on the Texas Gulf Coast. A yard sale was being conducted in the front yard of the place and the Fishers stopped to browse. Of even more interest to them, however, was the "For Sale" sign on the house. The place was pretty run-down, but Clouis, a dedicated "fixer-upper," and Marilyn welcomed the challenge of restoring the place back to its circa 1881 splendor.

The previous owners neglected to tell the Fishers that the house came complete with a ghost, but it wasn't long before Clouis figured that out for himself!

At the time the Fishers and their three children moved in, the house was badly in need of rewiring. The wiring would not even support an air-conditioner, which was badly needed during the hot summer of '79. One July night stands out even now in Clouis' memory. It was about 1:30 a.m. when he awoke with a start and realized that a light was faintly glowing in the room. He described what he saw to be a "glowing fog" that floated into the room, sort of circled around, and then went out, and into a large room next to the bedroom. The night had been unusually hot. But suddenly, Clouis felt an arctic blast of cold air enter the room. He said he was literally petrified.

Clouis did not mention the strange incident to Marilyn, who had slept soundly through the night. Nor did he mention his strange experience with any friends or other family members. He just tried, with little success, to put the occurrence out of his mind. Soon after this initial encounter, Clouis also began to hear strange, unexplainable noises as well.

Several weeks after the purchase, Clouis, who is a Realtor, attended a company sales meeting in nearby Corpus Christi. A new employee, a woman he had never seen before, walked into the room. After she was introduced to Clouis, she very matter-of-factly inquired, "Have you seen the ghost in your house yet?" It was then that Clouis realized, with some relief, that he hadn't been imagining things.

The lady went on to explain that in 1946 she had come to Rockport as a young single school teacher. She had rented a small upstairs apartment in the spacious old house that Clouis had bought for his family. Soon after she moved in, she came home from school one afternoon and went straight upstairs to her apartment. She heard footsteps of someone walking outside her room, and then the footsteps went down the stairs and out the front door. Frightened, because she thought she was alone in the house, she cautiously went to the front window and peered out to see who had exited the house. No one had come out the front door! A careful search revealed no one was around. She mentioned what she had heard to the daughter of the owners from whom she had rented the apartment. She told her it was just "our ghost." The family thought it might be the spirit of a woman.

After Clouis and Marilyn learned they had a ghost, they began to understand why they had heard the sound of footsteps, and why other unusual things had been happening at the house. Clouis says the antics of the spirit are actually more annoying than frightening. While the Fishers have never seen their resident ghost, except for an occasional glow of light, Clouis and Marilyn both believe it is the spirit of the first man who owned the house, Leopold Bracht.

It seems the Bracht brothers came to Rockport back in the mid-1800s. Leopold ran a successful mercantile business and thus was able to provide a large and spacious home for his growing family. The house was actually built at another location by a builder who hoped to sell it. Today we would refer to it as a "spec house." But the house did not sell right away, standing unoccupied for several years. When Leopold Bracht bought the structure, he had it cut in half and moved to its present site by mule train! This was in 1889, when the structure was about eight years old. Here it was reassembled and made ready for occupancy. In the early 1900s, Bracht remodeled the house considerably, modifying the mansard roofline into a two-storied, gabled-roof house with wrap-around porches on two floors. Space was added to the living areas until it reached its current size of over 4,000 square feet . . . the better to accommodate the Bracht family of six daughters and one son!

Marilyn Fisher told me that a few years after they had moved into the house, one of the Bracht daughters, then a very elderly lady past ninety, called and asked if she could have someone bring her over to see the house in which she had spent much of her childhood. Marilyn said they had a wonderful visit, and the lady told her many interesting stories about the family and the old house. She said her father, Leopold Bracht, was very strict with his daughters. He kept very careful watch over them. In fact, two of the girls never married. It seems the girls had to observe very strict curfews or Leopold would be very angry.

Soon after the Fishers moved in, their daughter, Laura, who was in high school, started dating. She had several dates with a very nice young man from Rockport and always tried to be in by the deadline that Clouis had set of 10 p.m. Several times as she arrived at the house, just in time, the front porch lights would start to flicker on and off, off and on! Laura found this both annoying and embarrassing, and when she went in the house, she went upstairs to tell her father she didn't appreciate that, only to find that Clouis was in bed, fast asleep! The same thing happened numerous times, and they had no explanation, except that Leopold Bracht was keeping tabs on Laura just as he had on his own daughters!

Almost from the time they moved into the house, Marilyn said, the side door, which enters the kitchen off the front porch, would open every afternoon at 5:15 sharp. Even if the door was locked, it would somehow manage to swing open! Now, Mr. Bracht had owned a mercantile store a few blocks from his home, in the business section of

The Bracht-Fisher home, Rockport

Rockport. He apparently closed at five o'clock, and it would be just about 5:15 when he would arrive at home, using the side entrance. Even after they installed new locks, the screen door would often still shake as if someone were trying to gain entrance. A good "talking to" with Leopold finally put an end to that particular problem.

The Fisher family cat, Samantha, a big black feline, was just a kitten in '79 when they bought the house. But ever since she has been a resident of the place, she has been especially sensitive to Leopold's presence. At times, she just bristles, the hair standing up in a ridge behind her neck, for no apparent reason. And sometimes she will hiss and make a sharp swat with her paw at some unknown entity. Then Clouis will say, "Well, I see it's gotten to old Samantha again" (referring to the ghost).

The Fishers have just learned to accept the presence of Leopold, who has been with them the entire fifteen years they have lived there. Sometimes he doesn't make a sound for weeks at a time. Then, for no particular reason, he will make his presence known. He seems to get especially active whenever the Fishers are into a project, changing or remodeling some part of the old house. Leopold must have liked it just as it was when he lived there, and he doesn't want any changes made. Although he did not die in the house, Bracht spent most of his time there and was probably very happy there as head of the household. It is just the most natural place for him to turn up. Fisher says many times he and Marilyn have both felt someone was staring at them. This most often happens when they are in the kitchen standing in front of the kitchen sink. When they turn around, they feel as if they almost see something out of their peripheral line of vision, but then, there is never anything there. The strange feeling that something, or someone, has been watching them still remains, however.

Clouis told me about one night when he had just finished rewiring the house. The family was sitting around the dining room table having supper when suddenly the dining room lights went out. His daughter, Laura, looked up at the light fixture and said, "All right, Leopold, that's enough out of you tonight." Evidently the ghost got the message because the lights came right back on again!

When the Fishers' son, James, was in high school, he had three of his friends over to visit one evening. The boys were around 16 or 17 at the time. One of James' friends had brought a Ouija board along to provide some entertainment. Clouis said all was quiet and peaceful when suddenly he and his wife heard a terrible racket as the boys ran down the stairs and out the front door, slamming it hard behind them! When the youngsters calmed down, they explained that they had started talking to Ouija and asking it some questions, when suddenly the bedroom door, which they had locked from the inside, flew open! There must have been something else that happened, but they would never discuss it. Two of the boys would not even come back into the house. Clouis said one of the young men, the son of the local Baptist preacher and now a young man in his mid-20s, still tells the Fishers he will never, never, forget that night!

Currently, the Fishers are doing a lot of work around the house in anticipation of turning the spacious dwelling into a bed and breakfast inn. Leopold is not always happy with the new project! Recently, Clouis has been adding extra bathroom space to the upstairs area where the guests will be accommodated. He leaned the door for the new upstairs bathroom against the stairs, and went downstairs for a minute. He heard a tremendous crash, and felt sure the door had fallen over. A careful search revealed nothing was out of place; nothing had fallen. Yet the noise had been very real, and very, very loud!

Leopold has been destructive only once. When the Fishers hung a watercolor picture of purple iris in the newest bathroom, they came home to find it on the floor, the glass shattered. The heavy multistrand wire on the back had stretched taut and broken at one end, but the picture hanger was still in the wall. Now, the picture had hung for some time in another room. It was just after it was moved to the new location that it was forcefully removed from the wall.

The Fishers have both resorted to talking to Leopold, telling him that the place is going to be nicer and more attractive than ever when the work is all done. They stress that they are trying to bring it back to its original state of elegance, when Leopold and the rest of the Bracht family lived there. They hope by acknowledging his presence, and making him feel a part of the project, that his spirit will be happier. They hope maybe he will calm down so that the bed and breakfast guests can spend peaceful, restful nights in the pretty old home that's painted a cheerful yellow with white trim. Its spacious rooms and cool, inviting porches will offer a wonderful haven for Gulf Coast visitors.

If you would like to stay with the Fishers, and Leopold, of course, you might call them at (512) 729-3189 for rates and reservations.

The Night the Karankawa Came Calling

Sue Casterline lives in a small community known as Estes Flats, just south of Rockport. Her house is situated in a stand of very ancient, very large live oak trees. She told me that early settlers in the coastal plains area usually tried to locate their homes around large live oaks. Because salt water will kill them very quickly, when a stand of very large oaks is found, it is a good indicator that the land is sufficiently high enough not to flood during hurricanes, which so frequently hit that part of the state. Sue believes the coastal area's first settlers, the Indians, might have located their village near large oak trees for this same reason.

A short distance, something like a couple of city blocks, from Sue's home, a landowner decided to build some boat storage barns about twelve years ago. The ground had to be leveled first before the actual building process could begin. One portion of the land formed a good-sized hill. No one realized at the time that this had been an old Indian burial mound until the bulldozers came in and uncovered some skeletal remains and some artifacts. Archaeologists were dispatched from a nearby university, and they determined that the mound probably represented the sacred burial grounds of a community of Karankawas. Nothing was actually removed from the mound, and the bones were resettled into their previous resting place as carefully as possible.

Soon after the mound was disturbed, Sue's mother came to visit her. Sue said that both she and her mother were a little bit psychic, especially when it came to feeling or seeing something concerning one another. One night Sue's mother was awakened very suddenly from a sound sleep. She distinctly saw the figure of an Indian man standing by the side of her bed. He was bare-chested, and had long hair. He seemed to be bending towards her, intently studying her. She cried out, and the figure disappeared immediately. When she told Sue why she had cried out, she said the figure she saw was so real that she did not think she could have possibly dreamed it.

Four or five days after this incident, Sue was alone at home, doing the laundry. She had been in her garage, where the washer was located. She had just walked through her kitchen, back into the house, and noted all was in order. She went into her bedroom to check on her new baby, and then walked back through the kitchen to check on the progress of the laundry. This time she was astonished to discover all nine drawers in her kitchen cupboards were standing wide open. She said she was astounded, but not at all frightened. In fact, she felt like someone or something was just playing a joke on her, and she found it amusing.

The following weekend a friend came to see Sue. She told her friend about her mother's strange experience with the Indian, and then of her own strange experience with the kitchen drawers. Her friend said, "I just can't believe any of that." Suddenly, from off a shelf in a pantry, which was clearly visible from where the two women were sitting in the dining room, a big squeeze bottle of mustard literally flew off the shelf and crossed a narrow hallway to the center of the kitchen floor. Sue said it did not fall from the shelf; it was hurled! While it wasn't scary, she said, it definitely succeeded in "making a statement."

It has been a number of years since the Indian man appeared in Sue's guest room and the kitchen cupboards went berserk. But then, no one has disturbed the final resting place of the Karankawas again, either.

Someone's in the Kitchen at Beulah's

The Tarpon Inn, located in the waterfront area of Port Aransas, has long been a favorite resting place for visitors to Padre Island. In fact, the historic inn has already celebrated its 100th birthday!

The town of Port Aransas sits on the northernmost tip of Padre Island, a barrier island which protects the bay and harbor of Corpus Christi. The harbor was discovered by the Spanish on Corpus Christi Day in 1519, hence its name. It was not fully explored until a Frenchman mapped the area in 1720. Padre Nicholas Balli acquired the title to the land, which is a 100-mile-long strip of sand dunes and grass, for the sum of 400 pesetas paid to King Charles IV of Spain in 1880. The padre set up a cattle ranching operation on the island, and in time, the land took on the nickname "Padre Island" rather than its official name of Isla de Corpus Christi.

According to Rand McNally's *Weekend Escapes, Southeast Texas Edition*, in about 1855 an English settler built a ranch house up at the northern tip of the island. He established a small town, eventually to be called Port Aransas, which sprang up around his homestead.

During the Civil War, the site of the Tarpon Inn was occupied by a barracks for Confederate troops, and in 1886 the Tarpon Inn was built from materials which had been salvaged from the old barracks. The inn was named for the tarpon, huge game fish with extraordinarily large scales that were found in the waters around Port Aransas.

The first Tarpon Inn was destroyed by fire in 1900. It was rebuilt in 1904 and was destroyed by a hurricane in 1919. In 1923 it was rebuilt in its present form, a two-storied, long frame building, with long galleried porches both upstairs and down. The original building was painted white. Today, it is sky-blue. Mr. J.M. Ellis, the builder in 1923, wanted to assure the hotel would not fall victim to another hurricane, so he sank pier pilings in sixteen feet of cement for the foundation and then put a full pier at the corner of each bedroom for added strength in case of a storm. Hence, the hotel has withstood many storms and quite a few rambunctious young people on spring breaks as well!

A lot of well-known personalities have stayed at the inn, but the one they still talk about most frequently is President Franklin Delano Roosevelt, who came down for a few days of tarpon fishing and left his signature on a tarpon scale which is proudly displayed in the hotel's lobby.

Right behind the inn is a lovely little garden area. Here there are two frame buildings, each a part of what is called Beulah's Restaurant. The long building at the rear of the property, which mostly serves as a bar and overflow dining room for the larger Beulah's, was at one time the original Tarpon Inn's location, the site that burned.

Beulah's Restaurant has had several names over the years. At one time it was the bar to the original Tarpon Inn, and after this, it was known for a time as the Silver King. Since mid-1992 it has been called Beulah's. The head housekeeper at the Inn for many years was Beulah Mae Williams, and it is in her honor that the restaurant was named. She resided in a very old, long frame building that still stands behind the restaurant on a little side alley. Beulah is currently living in a retirement home in Lamar, Texas.

Ms. Julie Caraker, who manages Beulah's, describes the place as one in which the atmosphere is "upscale, down-home," and combines

Beulah's Restaurant, at Tarpon Inn in Port Aransas.

good home cooking with the added flair of gourmet cuisine. After a recent visit and a delicious lunch, we can attest to this being a pretty accurate description. The food is excellent, attractively presented, and not inexpensive.

When I first approached Ms. Caraker, via telephone, and asked her, point blank, if there might be a ghost at the establishment, she did not seem at all taken aback. She quite freely described her feelings and experiences.

Paula Bonillas, of Corpus Christi, and her husband, Steve, own a restaurant by the name of Blackbeard's in Corpus Christi. Their place is haunted, too. Knowing of my research project, Paula had sent me a copy of an intriguing article that had run in the *Silver King Newsletter* some years back. That is why I decided to contact the present management of the restaurant and learn more about the place.

The *Silver King* article stated that Beulah's (then the Silver King) was haunted. It mentioned that while Beulah Mae Williams had never seen the ghost, she had definitely heard it. Beulah cited one particular day when she was walking outside past the kitchen and had heard quite a clatter within, such as would be going on during a very busy day. She knew the restaurant was closed, however. Curiosity beckoned, and she went inside and found everything in its place. There was no explanation for the din she had heard. It had to be the ghost that she had heard other employees mention. This ghost must have been hard at work in the kitchen that day!

The article went on to say that Mr. Kent Marsh, an evening chef at the Silver King, had witnessed what he called "an eerie haze" in the form of a "woman of middle age and medium height." Mr. Mike Buvosa, a former employee, also saw the apparition and thinks she is from a past era since her hair was pulled back in a severe bun, a style not often worn today.

Ms. Caraker informed me that the fire in the original Tarpon Inn building had caused massive damage. It is rumored that the cook lost her good pearl necklace in the fire, and she still comes back in search of her lost gems. This might explain the hazy figure seen in the kitchen by both Marsh and Buvosa. However, Ms. Caraker believes the "main ghost" is a man who once worked as a cook at the restaurant. Caraker said a lady who said she was a psychic from Colorado stopped at Beulah's recently and asked Julie if she knew the place was haunted. When Julie answered that she did indeed believe that there was a resident spirit, the psychic asked her if the ghost's name started with an "S." Julie said she believed the ghost was a former cook who was named Samuel, but everyone always called him Sammy.

According to Julie, Sammy still comes around, often at breakfast time, to help her cook. Recently, after the kitchen floor was freshly mopped, Julie was astonished to see large footprints following her much smaller ones on the kitchen floor! Sammy was following her all around the kitchen as she worked!

The mischievous side of Sammy often comes out. He turns lights on and off in the original portion of the old inn, the part of the building that was no doubt his bailiwick.

Mark Wilks, another employee at Beulah's, spoke with us on a visit we made to the inn in August of 1993. He also believes there is a ghost there. He told us about an incident that took place a number of years ago when he and his wife, Janet, were just teenage friends. Janet had left her bicycle leaning against the wall of the restaurant one afternoon. Later that day, she asked Mark to accompany her to get it. Since it was beginning to get dark, she was afraid to go alone. Just as the two retrieved her bike, they heard the "wildest clatter imaginable" coming from inside the kitchen. Mark said it was so loud he was sure that they could hear it across the bay in Aransas Pass! It sounded as if all the pots and pans were being thrown across the kitchen and knocked down from their racks. They knew the place was closed for the day, and that no one was inside. Mark says that even now Janet will not go into the kitchen, and she's always uneasy even in the cheerful restaurant and bar section of the building.

And Julie Caraker said that whenever she goes into the little room behind the bar in the old building she gets "prickly sensations" and knows that the ghosts are still there!

Paula and Steve Bonillas told me about a recent visit they made to Beulah's. As they were enjoying their meal, a door near their table suddenly flew open from the inside. Although there was no breeze, no person to open the door, and no reason for the door to open, it just did. When they questioned their waitress, she matter of factly stated it was "just the ghost." Paula told me I would just have to see for myself why that particular door cannot open by itself. Well, I did. And it can't.

The Graveyard Ghost

Julie Caraker, whom we met at Beulah's Restaurant adjacent to the Tarpon Inn, had an interesting ghost encounter when she first came to Port Aransas. She rented a little white frame house that had once been a church. It washed ashore after a storm, was renovated and converted to a house, and now is located on Oaks Street, just a short distance from the inn. Right in front of the house, just a few feet from the front porch, is a tiny little private graveyard that belonged to a family named Mercer. Since the graves are old, they must have been early settlers to the area. The mother, Emma, her husband John, and their son John, plus two infants, are all buried there. Emma's dates, "Born, Jan. 24, 1856, Died, Jan. 28, 1906" are clearly discernible. Some of the other markers are harder to read. Emma was apparently the last person to be buried in the small plot.

Soon after Julie moved into the cottage, strange things began to happen. She said she was very tired the first day, after moving, and wanted to take a bath to freshen up. She dreaded cleaning up the bathroom, however, because leaves and debris had blown in the partially opened window and accumulated in the bathtub. Imagine her surprise when she opened the bathroom door and found the tub all cleaned up! She says now she is quite sure the "ghost" did the cleaning!

A collector of antiques, especially vintage clothing items, Julie said often her little displays of old gloves and fans and accessories would be rearranged, quite noticeably. Nothing was ever missing or harmed, however.

Julie said both she and her young son, who was about eight years old at the time, had actually seen the ghost. The apparition was the figure of a woman, wearing a long white petticoat that showed from under a long black hooded cape. It was on a dark, foggy evening the first time she saw the figure walking between her house and the little cemetery. She said she had talked with other people who also had seen the same figure.

Her little boy was never afraid of the ghost, nor was she. He often referred to her as "our guardian angel."

Home and little cemetery, Port Aransas

Ghosts of the Lower Rio Grande Valley

THEY ARE HERE
Docia Williams

Graceful fronds fan tall palm trees
That gently sway in the evening breeze,
As twilight falls on far-flung reaches
Of coastal swamp land and sandy beaches
The sunlight fades, and darkness falls
And ghosts come out, to make their calls
Back to where, in the days of yore
They lived, and breathed, and walked the shore;
And dreamed their dreams, as now we do,
And loved the homes that they once knew . . .

Their stories now I bring to you.

Fort Brown, Where
Old Soldiers Never Die

Way down at the very bottom of the Rio Grande Valley at what one might call the "jumping off place," lies a beautiful city of some 95,000 souls, called Brownsville. The city sits just across the Rio Grande from its sister city, Matamoros, in the Mexican state of Tamaulipas. The two cities are in one of the most interesting and intriguing regions in Texas, dating back to Spanish Colonial days, and covering periods of exploration, wars, revolutions, banditry, and "you name it . . . it was there."

General Zachary Taylor established Fort Brown in 1846 to maintain the United States' claim to the Rio Grande as the international boundary, the line won some ten years earlier by Texans in their battle for independence from Mexican domination. The old fort housed troops during the Mexican war, defended the border, and later exchanged hands during the Civil War. By a strange quirk of fate, the last engagement of the Civil War, the Battle of Palmito Ranch, was fought near Brownsville in May of 1865. Confederate soldiers under the command of Colonel John S. Ford, not having heard of Lee's surrender a month earlier, completely routed and captured a Federal force in a fierce running two-day encounter. Only after the battle did the victorious Rebels learn of Lee's surrender. The victors then became the formal captives of their former prisoners! That battle was the final one of the Civil War.

Fort Brown's hospital was where the famous Dr. William Crawford Gorgas did much of his yellow fever research. During the Spanish American War, he was appointed chief sanitary officer in Havana and did much to clear that city of yellow fever. Then he was sent to Panama, where in five years he succeeded in greatly reducing the death rate from yellow fever during the time the canal was being built. Later, Gorgas became Surgeon General of the U.S. Army and was promoted to the rank of Major General.

Today the hospital has been converted to an administration building for the University of Texas at Brownsville (formerly called Texas Southmost College) and is called Gorgas Hall. Other campus buildings from the original fort days, which ended in 1920, are the Medical Laboratory, the Military Police Headquarters, the Post Guardhouse, the Morgue, and the Post Headquarters.

The former fort has its ghosts, too.

Yolanda Gonzalez, librarian at the Arnulfo L. Oliveira Memorial Library on the University of Texas campus, was kind enough to share some interesting happenings with me. "There are supposed to be ghosts everywhere," she says, as she related personal sightings and experiences she has had. She believes the college's ghosts are friendly, and she doesn't fear them. On several occasions, she has seen books in glass-fronted cabinets move slowly, as if someone were searching the shelves for a certain book.

One night while working late putting up a display to go on view the next day, she saw a door to the Hunter Room open, then close. She thought the janitors might have opened the door, and ignored it until she saw both janitors come in together from having dinner. The three then investigated and found the door was still locked. Gonzalez said they told her it was "just the ghosts of the college."

According to an article which appeared in the October 31, 1993 *Brownsville Herald*, one of the most widely told stories concerning the old fort was related by a janitor, who early one morning walked out of the building and heard the "thundering of horse hooves and the stomping of marching soldiers." When he looked out, he saw an entire regiment of soldiers on parade, saluting the American flag!

Ms. Gonzalez talked at length to the janitor who had viewed the strange dawn ceremony. She said he described in great detail how the soldiers and horses looked, and said a bugler was standing near the flag. He said the sound of the horses' hooves was so loud he got scared and tried to run away.

Later that same morning, the janitor found a button from a uniform, and a buckle. He kept the button but gave Gonzalez the buckle, which she took to the Historic Brownsville Museum. The museum director, Bruce Aiken, authenticated it as being a buckle used in some type of harness like a backpack or horse harness. It could have been used anytime from the 1860s to the 1910s, he said.

The ghostly soldiers also bothered another college employee. When John Barham, former Dean of Continuing Education, first arrived in Brownsville, he was given a room in the old commandant's house until he could find a place to live. Barham, now Provost of Suffolk Community College in Long Island, N.Y., said that for three mornings he was awakened by the sounds of marching feet and of prancing horses' hooves. He said he could distinctly hear the hoof beats and the jingling of spurs.

Barham told the college officials he had been awakened by the ROTC cadets marching early every morning. Imagine his great surprise to learn that the college didn't even have an ROTC program! He later learned the old parade ground ran right in front of the former commandant's house where he was staying.

Gorgas Hall, the former fort hospital, has its share of ghostly visitors, also. Numerous people have reported sighting a lady dressed from head to toe in white in the style of nursing uniforms a hundred years ago. She walks into locked offices and sits behind desks. No one has been able to engage her in conversation thus far.

Several janitors have sighted a woman dressed in black mourning attire. She asks for directions to the hospital and inquires about the condition of her son. Several janitors have seen the same woman, and sometimes the incidents have taken place several years apart! Some of the janitors who saw the lady and didn't realize that Gorgas Hall had been a hospital during the old fort days, directed her to the hospital across town. Only later did they realize they had encountered a ghost!

Then there's the puppy story. A little stray puppy has been sighted by many people over the years. He will follow a group of friendly people as they walk from class to class. When they stop and sit down, the puppy literally disappears! Administrators point out that the walkway which spans the length of the campus, connecting all the buildings, is at almost the same location as a similar dirt road that ran the length of old Fort Brown. The similarity was discovered after comparing old pictures of the fort and modern photographs of the college. No doubt, the friendly pup is just trying to find his way home!

Concerts on a Phantom Organ

Some people seem to think a building or house has to be very, very old to be haunted. Wrong! A very modern building can be haunted, too, because of something that happened there, or because of something that happened in that locale before the building was erected. And then, there are the houses and buildings that have been unknowingly built over graveyards. They can really have problems!

No one knows what caused the Brownsville offices of the Community Development Corporation at 833 W. Price Road to be haunted. A June 13, 1982 edition of the *Brownsville Herald* carried a very interesting story about the building by Greg Fieg, a staff writer.

It seems that the building, a very modern office complex with acoustical ceilings, wall-to-wall carpeting, and all modern conveniences, became so wrought with ghostly happenings that many employees quit, and the people in the Community Development Corporation were planning to move at the end of the summer to another location.

Eerie organ music, vibrating furniture, flashing lights, and strange unexplained noises in their offices were bad enough, but Executive Director Nick Ramon also saw a tall, black-hooded figure that stalked the halls of the building. Ramon said when he saw the strange figure he ran out the door, but more than just being frightening, he felt the figure was extremely tragic and was suffering. "I felt sorry for him," Ramon was quoted as saying.

Other employees at the offices saw strange shadows, as though a figure had moved from a chair just as they approached. There were other unusual occurrences such as low voices calling from dark, empty rooms, toilet paper rolling inexplicably across the restroom floors, doorknobs jiggling when no one was around, papers that would turn up missing and then reappear, and a radio that would turn itself on and off. Often some of the rooms would become unbearably cold, and staff members would sense some "presence" had entered them.

The staff members finally got so nervous that many of them kept vials of holy water, crucifixes, and various icons in their offices. They even called upon a priest, Father Timothy Ellerbrock, formerly of Christ the King Church, to help. He visited the offices, but his praying and rituals did not seem to help.

Ruben Reyna, who was fund-raising coordinator at the time the story appeared in the *Herald*, said he was playing his guitar in the staff conference room late one night when he heard strange organ music accompanying him. It sounded like an old pipe organ. It would build to a climax like in the old silent movies, then come to an abrupt stop. Yolanda Gonzalez, who worked in the same building for another firm, said she also had heard the organ music. She said it sounded like church music, but it was like the organist was practicing and never quite finished the piece. She said it was certainly a real organ that she heard! Well, there isn't a church within a half-mile of the building complex.

One night Reyna said he was frightened by "thumping noises" when he was alone, and as he fumbled for his keys to lock up and leave the building, he felt as if he were pushed, bodily, out of the office by some unseen hands.

The executive director, Ramon, has seen a flashing light, a furious "tempest" raging inside the office water cooler, and other strange things that defy explanation, in addition to the black-hooded figure. One woman employee is convinced that "something" chased her down a hallway. Augustin Sauceda, a housing counselor, said a voice once called out his name from within an empty office. He thought at first it was Nick Ramon. The voice called "Augustin . . . Augustin." When he looked inside and saw no one in the office, he then recalled that Ramon was out of town!

Too many things happened to too many people in that building. They were more than glad to change their office address!

The Pasture of Souls

This story came to me through the generosity of Yolanda Gonzalez, librarian at the Arnulfo L. Oliveira Memorial Library on the campus of the University of Texas at Brownsville. It appears in *Studies in Brownsville History*, edited by Milo Kearney. The story was told by Felipe Lozano in his Brownsville barbershop to his customers in 1963 and was recorded by Peter Gawenda.

Way back, when Brownsville was still a small town, there used to be an empty area next to the old graveyard. People used to call it *el pasto de las almas*, meaning the pasture of souls....

It all started in 1849, when during an epidemic of cholera more than one hundred people died within a few weeks. As Brownsville did not have a priest yet, and as the padre from Matamoros was busy across the border, many bodies had to be buried in mass graves or unmarked graves without the blessings of the church. And as the graveyard was too small anyway, the bodies were hurriedly buried right outside.

In later years, the 1860s and 1870s, when [Juan] Cortina [the Mexican Revolutionary guerrilla fighter] raided the town and countryside, or when bodies of unknown desperados were left behind after shootouts, they also were buried beside those outside the graveyard.

But around 1880, the night before All-Souls-Day, several people observed a very strange phenomenon. As it is a custom to care for the graves of loved ones before All-Souls-Day, people were still planting flowers or arranging decorations on individual graves. A thin fog had started to settle around the graveyard and dusk was slowly replaced by darkness when suddenly a light popped out of the ground, right there where the *desconocidos* (unknown people) were buried. The light looked like the flame of a candle and it seemed to float back and forth very slowly. And after a few seconds it was gone.

Only two or three people had seen it, but the word got around quickly. And when suddenly another light appeared, then a second, a third and even a fourth one, and when the lights seemed to float towards the graveyard, everyone ran as fast as they could. Although people were afraid, some dared to pass the graveyard during the following nights. In some of the town's cantinas the very brave or maybe the very drunk made bets that they would go visit the *pasto de las almas* at midnight. And those that really did, would return pale and sober.

Very quickly the word spread that the flames were the souls of those who could not find rest because they had been denied the last rites or were buried outside of the blessed earth. For several years afterwards the gruesome appearances would occur, especially around All-Souls-Day, until finally a priest blessed that piece of land and a mass was read. Later, when the graveyard was expanded, this lot was included.

Nowadays only on very rare occasions can one see one of these flames pop out of the ground, then slowly wander over several graves, then stop, or slowly float back, and then disappear. If you should ever see one, please say a prayer, so that the wandering soul might find rest.

La Abuela

This is another story told by Felipe Lozano in his barbershop in
Brownsville in 1963 and written down by Peter Gawenda for inclusion
in the book, *Studies in Brownsville History,* edited by Milo Kearney:

Before the turn of the century several incidents occurred
on ranchitos around Brownsville in which children and young
mothers were helped by an old woman. Two of these stories
are as follows:

The Garzas lived in one of the ranchitos right outside of
Brownsville. Every morning they would head out into their
fields and work all day long. Their only child, the four-year-old
Consuelo, would be with them and she would usually play at
the edge of the field or under the mesquite trees. She would
chase butterflies. Very often one could see her interrupt her
activities to look for her parents, and only after she saw them
would she continue her play.

One day, though, when chasing a butterfly, she started
wandering off, and neither the parents nor she herself realized
that she was getting lost in the mesquite brush. When dusk set
in, the parents called their daughter, but they did not receive
any response. As they always walked the same way to the
fields and then home again, they finally hoped that Consuelo
had already found her way to the house. But this was not the
case; the parents looked and called in vain. They walked to all
of the neighbors, but no one had seen or heard Consuelo. The
father went to the sheriff's department for help, and that same
night a search party was assembled to look for the girl. Three
days later the search was discontinued, and Consuelo was
given up as having died either from hunger or from attacks of
coyotes or snakes. The parents and relatives were broken-

hearted, and especially the mother, who blamed herself for not having watched the four-year-old. On the fifth day, right after the parents had returned from church and were preparing to again search for their daughter, an old, frail-looking woman in a strange outfit approached the house, led by little Consuelo. The girl showed no signs of hunger or thirst and was in excellent spirits. In fact, she was "flowing over," telling her parents about the nice treatment by the "abuela" (this means "grandmother" in Spanish). As the parents were so busy caressing and kissing their daughter, they had completely forgotten to take notice of the old woman. When they finally turned around to thank her, she had disappeared. All three ran first inside the house, then to the back, but in vain. The girl's "abuela" was gone.

The grateful parents made a novena at the church and the father set up a marker where the girl had been returned from the mesquite brush. But the old woman never returned, although the girl would always remember her "abuela," even when she herself was already in her seventies. She would always remember a beautiful smile.

Another incident happened right across the river on the road from Matamoros to Reynosa where a woman was about to deliver a baby in one of the desolate little farms. The young woman's husband had gone to town on his horse to get the midwife, but was held up for some unknown reason. As the young woman was in pain, she screamed several times, and suddenly an old woman wearing an old outfit walked into the hut. Without saying a word she quickly boiled water, put cold compresses on the young woman's head, massaged her abdomen to ease the pain, and then helped a healthy little boy into this world. The old woman then washed the baby, cleaned the young woman, and left the son with his mother.

By the time the young father returned with the "partera" (midwife), he found only his wife and son, both sound asleep. The mother always remembered the beautiful and very soothing smile of the old woman, who was lovingly referred to as their "abuela."

In all such incidents, the outfit of the "abuela" was described to be similar to an old Indian costume as can be seen carved on some of Mexico's ruins. Some of the people therefore believed that she must have been, and maybe still is, the good spirit of an Indian medicine woman.

The Man With the Shovel

This is another story from *Studies in Brownsville History*, edited by Milo Kearney. It was told by an old gentleman referred to as "Jefe" in the barbershop on Marketsquare in 1968, retold by a student in 1982, and recorded by Peter Gawenda.

Several times during the past one hundred twenty years a strange appearance has saved people's lives and at other occasions the reputation of young ladies. Two of these incidents are still being told in detail.

It must have been in the year 1892 or 1893, when a man named Alfonso or Alonso returned from one of his usual visits to one of the town's cantinas. It was a very stormy night, and he tried to get home as quickly as possible. He had only five blocks to go when he suddenly saw this man without a head, surrounded by a pale bluish light. The man had a shovel in his hands and was drawing a line across the street. Alfonso sobered up immediately, and was ready to run, but the figure had disappeared. Hesitantly he kept on walking, but when he approached the mark across the street, his feet seemed to become as heavy as lead, and no matter how he tried to move, he couldn't. While he was still attempting to move, suddenly a tremendous lightning bolt turned the night into day. And then he saw this large object crash onto the ground only thirty or forty feet in front of him. It was the roof of one of the houses right there on Second Street.

Needless to say, he was the first in church the next morning to attend the six o'clock mass. Very faithfully did he light a candle every Sunday for the following year, thanking our Lady for this miraculous rescue. He knew that our Lady must have had her hand in his survival, as his wife prayed to Mary every day.

Another incident happened in the early 1930s. A very hot-blooded admirer of a Brownsville girl had come from Matamoros and was walking down St. Charles towards Second Street. He knew that the girl's parents had left town to visit a sick aunt in Port Isabel, and he was looking forward to this night. The weather was bad; again it was very stormy and nearly pitch dark. Suddenly he saw a strange figure with a shovel. The figure had no head and was wrapped in a black cloak. A strange bluish light surrounded the figure, which was drawing a line across the street. Thunderstruck, the young man, named Salvador, stopped, but the figure disappeared.

Quite scared, Salvador started running towards the house of his girlfriend. But as if held by a magic force he was stopped at the line. Again and again he tried to cross the line, but in vain. He therefore turned around, ran back to Third Street, ran down Third, turned onto Levee and suddenly saw the figure. Again a line was drawn across the street, and Salvador was held at the line. And when he tried to approach the girl's house through Elizabeth Street and once more saw the headless man with the shovel, fear overwhelmed him, and he quickly returned to his home in Mexico.

Quite often he had to think of his frightful experience, which he confessed to the padre on his deathbed. It is said that the headless man with the shovel has drawn lines to prevent people from falling into the flooded Rio Bravo, or into water-filled ditches, but it has also prevented young men from approaching unprotected young ladies. In one instance the figure is said to have prevented the abduction of a girl to Mexico. In this last case the boy was so frightened after seeing the headless man, that he tried to escape into Mexico. The people that fished his body out of the river said they never had seen such fright in any dead man's face.

The Brick-Throwing Ghost

In August 1879, Brownsville made headlines throughout Texas when several newspapers carried a story which involved the home of the Glaevecke family. The *Daily Express* of San Antonio carried the following story on Tuesday morning, August 26, 1879, under the headline: "Brownsville's Big Sensation, Spooks and Brickbats, a Prominent Citizen's House Bombarded."

Brownsville is just now dazed with wonderment at a startling manifestation of a spiritual character, which if not convincing to the skeptical are none the less violent to those who come within the range of the unseen battery [sic]. Last Monday the family of county clerk Glaevecke complained to him that the servants could not enter the yard without being attacked with a volley of brickbats, which a neighbor's servant would fire at them. There had been between the servants of the family of Mr. Glaevecke and that of Mr. Yznaga, a neighbor, some little difficulty, and to this cause was ascribed the attack. Mr. Glaevecke paid no attention to the complaint at the time, only remarking that as long as they were not seriously hurt the family had better not interfere. But after dinner the old man suddenly changed his mind; for on taking his chair into the back garden to enjoy a smoke, he was assailed by a shower of brickbats, he receiving two wounds. He immediately reported to the police authorities the circumstance and asked that an officer be put on the watch, that the offender might be arrested. The officers were unable to discover from whence the missiles came, but they continued to come . . . in fact they came so thick and fast that Lieutenant Herrera, who was stationed on the tip of the roof, was obliged to descend and seek safety within the walls. This state of things continued up to Thursday, when Mr. Glaevecke swore out a warrant for the arrest of a servant belonging to Mrs. Yznaga on suspicion. In the meantime, Mrs. Glaevecke and her daughter had become so alarmed that they fled to the rancho for safety, leaving behind the elder sister, who is more courageous. The arrest of the servant had no visible effect upon the throwing of bricks, and they continued as before, with remarkable precision, generally coming through the open doorway, and when the doors were closed they came crashing through the windows. On Friday one was fired through the doorway, killing a parrot; while at supper one came booming over the table, scattering the china in all directions. On finding that the arrest of the neighbor's servant had no effect, Mr. Glaevecke ordered his release; but Mrs. Yznaga, who is sorely perplexed, ordered him to Matamoros, until quiet shall be restored. This morning Mr. Glaevecke caused the arrest of another of the Yznaga's male servants, and for a time it seemed the firing ceased; but it was only temporary, and about ten o'clock today it recommenced.

In company with Mayor Carson, Sheriff Brito and others, a *Democrat* reporter visited the premises and witnessed an ocular demonstration of the singular performance. He found abundant evidence of the attack. On all sides were brick and fragments of brick, and sixteen shattered windows and broken crockery on every hand confirmed the rumors that had prevailed. He found Mr. Glaevecke haggard, his daughter careworn, and the servants trembling with fright. A boy servant, Anastasio, bore many wounds; his head was bandaged and one of his feet was swathed in linen and arnica, while his limbs and body bore abrasions and contusions. He seems to have been singled out by the enemy for an especial target, and whenever he appeared in the yard he received their fire. Mr. Glaevecke also had a wounded hand.

The objective point seems to be the kitchen and the dining room, and this morning the firing was incessant, so that the family was obliged to abandon the kitchen and send to a neighbor's for breakfast. While we were investigating, a brick struck the house with considerable force, shortly followed by another. John Clark dodged into a corner, the servants scattered, the mayor tried to appear unconcerned but failed. The reporter was unmoved; he had come to see, and this was what he wanted.

With the air of a veteran he walked to the door to obtain a better view. A full grown brick howled over the alley like a cannon ball; two more rebounded from the roof. The reporter had gratified his curiosity and was willing to go. Mayor Carson suddenly recollected that he had business at the office, and we were hastily joined by Mr. Clark, who appeared to think His Satanic Majesty had visited Brownsville to protest against the observances of the Sunday law.

At the time these missiles were thrown there were three policemen in the yard, who saw nothing of them until the concussion was heard. And of all that have been hurled none have been seen by those on watch till they reached the house. Not only have policemen been thus baffled, but squads and throngs of neighbors who have been on the qui vive have been also deluded. This afternoon the daughter received a contusion on the head while overseeing the dinner, and the doors had to be closed and windows protected.

Among the many who were attracted to the strange scene this evening was Mr. Yturria, the extensive wholesale merchant on Elizabeth Street. While awaiting developments he was hit, without warning, on the head by a brick, which inflicted a severe scalp wound. And tonight we learn that the fusillade is more brisk than ever.

The missiles fell at intervals during the day and up to about nine o'clock at night, which would seem to indicate that it is the work of human hands. On the other hand, every vigilance has been employed to discover the author without avail. Policemen and citizens have been hit while watching, and sufficient numbers have been on the alert to cover ordinary range. Clerk Glaevecke discounts the idea that any supernatural agency is employed, and firmly believes it is the work of the neighbor's servants, who will be arrested tonight.

THE LATEST
Quoted by the *Daily Express* from
the *Democrat*, a few days later:

The firing of brickbats at county clerk Glaevecke's house ceased on Saturday night, and the invisible fiend rigidly observed the Sunday law, and the occupants had begun to think that peace had come with the arrest of Mr. Yznaga's remaining servants. But on Monday, at about 10 o'clock, it recommenced. Mr. Yznaga returned home on Sunday, and aided Mr. Glaevecke in every way to discover the perpetrator, and arrest him. He called together all his servants, and while thus gathered the firing began again, which would seem to disarm any suspicion that might be directed against them. On Monday night but two were fired. On Tuesday the boy Anastasio was again hit on the head, and a hot brick fell in the yard, and several have been thrown today. The cook has become thoroughly alarmed at these strange manifestations and has quitted the house. No one has yet been able to discover the bricks in the air, or until they reach the house, and the trees and foliage surrounding the house are untouched by the missiles. Truly, it is a strange proceeding.

The quoted articles appear in *Studies in Brownsville History*, edited by Milo Kearney. No other articles about the strange occurrences at Clerk Glaevecke's home were available. My personal opinion is that a very bad poltergeist set off the brick bombardment, and we have to hope he finally tired of his mischievous activity and let the family get back to the business of peaceful living once more.

A Dead Dog's Devotion

An acquaintance of mine who lives in the Valley shared a personal experience with me recently. She requested that I use all the facts, except for her name, and I shall respect her wishes. I will call her Mary.

Now Mary is an elderly widow who lives in a tiny white frame cottage in a small community south of McAllen. Her husband had been a citrus farmer before his death. They had no children, but Mary was very devoted to a little gray toy poodle whom she called Buttons because of his shiny little shoe-button eyes. The dog slept in a little basket beside Mary's bed. Sometimes if Mary overslept, Buttons would wake her up by rearing up on the bed and scratching at the covers to uncover Mary's arm. He would often make a little whimpering noise as if to say, "Wake up! I need to go outside!"

In time, little Buttons became very old and arthritic, and then he developed a heart problem. Mary was heartbroken, but she knew she had to have her beloved pet put to sleep. She vowed never to get another dog to whom she would become so attached.

Several months after the dog died, on a rainy November night, Mary was awakened in the middle of the night by feeling the covers being tugged from her arms. And she heard the unmistakable sound of Buttons' "let me out" whimpers. As she awoke, she looked at the side of the bed, and there in the glow of her night-light she could plainly see two shiny shoe-button eyes staring at her.

Astounded, she turned on the lamp beside her bed. But there was no dog there . . . nothing at all. Mary had been so sure she had seen and heard her little poodle. Unnerved, she decided to get up and go out in the kitchen and make a cup of hot chocolate to calm herself. As she walked through the hallway into the kitchen she was almost overcome by the smell of gas coming from her gas range. Evidently the pilot light had gone out and the odor of gas filled the room. She raised the window and opened the outside door, but it took some time for the noxious fumes to disappear.

Mary always wondered if, had she slept all night in that tiny little cottage with all the doors and windows tightly closed, she would have been "put to sleep" by the gas fumes coming from her kitchen if not for the protective spirit of her little poodle, Buttons, coming back to alert her.

Is There an Explanation for This?

The story I am about to tell you is so unusual that I frankly didn't know what else to call it. Since it isn't exactly (or is it?) a ghost story, I didn't know just what to do with it, but I want to share it with you. It is a true story of an ongoing situation, and therefore I am changing the names of the principals and not mentioning the name of the town, which is in far South Texas.

It was just a few weeks ago that I heard of the experience a young woman I will call Betty Chambers. She and her husband live on a farm a short distance from the town where she serves as the elementary school's librarian. One summer night about a year and a half ago, she woke with a start, from a sound sleep. The room in which she and her husband slept was not very dark, as there is a giant security light mounted outside the bedroom window. Usually the Chambers kept the drapes drawn to darken the room, but tonight they were open and the room was well illuminated. Betty glanced to her right, and there, standing beside the bed, was the figure of a little boy. He looked to be no more than 7 or 8 years old. He had very fair skin that had an almost translucent look to it, big blue eyes with dark circles beneath them, and blond hair. Although he appeared real, Betty said he also looked to be of another era. He wore a collarless buttoned-up white shirt, dark knicker trousers, and had long socks tucked up into the knickers. He looked to be wearing old-fashioned high-buttoned boots. His attire was that of the early 1900s. Betty said she was very startled to see the youngster standing there, staring at her, and yet she was not particularly frightened by the figure. She called out, "Who are you . . . what do you want?" When she spoke, the figure disappeared! Her husband, Bill, awoke and asked her what she had said. Betty told him that she had seen a little boy standing by the bed, and her husband said, "You must be having a bad dream. Go back to sleep." And with that, he rolled over and it was only a few minutes before his deep, even breathing told her that he was fast asleep.

Betty didn't mention seeing the youngster again, but she certainly did not forget the incident, and she thought of the strange nocturnal visitor many times over the rest of the summer.

When school started in late August, Betty was in her library with a group of first-graders clustered about, when the first-grade teacher came to the door with a little boy. She called Betty to come over and meet the youngster, who had been late in enrolling. As she bent down to say hello and take his hand, she said the child looked up at her and she knew. There was no doubt. The same fair skin and blond hair, the same deep-set blue eyes, with the same dark circles beneath them. And unlike the other blue-jean clad little boys, his clothes seemed "different" too, sort of old-fashioned, Betty said.

Betty said she must have had a totally stunned expression on her face, because the first-grade teacher said, "Are you all right?" Betty said she just managed an "uh-huh." The teacher told her the little boy was named Geoffrey, and she introduced him to Betty. Betty asked him, "Are you new here in town?" The youngster replied in a very strange manner for a first-grader. He looked up at her and said, "Yes and no. I know you. I've always known you." Betty said it gave her the cold chills as she recalled seeing that very same little white face, those same dark-circled blue eyes, in her bedroom on that summer night visit.

Betty went on to tell me that all year little Geoffrey would try to sit as close to her chair as he could. He didn't seem to want to mix with the other children, and she would catch him just staring at her. Sometimes he would lean over and say to her... "You know, I've always known you."

The books the youngster seemed to like most were old-fashioned books, with illustrations from the late 1800s and early 1900s. He showed no interest in Ninja Turtles and space adventures like the other children.

This year the youngster is again at school, and he still comes to the library story sessions. Betty says he is beginning to mix more with the other children, but there is still something very strange, very disturbing, and rather sad, about the little boy. And he still continues to tell her... "Don't you know? I've always known you."

Has anyone any explanation for this? I have had several psychics suggest that this is a classic case, supportive of reincarnation. Have you a better explanation?

CHAPTER 3

History and Mystery in Far South Texas

BRIGHT SHINES BAILEY'S LIGHTS
Docia Williams

Oh, there are lots of phantom lights
That light the still and foggy nights;
Lights that bob along a fence,
Or in the forests, dark and dense.
Lights, no bigger than a ball,
And lights, we've heard, near six feet tall!
Lights like those on Bailey's Prairie,
Big, and bold, and downright scary...
That's seen to come, and seen to go
'Bout every seven years or so.
Oh, so strange, these ghostly lights
That come to haunt our Texas nights!

The Light on Bailey's Prairie

Down near Angleton there's a place known as Bailey's Prairie. "Brit" Bailey, for whom it is named, was one of the most colorful of Texas' frontier characters. What was the truth, and what was fiction, has all gotten sort of tangled up over the years as different tale spinners talk or write about the colorful figure.

Brit, a hard-living, hard-drinking, sometimes controversial but always highly interesting Texas frontiersman, still seems to appear from time to time! At least that's what folks around Bailey's Prairie say. Bailey's appearances, which take the form of a big ball of light, known as Bailey's light, seem to take place about every seven years. Old Brit has carved himself a unique and permanent niche in the "Hall of Fame" of Texas "ghostdom."

Having read numerous accounts of Bailey's life, death, and subsequent hauntings, all of which did not always agree, I was delighted when I was contacted by his great-great-granddaughter, Mary Lou Polley Featherston, of Port Arthur. Her letter stated, "I was a Polley, great-granddaughter of Mary Bailey Polley, daughter of Brit Bailey. She married Joseph H. Polley who was also one of the Old Three Hundred. (This refers to Stephen F. Austin receiving permission from the Mexican government to bring 300 Anglo families into Texas in April of 1823.)

James Briton "Brit" Bailey was born on August 1, 1779, in North Carolina. He took pride in being descended from Robert Bruce of Scotland. As a young man, he moved about a good bit, and lived in both Tennessee and Kentucky. During the War of 1812 he served as a U.S. Navy captain.

In 1812 he packed up his wife, Edith Smith Bailey, and their family of six offspring, and came to Texas where they settled on a piece of property along the Brazos River in what is now known as Brazoria County. This land grant was under Stephen F. Austin's jurisdiction. At first, it's said that Austin tried to oust Bailey and his family when he

(Austin) learned that Bailey had served time in the Kentucky state penitentiary for forgery. Bailey often stated it wasn't serving in the pen that caused him embarrassment; it was the term he'd served in the Kentucky legislature that set heavy on his conscience. After paying his debts to society, Bailey packed up his family and came to Texas, just wanting a new start where they could be left alone. The settler finally got squared away with Austin, and while they were never really friendly, Austin accepted Bailey in July of 1824 as one of the "Old Three Hundred." He was able to live and die on his original land claim, a "league of land."

In 1824 Austin used Bailey's cabin to meet with settlers who lived along the lower Brazos, where they took an oath of loyalty to Mexico's federal constitution in 1824. At the same meeting a company of militia was organized, and Brit was appointed as a lieutenant. That same year he took part in the Battle of Jones Creek. This was a no-win fight between Captain Randel Jones and his group of some twenty-three settlers, and a party of thirty or so Karankawa braves who were camped on a tributary of the San Bernard River. The Indians had massacred some settlers, so Austin authorized Jones to go after them. Both sides suffered losses in the skirmish, and no one came out the victor.

Because he was a good talker, Bailey was often called upon by Austin to negotiate with the Indians.

Tired of the cramped conditions of his little cabin, in 1827 Bailey contracted with Stephen Nicholson and Peter Reynolds to build him a frame house 18 feet square, with 9-foot galleries on all sides. The finished house was painted bright red! Bailey paid the builders the sum of $220 in cash and the balance in cattle and hogs. A visitor to Bailey's place in 1831 wrote to a friend that Bailey's red house "sure had a novel appearance."

Bailey became very successful as a cattle rancher and cotton grower and gradually expanded his land holdings until he owned a great deal of real estate from Houston south to the Gulf Coast.

The Mexican government evidently thought highly of Bailey, because in 1829 General Viesca commissioned him a captain in the militia.

Brit could be the epitome of the solid citizen; responsible and trustworthy, a good businessman and a good leader. But he had two faults. He loved his liquor, and he had a very short fuse. He thoroughly enjoyed a good fight, and when he was bored or just a little too liquored up, he'd pick a fight just for the sheer fun of it!

His short temper showed itself on many occasions. One time, when a horse he was riding wasn't behaving to his liking, he reached down and bit the critter's ear until the blood flowed. The mustang, not taking kindly to such ill treatment, bucked and threw Bailey to the ground. Not to be bested, Brit promptly took out his hunting knife and slit the poor horse's throat!

One afternoon when his family was away, old Brit got pretty well inebriated. He hadn't counted on the circuit-riding preacher knocking on his door to seek lodging for the night. Brit greeted the churchman with his customary greeting, "Walk in, stranger." He told the preacher he could stay the night if he would agree to abide by the house rules. Not quite knowing what the "rules" were, the man of the cloth hesitated a minute, but needing a place to stay, he agreed, feeling quite sure the "house rules" couldn't amount to much. After supper, Brit picked up his rifle and told the preacher to disrobe and then get up on the table and dance a jig that was called the "Juba," an African dance popular with the local black population. The preacher told Brit he didn't know how to dance, but a shot aimed at the preacher's foot convinced him he could dance pretty well after all! He stumbled around on the table top, "jigging" as best he could while one of Brit's black servants played "Juba" on the fiddle!

It was said that Brit was just about the hardest drinker in all of Austin's colony, a dubious honor. The Bailey family history records tales of some of his most noteworthy sprees. One Saturday night, Brit, accompanied by a black boy named Jim, rode into town for a little partying. There was a revival going on, and most of Brit's usual drinking companions had been dragged to the camp meeting by their wives. Brit was pretty let down. He and Jim rode on back out to Brit's place, and after sitting under the old oak tree pulling on his jug for a good long while, Brit decided to liven things up a bit. He really lit up the night when he set fire to the corn crib, and sat drinking and admiring the flames till all his corn had gone up in smoke. It's said he probably would have set fire to the house as well if his favorite daughter hadn't arrived and talked him out of it!

There are all sorts of tales about Brit's drinking escapades, and unfortunately, most of them are true!

Finally, the hard-drinking character took sick and died of what they called cholera fever on December 6, 1832, at the age of sixty-three. At the time of his death his marital status was a subject of controversy, also. When he arrived in Texas in 1821, he brought his wife, Edith Smith Bailey, and their six children. However, an 1826 census of the Austin Colony lists his wife's name as Nancy. In his last will and testament he left his property to his "beloved Nancy and our two girls, Sarah and Margaret." The three surviving children that Brit and Edith brought with them to Texas were disinherited, without any "just cause." In 1838 Elizabeth Milburn and Mary Polley petitioned to have the will declared null and void, claiming they were Brit's legitimate children and that Nancy was only "represented" to be Brit's wife. (She might have been a common-law wife.) The plea was first denied, and then the will was set aside in January of 1839, some seven years after Brit's death.

Now, Bailey made some mighty strange requests concerning his burial, too. For one thing, he insisted he be buried standing up because he had "never stooped to any man while alive, and didn't intend to change after death." He wanted his gun placed over his shoulder, and his powder horn nearby. He wanted to be buried facing west, because he'd been moving in that direction all his life, and wanted to be facing in that direction when he crossed over into the next world. And one last request, he wanted a big, full, jug of whiskey planted right at his feet!

Nancy Bailey saw that his instructions were carried out. A huge hole, over eight feet deep, and "big around as a wash tub," was dug in a pecan grove near the red house. The remains were placed in a pine coffin, and provided with a gun and ammunition as requested. But when Bubba, a favorite slave of Bailey's, a giant of a man, came up with a huge jug of whiskey to plant at Bailey's feet, Mrs. Bailey would have none of that. Bubba insisted that it was what his master had requested, but on that one request, Mrs. Bailey flatly refused. It is said she jerked the jug away from Bubba and threw it out the window. She said Brit had had more than enough of that stuff on earth, and she didn't think he needed any wherever he was headed to in the great beyond. And that's evidently what caused all the trouble to start out on Bailey's Prairie!

Bubba used to talk a lot about old Brit. And he would always conclude his stories saying that "Marse Bailey don't stand easy in his grave. He's still out huntin' dat jug of whiskey."

A few years after Brit died, the place was sold to John Thomas, who brought his wife, Ann, there to live. He had heard tales that the old red house was haunted, but he hadn't told his young wife. Soon after they moved in, business called John away. On a very dark night, Ann and a servant girl were sleeping in the bedroom when something suddenly awakened Ann. The night was very dark, but darkness had never frightened her. No, there was something different, a "presence" that she felt. She gazed towards the door and could barely make out the form of a big man. She instinctively knew that this was no mortal man. She knew she was seeing a ghost! As the figure seemed to drift towards her, she was far too frightened to scream. As it came to the foot of her bed, it seemed to stoop and grope around under the bed. Then the figure retreated to the doorway and disappeared.

The servant girl, named Malinda, had also been awakened by the figure. She was too petrified to cry out. She told Mrs. Thomas that she (Mrs. Thomas) was sleeping in the very bed in which Brit Bailey had died four years before! This thought brought no comfort to the frightened Mrs. Thomas, and she promptly changed bedrooms!

As soon as John Thomas returned from his trip, Ann told him of her experience, which he explained away as a nightmare, or just a figment of her overactive imagination. But she said she wouldn't sleep in their bedroom again. He said he would go sleep in the room and show her that there was nothing to fear. In fact, he said, Old Brit had been a friend of his, and if he made another nocturnal visit, John joked he'd just get up and shake the old man's hand!

Well, in the bedroom opposite to where she now slept, a few nights later Ann heard a terrible, unearthly scream. She could, and did, move this time. She burst into the room, and found her husband sitting on the side of his bed, rigid with fear. His face was streaked with sweat, and he was just able to gasp... "I saw him! It was old man Bailey. I saw him plain as day!" It wasn't too long after that that the Thomases moved away from the big red house.

As the years rolled by, the old house that had belonged to Bailey stood vacant and forlorn. But something was still around. As new dwellings rose up on the other side of Bailey's Prairie, people began to report seeing strange lights. In 1850 Colonel Mordello Munson was awakened by the mournful wails of his hounds. When he went outside to investigate, he found his dogs crawling on their stomachs, cowering in fear. Then he saw a great column of light, the size of a big man! It was some distance away. Although he and a friend pursued it for most of the night, on horseback, they were never able to catch up to the elusive and mysterious light.

People living around the Prairie still talk about the lights. It is my understanding that Catherine Munson Foster, the well-known Brazoria-area folklorist and writer, now owns Bailey's Prairie. She wrote about it in her book, *Ghosts Along the Brazos*. She says the light would most often appear on late fall nights. It would circle around as if searching for something. Everybody who knew about Brit Bailey and his strange burial rites were convinced that his ghost was still abroad, searching for his jug.

Gradually the lights have lessened in size and intensity, until they seem to appear only once in a great while. Around West Columbia these days they say that Brit can only work up enough strength to shine his strange light every seven years. Some folks say he has caused cars to stop dead on the road, and some even say he caused a gas blowout when oil well workers worked too close to the site of his grave, an unmarked site somewhere up on Bennett's Ridge that no one can seem to locate now.

If you accept the seven-year theory, then figure that Brit should be around again in about 1995. That is, if he is still searching. After so much looking for years and years, he may have found his lost jug by now and be well settled down into an eternal stupor.

The Legend of Knox Crossing

While researching the South Texas ghost situation, it became my privilege to enjoy a highly interesting correspondence with Wilbur Butler of Beaumont, who shares my interest in "spirits."

Wilbur first heard the story of Knox Crossing from his mother, Wilma. He said it had been so long ago he can't even recall when he first heard it, but it must have been over forty years back. His mother was a schoolteacher at Choate, a little community on Highway 239 between Kenedy and Goliad. She taught in the Mexican school. In those days, the Anglo and Hispanic children attended different schools, Wilbur explained.

Mrs. Butler said back in the early 1930s, one of her students, who was named Pedro Chavez, told her what had actually happened to him, and of course, she repeated the story to her family. Young Wilbur and some of his teenage friends investigated the area where Pedro had his strange encounter, but they never had a sighting. Years later, Wilbur and his wife and children visited the area and this time came back convinced that there was something to the story after all. Wilbur sent me the story he had written about Pedro's strange experience and has given me the permission to quote it to you, just as he wrote it:

There is no such thing as a ghost, is there? This is the question that seventeen-year-old Pedro Chavez pondered as he walked along. The dirt road beneath his feet, lit only by the light of the moon, paralleled the San Antonio River down near the farming community of Choate, Texas. In the moonlight Pedro could make out an opening in the shadows in the trees up ahead. He knew the area well, and so he knew the break in the shadows, that indicated another dirt road intersecting the one on which he traveled. He must now follow its path on his way home, just as he had many times before.

It was late at night, for Pedro had stayed at the dance much too long. On previous occasions he had always left early enough to pass this way well before midnight. But he had so much fun dancing with all the girls, he let time get away from him. Anyway, as he danced, he kept telling himself, "There's no such thing as a ghost." It was easy to convince himself as the music played and he held pretty Maria in his arms. Now alone, as he trudged along the dark dirt road, it wasn't quite so easy to believe!

As he neared the intersection of the roads, his pace grew slower. Stopping to check the time, he fumbled in his pocket for the watch he had borrowed from his father. By the light of the moon he could see it was 11:58 p.m. Pedro kissed the small gold cross that dangled from the watch fob, and made the sign of the cross across his chest with one hand as he stuffed the watch back into his pocket with the other. He now quickened his pace, hoping to get across the river before anything happened. As he reached the intersection, he stopped and peered around the corner. His knees trembled as he stood and looked over the river bridge in front of him. It was an old wooden structure with a heavy wood framework on both sides and across the top.

He had come to Knox Crossing, well known for its apparitions. Pedro had crossed over this bridge many times before and nothing had ever happened. But tonight a cold wind seemed to pass through Pedro, as he stood there, his heart pounding and his breathing becoming labored. Yet, he saw nothing. Just maybe, if he walked quickly and quietly, nothing would happen.

Pedro stepped out onto the plank floor of the bridge. He had gone only a few paces when a light appeared at the other end. The light seemed to float in midair. As Pedro continued, he kept to the opposite side of the bridge from the light, which now began to move, as if coming to meet him. While the light was still some distance away, he began to see a form taking shape behind it. The light appeared to be suspended from a frail arm held high above a body. As his eyes moved down the arm to where it joined the body, Pedro noticed a beautiful white flowing gown. But something was wrong! As his eyes searched the darkness to find the identity of the young woman who carried the light, he realized there was no head above her shoulders! The cold steel of a knife blade being driven between his shoulder blades could not have chilled him more! Closer and closer she came. He could see her quite plainly now. Pedro could hardly force his eyes from the void where her head should be. It just wasn't there! Close enough now to reach out and touch her, she passed on by. Pedro's eyes now focused on her other arm and hand, which she held at her side. She was clutching something. Only then did Pedro realize, she carried her head by its raven black hair! The very moment his eyes met the eyes of the head she carried, a fiery green glow pierced him to his very soul. Unable to move, he could only watch as the figure moved on past. The head she carried slowly turned as she moved away, keeping its hollow green eyes focused on him.

It seemed to take an eternity before Pedro could move, and even then he dared not look back. He had reached the end of the bridge before he finally regained his senses. Standing there, he looked back across the bridge and thought, "Did I really see her, or did I just imagine the whole thing?"

Fifty years after Pedro had told the story to his teacher, Mrs. Butler, her son, Wilbur, and his wife, Ann, accompanied by two of their children, Stacy and Beau, decided to check out the old bridge at Knox Crossing. Wilbur said they parked their station wagon near the same intersection that Pedro had described and then just sat in the darkness to see if anything might appear. Wilbur said he had grown up in that area, and over the years had visited the place without seeing anything unusual. But this particular night they were not disappointed. Just before midnight they turned off the car's engine and lights. They quietly held a conversation when suddenly all four of them froze without warning. Butler says a light suddenly appeared in the field to the left of the road and floated above the tall weeds there for a short time. Then it began to move in the direction of the dirt road which leads to the old river bridge. Butler stated, "As it came to the road it changed course, and rather than going in the direction of the bridge as one might expect, it came directly at us, traveling at an electrifying rate of speed."

Wilbur said not one among the four of them had Pedro's nerve to stay and see what mysterious forms it might hold. "We drove away like a bat out of hell with a ball of fire tied to our tail!" But unlike Pedro, the Butler family never doubted what they had seen. Four sets of eyes had seen the same mysterious "ghost light."

A Postscript to Wilbur's Strange Story

Wilbur Butler knows that he and his family saw something highly unusual that night they went ghost hunting near the old Knox Crossing Bridge. Recently, a friend of Wilbur's, Nancy Vernon of Rockport, sent him a Xeroxed page from the late Ed Syers' book *Off the Beaten Trail*, which describes an eerie ghost light more or less in the vicinity of where the Butlers had their strange sighting.

Syers stated, "There are some valid ghost believers in the brush country below San Antonio; though over the past, they have reacted with an insensitive vigor, reaching for firearms or clubs. Take the old moss-covered bridge between Kenedy and Runge and what stalked below. Kenedy's Beauregard Moye, who looks like a white-haired cowboy, and is, took me out.

"Long ago, he and the other boys chased "The Thing" night after night, towards the dark timber edging Pleas Butler's pastures (note: Pleas Butler was Wilbur's great-uncle), trying to get between it and the river.

"It kept changing size," Mr. Moye reflected. "Big as a wagon in the trees, then above them, like a barrel on fire. Get close? It'd turn off like a light.

"Otto von Schroeder, a fast dead shot (and a neighbor of the Butler family, according to Wilbur), and strong as they came, got it down once and tried to stomp it. In the confusion, he might have thrown a couple of shots, but he never could get a real grip on it.

"It retaliated angrily, soon after, by drifting right through three-strand wire, burning too bright to look at, and chasing Miss Sallie Ricks' buggy into a ditch. Miss Sallie wasn't hurt, but she was considerably put upon; and Mrs. Moye has kept an eye on that bridge for her ever since. But he still doesn't understand." Wilbur says after reading this account in the Syer's book, maybe what he always thought was Pedro's headless woman's lantern might just be "the Thing" that Mr. Moye just didn't understand. We don't either. Do you?

Reeves Thicket's Ranch House
and the Interesting Tales it Could Tell

Between Victoria and Goliad, off Highway 59, there's a small community called Reeves Thicket. It used to be one huge ranch, but over the years the land has been subdivided and sold off in large lots where over 300 families reside today. The original ranch belonged to one man, John Reeves, Sr., who came here from Pikes County, Georgia, in the early 1840s. It is believed his wife probably died in childbirth, because Reeves came to Texas alone, leaving his father and oldest son, John Jr., behind for a time. Finally, after he acquired considerable land holdings and established a law practice, he sent for young John and his father to join him. John Jr., brought his wife, Cady, and their nine children with him. Later, another child, their tenth, William Worth, was born after they had settled into their new Texas home.

After a few years, John Jr. and his family moved to the banks of Coleto Creek, in the area now known as Reeves Thicket. John Sr. was pretty old by then (he was born in 1779) and needed looking after, so John and Cady cared for him until he passed away in 1863. His grave is one of those in the rather sizeable Reeves family cemetery that sits on what is known as Reeves Hill today.

John Reeves, Jr., died in 1868, and at that time, one of his sons, Jonathan, whom they called Tobe, moved the family home from the banks of the Coleto Creek to its present location. It was a big house and had to be moved uphill about half a mile. Evidently it was slowly (how else?) moved uphill by being placed on huge logs, which were rolled along by teams of sturdy mules. The place that we visited recently is smaller than its original size. According to the present owner, it suffered considerable storm damage a number of years ago.

Today's owner of the Reeves ranch house, the old cemetery, and quite a few acres of the original holdings, is a direct descendant of the founding Reeves family, and he is "obsessed," as he puts it, with taking care of, and preserving, the old family homestead. A young man in his mid-30s, Charlie Faupel is a storehouse of knowledge of regional history, both factual and legendary. During a recent visit to the ranch, he was kind enough to tell us a lot of interesting things about the house and the land surrounding it, and about the spirits he feels still guard the place. According to Charlie, Tobe was probably the most colorful of the Reeves family members. He took over the ranch shortly after the Civil War ended, endured drought, hard times, outlaws, and a yellow fever epidemic. Tobe was called the "law west of the Coleto" and he was said to have administered justice in his own way. For instance, one hot summer day in the 1870s he'd been out with his men rounding up some cattle. When they got home, they found someone had stolen some of their horses. Along with some of his ranch hands, Tobe rode out to catch the culprit. They crossed over Reeves Creek and rode over to Fleming Prairie, where they found the horse thief. A shootout was the result. Tobe remained on his horse; the thief took cover and managed to shoot Tobe's left ear off. This really made Tobe angry, according to Charlie (well, who wouldn't be mad about losing an ear?). Now, Tobe had planned to be "fair" with the culprit and give him a hearing before hanging him, but he was so enraged that he just up and shot him right there and buried him somewhere out there on the land. Charlie says there's some evidence of that gravesite today, and there are probably numerous other graves scattered over the vast estate.

There was quite a big outlaw gang around in the 1860s and '70s known as the "Brookins gang." They lived on the Coleto and made raids on ranches in the area, but it is said they gave Tobe Reeves' place a wide berth!

When the Reeves family first settled the area, they decided to call their ranch Reeves Thicket because of the thick brush that dots the countryside. It was in an area once crossed by the Old Spanish Trail, and signs of the trail are evident even today. There was also an old wagon road that followed Coleto Creek. Charlie Faupel said his great-great-grandfather Tobe was a "really, truly" cattle baron of his time, and he showed us the old live oak hanging tree that was used to put more than one desperado out of business. It has a huge limb that sort of stands out, and this was probably the hanging limb. Charlie says it's hard to get a horse to ride by the tree. In fact, he says, there are lots of places on the ranch that just naturally spook a horse, sensitive as those creatures are to otherworldly beings!

Charlie loves to talk about his rambling old wooden ranchhouse and the surrounding land, which he inherited and in which he takes great pride. He says it is strange, but his feeling for the old house is like the house owns him, and he is sort of possessed by it and the ties it has with his ancestors. Well, it is very old. And very charming. And not many people can boast of living in a house that so many generations of their family have lived in, and died in, as well. Charlie said if his old bed could talk, it could tell lots of stories, as it came by wagon over 135 years ago from Georgia, and was where the colorful Tobe died of pneumonia in 1890, and where his grandmother, Isabel, was born in 1901. There are pictures and mementos everywhere depicting important events in the Reeves' family history: old photographs, portraits, and memorabilia of all kinds.

The house wasn't always a homestead, however. Charlie says for a time it was sort of abandoned and used to store feed and hay. Six generations just sort of wore it out, but Charlie, of the seventh generation, is doing all he can to keep up the place. That's why the spirits which Charlie thinks are peaceful and just kind and gentle presences are there,

Reeves Thicket "hanging tree"

because they are happy he is looking after the place. He also revealed that the house was placed atop the hill overlooking the creek where once the family slaves had been buried in unmarked graves. He thinks his office and bedroom are probably located right over the old slave cemetery!

Charlie told me that Union soldiers once rode right through the house on their horses, and once the roof caught fire during an Indian attack. There's still a lead bullet embedded in the front porch banister, and there are also three bullet holes in the dining room wall. A large section of the house was destroyed by a storm in 1942.

Today, Charlie believes that UFOs make regular visits to Reeves Thicket. His cousin Susan Purcell, with whom I later spoke, believes this as well. Not in the realm of ghosts, but very fascinating nonetheless, Charlie says the big attraction at the ranch, besides his pet llamas, is frequent sightings of what must be described as unidentified flying objects. The bachelor owner of Reeves Thicket Ranch and his frequent visitors enjoy sitting on the long front porch of the ranchhouse to watch the hovering lighted objects. They will hover for quite a long time, sometimes, and then dart off with great speed, into space. Various law enforcement agencies have been told of the sightings, and they are interested, but what could they do, other than show interest? It would be difficult indeed to arrest anything that elusive or that fast moving, and what would the charges be, anyhow, other than "trespassing on Reeves Thicket Outer Space?"

Yes, Reeves Thicket is a very fascinating place. The old ranch house is interesting, and the owner, Charlie Faupel, is a unique and interesting young man. So why wouldn't any watchful spirits out there be pretty fascinating, too?

A Strange Visitor to Reeves Thicket

Over at Reeves Thicket, Charlie Faupel's cousin Susan Purcell and her husband, Kim, have reported some might strange things, too. The thickly wooded ranch land holds many mysteries. The thicket used to be the hangout of a lot of unsavory characters, including Sam Bass and his band of outlaws. When somebody got crossways with Bass or one of his gang, that somebody usually got shot! Susan says she's sure that there are lots of unmarked graves scattered all over the place, and that is one reason why the horses so often get spooked when they are out riding over the place.

The Purcells, like cousin Charlie, often have seen what they refer to as UFOs flying over their property, often hovering for some time over a certain spot. And then, there's the strange little "man-creature" wearing a heavy long brown coat! When Susan's son was just a toddler, she used to take him for walks in his stroller. One time the infant gurgled and smiled and put his little arms out in front of him as if he was amused or delighted at something he saw. A look in the direction in which the baby was looking revealed a glimpse of a "small creature, about four feet tall, wearing a very long brown cloak, which appeared to be quite heavy." "It," whatever it was, was about sixty feet away from Susan and she didn't get a good look. Just one glimpse, then it was gone. A couple of weeks later she saw the same figure again.

Then, a few days later, Kim Purcell was out working on the place on his tractor. About noon one day he saw the same "little person" peeping around from behind a tree. A small figure, clad in the same clothing Susan had described, has also been seen around the banks of a pond on the property which is called Shell and Trigger Lake. Although there were stories around for a while that an old hermit was living around there, the Purcells don't think this person, or "thing" they have seen, quite fits that description. They wonder. Is he a midget, and if so where would he have come from and where does he live? Or is he a ghost? Or is he a creature from another planet, in view of there being so many sightings of UFOs in the vicinity?

Susan has seen the strange figure three times in all, while her husband has seen him twice. The second time Kim saw him was early one morning, about 2 a.m., as he prepared to depart on his morning paper route. He says he saw something and believed it was the same small figure that he had seen before. It was running away from Kim's parked pickup truck.

The Spirits at Sutton's Mott

What? A "mott?" When I first heard of Sutton's Mott, I must confess I wondered, what in the world is a mott? The word just wasn't in my vocabulary! It didn't appear in either my Webster's Collegiate or New World dictionaries. I finally found the word "mott" in my new Reader's Digest Illustrated Encyclopedic Dictionary. A "mott" is a Western U.S. term referring to a "small stand of shrubs or trees on a prairie." It apparently comes from the Mexican-Spanish word, "mote," meaning "shrub." So much for clarification!

Susan Purcell, about whom I wrote in the previous story, who lives over at Reeves Thicket near Victoria, told me for years people living in those parts have considered the thick stand of oak trees off Highway 77 that they call Sutton's Mott to be a "very haunted place."

Susan told me that lots of people have said hunting dogs, who usually love to get out in the open country and range around, won't go near the place to retrieve a dove or flush a quail. They'll just back off and whine and whimper, and the hair stands up on the backs of their necks when they get close to the place. And horses become terribly agitated, spooked, whenever they are anywhere near the grove. In fact, many cowboys who live in the area are not ashamed to admit they'll ride for miles out of their way rather than pass by the grove they call Sutton's Mott.

It seems a long time ago, sometime around 1850, there was a goat herder named William Sutton (they called him Old Bill) who lived up there where the thick stand of trees grew on an otherwise pretty barren area. He wasn't a particularly pleasant character to start with, and goat herds were not considered socially acceptable in a country where cattle ranching reigned supreme.

Apparently Sutton lived alone. Although he made a pretty good living off his goats, he also had a sideline source of income which netted him considerable cash. He loaned money to ranchers and then demanded a quick payback with a high rate of interest. It seems he got into a lot of arguments over his business terms when he went to collect some of his debts. One time, when tempers flared really high, old Bill Sutton shot a local rancher. When the son of the shooting victim learned what had happened to his father, he swore revenge on Sutton. The next Sunday, when Sutton attended Mass, as was his custom, over at the chapel at the Presidio of La Bahia near Goliad, the young man was waiting for him. When Sutton exited the chapel, the old goat herder was shot down right in the doorway. The young man had his revenge, and no one was particularly sorry to learn of Sutton's death.

Since the goat herder left no apparent heirs, there was no one who knew where Sutton might have sequestered his rumored wealth. Most people were pretty sure he had buried it within the thick grove of oak trees that they called the "mott."

Over the years, many people have come to try their luck at digging up treasure. All of them have left in a hurry! It is said that after they calmed down and quit babbling, many people have reported seeing terrible, frightful sights . . . headless forms hanging from the trees, suspended from great chains. All sorts of weird noises have been reported, too, until finally very few people will venture close to the thick grove of trees.

According to my friend Susan, the mott is still haunted. Old Bill, who was known to be pretty mean in life, is apparently just as mean as a ghost. Maybe he even called upon some pretty devilish fellow spirits to help him protect his gold! We believe he's still there, guarding his money.

If you would care to search for it, call me. I have a pretty good set of directions.

The Ghosts at Goliad

"Remember the Alamo!" "Remember Goliad!" These were the rallying cries shouted by General Sam Houston's forces on April 21, 1836, as they attacked the slumbering forces of General Antonio Lopez de Santa Anna at the Battle of San Jacinto. This battle won independence for Texas from Mexico's domination. Now, today, the whole world recognizes the shout, "Remember the Alamo!," but not nearly so well known, especially among non-Texans, is the poignant story of the massacre of Colonel James Fannin and his Texan forces that were stationed at the old Presidio of La Bahia at Goliad.

The establishment of the Royal Presidio of La Bahia ("the bay") in the year 1721 was in direct response to the encroachment by the French into the Spanish Province of Texas. The first La Bahia presidio was located on the banks of Garcitas Creek near present-day Lavaca Bay, on the remains of the ill-fated French Fort St. Louis which Robert Cavelier LaSalle had built. In 1726 the Spaniards decided to abandon this location and relocate in an inland position near Mission Valley, just above present-day Victoria. Finally, in 1749, the presidio was relocated to its present location just outside of the town of Goliad.

This presidio became the only fort responsible for the defense of the coastal area and eastern province of Texas. Soldiers from the presidio assisted the Spanish army which fought the British during the American Revolution. This action gives Goliad the distinction of being one of the only communities west of the Mississippi River that participated in the American Revolution!

Another little-known fact is that the cattle industry of Texas had its real beginnings at La Bahia, with the soldiers overseeing the herds from the missions of Rosario and Espiritu Santo, which were located nearby. Troop escorts for the cattle drive which supplied other Spanish settlements of the Southwest were commanded by the garrison at the presidio.

When Mexico won her independence from Spain, in 1821, the La Bahia became a station for Mexican forces. On October 9, 1835, a group of Texas citizens, led by Captain George Collinsworth, entered Goliad, attacked the presidio, and succeeded in taking possession of the fort. Later, at the presidio, the first Declaration of Texas Independence was signed by ninety-two citizens of Texas on December 20, 1835. In the Declaration, which was distributed throughout other municipalities in Texas, the settlers boldly stated their desire for full independence from the dictatorial government of the self-styled "Napoleon of the West," General Antonio Lopez de Santa Anna.

Texas forces were soon stationed at the old presidio, under the command of Colonel James Walker Fannin. One of the darkest days in Texas history was Palm Sunday, March 27, 1836, when Fannin and 352 of his men were executed a week after they were captured at the Battle of Coleto. First, Santa Anna had put every man at the Alamo to the sword. Joining that valiant force of 189 men in death were all the men stationed at Goliad. As the grim news of the needless execution of so many men reached the United States, volunteers streamed forth to assist the Texans who were at war with a dictator who was determined to fight a war of extermination!

Today, over one hundred and fifty years later, the old walls of the historic fortress and its adjacent Chapel of our Lady of Loreto

Presidio of La Bahia at Goliad, Chapel of our Lady of Loreto

sometimes echo with the mournful sounds of spirits returning from that troubled and turbulent time in the history of the great state of Texas.

Kevin Young, San Antonio historian and writer, was the museum director at La Bahia some years back. He recalls that his living quarters at the presidio were just a few paces away from where James Fannin and his men were summarily executed. Many a day, and night, Kevin said he felt "cold spots," and uneasy feelings like someone was watching him. He never actually saw a ghost, but he says he knows they are there!

Kevin suggested I contact the current museum director, Newton Warzecha. Only stationed there a little over a year, Warzecha said he has had no ghostly encounters "yet," but he didn't doubt the stories he had heard from many people who had reported either seeing, or hearing, the unearthly visitors to the old presidio.

The *Victoria Advocate* on Sunday, November 8, 1992, ran a very interesting feature article by a staff writer, David Tewes. Tewes had interviewed Jim Leos, Jr., a guard with Triple D Security Company who had been assigned to guard some equipment at the presidio that was to be used for the Cattle Baron's Ball. Leos, long used to nighttime duty, expected just a routine evening at the quiet old former fort. But just before midnight, strange things began to happen. The quietness of the night was broken by the "eerie, shrill cries of nearly a dozen terrified infants." It sent shivers down the spine of the veteran security guard and former deputy sheriff from Victoria. Leos said the cries indicated "pain and suffering." He couldn't locate where they were coming from at first. He finally realized the cries were coming from one of the dozen or so unmarked graves which are located near the Chapel of our Lady of Loreto.

As suddenly as the crying started, the sounds ended, only to be replaced by the singing of a woman's choir. Although he could see nothing unusual, the mysterious music sounded as if it were coming from the back wall of the old fort. Leos said the women were singing words, but he couldn't make out what they were saying, and the tune was also unfamiliar to him.

The strange singing ended in two or three minutes, but then a much more frightening event occurred. A small friar suddenly appeared! At first, there was a vaporous form arising from the ground in front of the double door that leads into the chapel. Leos said the little friar was only about four feet tall. The robe he wore was black, tied around the waist with a rope. He was barefoot and his face was concealed with a hood.

Leos recalled having heard other people talk about the same apparition. The words of warning came back to him: "Remain perfectly still because this is an aggressive ghost." The shocked Leos just froze where he stood and watched as the priest wandered around from one corner to the other of the old church. The figure then went to each corner of the quadrangle. Leos says he thinks the hooded figure was praying in Latin.

About an hour and a half after the friar disappeared, the apparition of a woman wearing a white dress, which looked somewhat like a wedding dress, materialized in front of one of the unmarked graves that are situated in front of the chapel. It was the same grave from which Leos had heard the cries of the babies, and Leos said the woman appeared to be looking for one of the infants.

The article in the *Advocate* stated, "Then she turned around and looked at me. She drifted maybe a foot or two off the ground and headed towards the back wall."

Leos said the ghostly figure just floated over the wall and out of sight as she headed towards an old cemetery established in the 1700s.

Although teased by his coworkers when he told of his nocturnal adventures, Leos is convinced that what he saw was real, and not the spinoff of a bad dream. After all, he doesn't ever sleep when he is on duty! And Leos knows he isn't the only person who has reported bizarre occurrences around the old presidio.

Many residents who live near the fort have related similar stories. Although Newton Warzecha hasn't seen anything since he has become museum director, he says, "I do not know whether there are spirits there, but I could understand if there are such things, because of all the violence that has taken place there." His assistant, Luiz Cazarez-Rueda, who sometimes lives on the presidio grounds, is rather guarded with his comments when questioned about ghosts. However, the expression on his face indicated to David Tewes, who wrote the article in the *Advocate*, that Rueda knew more than he wanted to tell.

Dorothy Simmons, owner of the Souvenir Closet in Goliad, was watching the museum within the fort one spring day for John Collins, a former director, while he was out running some errands. As she walked through the museum and got to the third room, she heard what she called "celestial humming." A beautiful soprano voice was singing. There was nothing scary about it. She could detect the music only in that one room. When she walked out, it stopped. When she returned, it began again. Although she tried to reason it was the wind, it just wasn't enough to account for the very real sound of music which she heard. Simmons says she believes that we can experience time warps or see just a fleeting glimpse of the other side.

Then, there was the time that Irma Valencia, owner of Irma's Cafe in Goliad, agreed to do some volunteer work at the presidio. It was a hot, humid summer day. As Irma began to clean the furnishings and to wax the floor after the last tourist had departed, only Luiz Cazarez-Rueda, the assistant director, was still there. He had gone outside to take down the flags. As soon as he left, Valencia said, she heard organ music begin to play, accompanying the celestial humming of a woman. She said the music was just all around her, but it stopped when Casarez-Rueda came back inside. At first she thought he had been playing a portable radio, but he said, no, he didn't have a radio. Then he asked her, "So you heard it too?" Although she had been there as a volunteer many times before, Irma said she had never heard the music previously. Once was apparently enough for her, as she has stopped going out to the presidio entirely.

It seems that visitors, often complete strangers to the presidio, have reported strange happenings, also. Cazarez-Rueda said a mother and daughter visited the fort about a year ago just before closing time. The mother soon came back to the entrance and asked Cazarez-Rueda if there were historical reenactors on the property, people dressed up in period costumes to add "atmosphere" to the place. He told her, yes, they were there sometimes on special occasions, but there was no one there on that particular day. The lady assured him she had just seen someone, a lady dressed all in black, with a black veil over her face. She was in the chapel, by the candles, and she was crying as if her heart would break. At the daughter's suggestion, the mother stepped forth to ask the lady what was wrong, to see if she could help. In that instant, the figure totally disappeared!

Cazarez-Rueda tried to get the visitor's name, but the lady didn't stay long enough to say who she was. She just said she wanted to get out of there, and didn't ever plan to come back there again!

There was an interesting article in the *Texan Express* back on October 31, 1984, written by Sandra Judith Rodriguez. She mentioned in her story that many people have reported hearing "mumbling noises," like a group of people praying, when they pass the Chapel of our Lady of Loreto in the evenings.

And several people from the La Bahia area have reported that every so often when they are in their cars, driving alone, they will suddenly see someone sitting on the passenger side of the car. This happens usually when they are just passing over the San Antonio River. In their confusion, some people have said they first thought somebody was in the back seat of the car and had moved to the front seat. They start to talk to the person, but the person does not reply. As they glance again, the person has disappeared. Some people even claim that the person they saw was headless! Talk about goose pimples!

And the La Bahia Restaurant crew, who work pretty late at night, have reported that some evenings when they pass by the old buildings they notice the chapel lights are burning. They know they had been turned off earlier in the evening. They also have reported hearing the cries of a baby, but no babies are ever found in the area.

During the restoration of La Bahia, one of the workmen stayed very late doing some paperwork. He had his dog with him. Suddenly the animal started growling and moving towards its master. The dog seemed very agitated and frightened. About this time, the man heard the cries of a baby outside the door. It seemed very close. He thought a mother with a sick child might be outside, seeking help. He waited for a knock but heard nothing, so he opened the door and peered out. He was surprised when he found no one there. He said the hair stood up on the back of his neck and he was all "goose pimply." He looked all around the presidio and could find absolutely nothing. He just left his paperwork and headed off to town as fast as he could drive.

And so the stories continue; a new one now and then, or a repeat of an oft-told tale. Who are these restless spirits? The crying babies, are they little lost souls of pioneer infants, dead and buried before they were baptized? Or, are they the offspring of Spanish militiamen and their wives? How did the little ones die? Did the Indians kill them in a raid, or was there an epidemic that snuffed out their little lives? The young woman in white ... is her own baby buried somewhere out there in an unmarked grave near the chapel? And who was the little friar in the black robe? Was he a chaplain brought to the presidio to serve the Spanish forces? Is his soul in turmoil because the Spanish forces had to depart when Mexico won her independence from Spain? Or is his spirit disturbed because so many brave men were executed right there next to his beloved chapel? The lady in black who cries in the chapel . . . was she the widow or mother of a soldier who served there? Why does her sorrowing spirit return to weep at the altar? And the music, angelic voices singing long forgotten canticles and hymns; are they songs of praise, or of supplication?

They are all there, caught in a web of timelessness, a multitude of lonely, lost souls, searching . . . sorrowing . . . seeking . . . singing . . . none quite prepared to let go of that life which they lived so briefly, so long ago, in a lonely outpost called La Bahia.

Poor Chipita

In the 1850s and early '60s Chipita Rodriguez lived on the Aransas River not far from the town of San Patricio. Her story is a very sad one and has resulted in her tormented spirit returning again and again to the scenes of her sorrows.

By far the best accounting of Chipita, her life, death, and continued returns to haunt the site of her death, is by Keith Guthrie, a writer from Taft, Texas, whose work, *The Legend of Chipita*, is outstanding.

Quite likely Chipita was a nickname. More than likely her real name was Josefa. She was the daughter of a hard-working Mexican named Pedro Rodriguez who left his Mexican homeland to seek shelter in Texas, away from the dictatorial Santa Anna. Pedro's young wife soon died of a fever, leaving him with a small daughter to raise.

Chipita's father used to tell her stories of her ancestors, the Aztecs. He spoke of the Aztec chief Cuauhtemoc, and his bravery when Cortes was plundering the village. The old chief chose death over telling the Spaniard where the Aztec treasures were hidden. Pedro told little Chepita over and over again as she grew up that to avoid trouble she must learn to "keep silent" just as the Aztec chief had done. Pedro eventually joined the Texas cause during the fight for independence from Mexico and was killed. This left young Chipita to fend for herself. "Be as quiet as the still water" became her watchword as she tried to remain true to her ancestors. Quiet and secretive, no one ever knew much about Chipita.

Somewhere along the way an outlaw took advantage of her. She became his common-law wife. Soon after she bore the man a son, he left her, taking the baby with him. All alone, she was left to make her way in the world as best she could.

Nothing much is known of what happened to her for a number of years until she turned up owning and running a small "inn," which was little more than a shack on the banks of the Aransas River. Her place, called Chipita's Inn, stood by Aldrete Crossing, which was a fairly busy ford crossing back in the 1850s and '60s. All she could offer was a place to sleep and a meager meal, but to weary traveler John Savage, one day in August of 1863, that was enough. Savage was a horse trader. He had just turned a profitable deal up in San Antonio and had $600 in gold in his saddlebags as he headed south to buy more stock. He had ridden hard, and he was tired. Chipita gave him a plate of hot food and pointed to the cot on the front porch of her little shack. He ate and then stretched out to sleep, his gun still strapped to his waist.

The John Welder ranch was about a mile from Chipita's place. The morning after Savage spent the night at the inn, a couple of Welder servants, and Welder's little daughter, Dora, set out in a wagon down to the banks of the Aransas River to gather up some firewood. One of the servants noticed a gunnysack lodged against a log a few feet from shore. She hooked the sack with a stick, but it was heavy and she had to call the other servant to help her. Together they could not move the gunnysack and whatever it held, but as they prodded it with a stick a portion of the material tore, revealing a man's arm to them. They rushed back to get Mr. Welder at the ranch, and he brought some men down to the river. The sack revealed a grisly find, indeed. The dismembered body of John Savage, his head cleaved apart by an ax, was in the sack. His pockets revealed a few coins, some matches and tobacco, and a pocketknife. No one knows whether Savage was buried there on the riverbank, or whether the Welders took the remains off to be buried somewhere on their place.

Savage's last known whereabouts were traced to Chipita's place. And the sheriff's men found bloodstains on her front porch, which Chipita said was chicken blood. No ax was found, either at her place or in the river.

Robbery was considered the motive for the killing. Strangely enough, some time later the $600 in gold, still in Savage's saddlebags, turned up downstream from Chipita's inn. Sheriff William B. Means was sure Chipita was to blame, and he showed up at her place soon after, leading a horse with an empty saddle. When they left, Chipita occupied the saddle.

Chipita was rapidly tried and convicted of the murder of John Savage. Her friend and neighbor Juan Silvera was later arrested as an accomplice. Chipita swore that she was innocent of the crime of killing John Savage. Many believed her, but they did think she knew, but would not tell, who had killed the horse trader.

According to Guthrie's book, numerous women of San Patricio felt sorry for Chipita and did not think she was guilty. They would come to the little jail and bring her food and visit with her. The day before she was sentenced to be hanged, she told her friend Kate McCumber, who had come to bring her some food and visit with her, that she had something she wanted to tell her. She made Kate promise she would not tell another soul for "many years." Kate kept her promise, and it was forty years to the day before she told her daughter what Chipita had told her back on November 12, 1863. Chipita told her she did not kill John Savage. She said after Savage fell asleep she took a little walk along the riverbank as she often did in the evenings. Hearing a commotion at the inn, she returned to her home to see by the dim light a figure of a man stooped over a prostrate body on the ground. The face of the man was revealed in the pale moonlight. It reminded her of her late father. Then she knew. The man who had killed John Savage was her son, whom she had not seen since he was an infant. The son took Savage's horse and the saddlebags of gold, leaving Chipita with a dead man on her front porch. She didn't know what to do. She was small, and Savage was a big man. She ran to get her friend Juan Silvera, who lived on the Aldrete Ranch across the river. She was sure he would help her dispose of the body.

Juan came to help his friend and together they dragged the body, which they had wrapped in gunnysacking, down to the river, which is where the party from the Welder ranch found it the next day.

Chipita swore to Kate that she was innocent, but she could not reveal her son as the killer even if it meant she would hang. If the story she told Kate McCumber was true, an innocent woman was hanged on Friday, November 13, 1863. She became the only woman ever to be hanged in Texas.

There were two other kindly women of the town, sisters Rachel and Eliza Sullivan, who believed in Chipita's innocence. They came early in the morning the day she was to be hanged, bringing warm water so she could bathe herself. Rachel brought her one of her own favorite dresses of blue and white organdy to wear. The sisters combed and braided Chipita's long hair before they departed.

At last the time arrived, and Chipita was taken by wagon down to the riverbanks where a grave had been dug near the mesquite tree on whose limbs she would hang. She had to sit on her own crudely made coffin as the wagon bounced along over a rutted road. She turned down the offer of a blindfold, calmly facing her fate, and still said, *"libre de culpa"* (not guilty) to the hangman. Her face remained without emotion, but she did ask, *"cigarillo?"* Deputy John Gilpin is said to have taken a corn shuck and some tobacco from his pocket, rolled a crude cigarette and handed it, along with a match, to Chipita. She took a long pull, let the smoke slowly ease out of her nostrils, and then a gust of wind blew the smoke into her eyes. But her face remained expressionless.

The rope was placed around her slender neck, and Deputy Gilpin whipped the horses out from under her. Her feet thrashed about as she strangled, as the weight of her small, frail body had failed to break her neck. There was no cover over her face to keep the horrors of her strangulation away from the witnesses who had followed the wagon to the hanging tree. As soon as Deputy Gilpin was convinced she must be dead, he cut the rope and dumped her little body into the coffin, which was then lowered into the waiting open grave. A bystander, Jack McGowan, added more details to the gruesome story. He said he heard a thump, and then a groan, coming from within the coffin! He said he didn't stop running until he reached his home, almost a mile away.

Since that grim day in 1863, Chipita's ghost has been seen by many people in the San Patricio vicinity. She is most often seen when a woman in Texas is being accused of a crime she did not commit. The ghost of Chipita is most always seen on nights when the full moon is waning and a low ground mist or fog turns the Nueces River bottom into a very eerie place. She comes to the place where she hung, and where her body was placed in an unmarked, unconsecrated grave. Mr. Guthrie told me in a recent telephone conversation that her apparition still appears on dark nights when the moon is on the wane.

Remember, Chipita was the only woman ever hanged for a crime in Texas. And she more than likely hung for a crime she did not commit. No wonder her spirit cannot rest in peace.

The Ghost at Little Egypt

Not very far from the Texas coast, in Wharton County, is the quiet little community of Egypt. It was so named by very religious early settlers, because farmers from surrounding areas would come there during drought seasons to purchase seed. The fertile area supplied grain seeds to many farmers, who recalled how Jacob had purchased seed from Pharoah in the Bible story (Acts 7:12), and so they named their own fertile spot Egypt.

The first settler in the area around 1830 was Captain William James Elliot Heard.

According to *1001 Texas Place Names*, by Fred Tarpley, the population of Egypt in 1902 was only twenty-six people. To that number, we must also add, "and at least one ghost!"

I recently spoke with Anita Northington, who is the widow of George Heard Northington, III, a descendant of Captain Heard. She lives in the old Texas plantation-style home that Captain Heard built for his wife, America, and their children, in 1850.

Numerous Heards and Northingtons have resided in the house, which was constructed of handmade brick made on the place. It has a broad front porch and is of the "dog-trot" type of construction that was so often used by early settlers.

According to Mrs. Northington, many ghost stories have circulated through the various generations, and she readily admits she has what she considers to be a friendly spirit. She sometimes hears "thuds ... or thumps," like something hitting the side of the house, and what might be footsteps on the inside. She doesn't seem to be the least bit afraid or disturbed, and in fact, she told me she feels a whole lot safer living alone in her old country house with a ghost for company than she would feel living in a big city with the crime that seems to be running rampant today.

In the 1930s, when Will and Essie Northington had the place, a man who once worked for them on the plantation came back for a visit. He was very ill and knew he might not live too long, and he wanted to make one last visit to the place that held so many fond memories. During his visit it was reported a large, heavy marble-topped table had moved around the living room by itself. Various other things of unexplainable nature occurred during his visit, convincing him the place was haunted.

Once when Anita's son and daughter-in-law and a party of young people who were all friends of theirs came for an overnight visit, there just weren't enough beds to go around. Some of the guests slept in the living room on bedrolls. One young man, a visitor from Russia, when asked what he thought of the old house, commented, "It is a very strange place." He went on to say that he had strongly felt the presence of "something" watching him all night long.

Anita told me that one time the cook got really spooked. It was her usual custom to ring a bell to summon hired hands, guests, and family members in for meals. This particular day she didn't. She came running out of the kitchen, hollering, "Miz 'Nita . . . that ghost done got me!" Then she went on to explain that she first noticed all the clocks had stopped running at straight up twelve noon. Then she saw the figure of a man without a head coming slowly down the stairs! It was pretty hard to get her calmed down and back in the kitchen that day!

Anita said one elderly man who once worked on the place told her, "You don't ever need to be afraid, Miss 'Nita. Nobody ain't ever going to bother you with that ghost around!"

Now who is the ghost that is said to haunt the old Heard-Northington country home there in Egypt? Anita believes it might be the spirit of a Confederate soldier who passed away in an upstairs bedroom. She was always told that two soldiers had been sheltered there for a time, and one of them had died there. They may have been among a number of soldiers evacuated from other parts of the Deep South after Sherman made his sweeping march through the area. There were no hospitals, and few homes, left standing in which to treat the wounded, so they were evacuated to Texas, many of them coming to the area around El Campo and Egypt.

Anita said that some Federal troops had moved into an area not far from Egypt that was called Post Bernard. Since the post was only about 8 or 10 miles from the house, there was need for hiding, as well as treating, the wounded soldiers.

According to family records, one of the soldiers had a wooden leg. Anita believes he is the one who died. She was also of the opinion he might have been a Presbyterian minister who had served with the Confederate forces as a chaplain during the war.

Mrs. Northington said that some former residents of the house had reported seeing apparitions, and some had reported seeing balls of fire running through the house, but she has never seen or heard anything that really frightened her. In fact, she believes her ghostly visitor is both friendly and protective.

The old landmark is open for tours, and Anita Northington welcomes visitors to her charming, historic home. If you would like to visit her, she would be happy for you to call her at (409) 677-3562 for information and directions.

CHAPTER 4

Corpus Christi's Resident Spirits

Corpus Christi

The Spanish explorer Alonzo de Pineda discovered a beautiful, broad, sheltered bay on Corpus Christi Day, in the year 1519. The bay was named Corpus Christi in honor of that special day.

It was not until many years later that a real city, which also took the name of the bay, grew up along the waterfront. The area was inhabited by numerous Indian tribes, and while the Spanish, and later the Mexicans, knew of the bay, no settlement was established there until 1839. The adventurous impresario and colonizer Colonel Henry Lawrence Kinney founded a trading post there, doing business with some of the settlers in the area.

The little post remained rather obscure until 1845, when its real growth began. Today, it is one of America's major seaports and an important recreational area as well. It is the home of the Texas State Aquarium and the U.S.S. *Lexington* Museum. Its shores are protected from the ravages of stormy seas by a beautiful seawall, which was designed by Gutzon Borglum, the famous sculptor who fashioned the presidential faces on Mount Rushmore.

The Ghost at Blackbeard's on the "C.C." Beach

Right within walking distance of the famous aircraft carrier the U.S.S. *Lexington*, often referred to as the "Great Blue Ghost" which is now permanently docked in Corpus Christi Bay, there's a restaurant called Blackbeard's. The popular spot on the North Beach (referred to as "C.C. Beach") has an interesting ghost legend, which the owner-manager, Steve Bonillas, revealed to us on a recent visit to Corpus.

The menu, which features a variety of tasty Mexican food, burgers, salads, and seafood, is printed with a cover story, the "Legend of Blackbeard's":

In the summer of 1955 this building was not green. Nor was it a restaurant. It was a bar. The North Beach area of Corpus Christi was a fun, active, and sometimes wild place to hang out. On a warm night people would crowd to the old bar, laughing and talking. The bar itself is still in its original position, but now it is a counter to the kitchen. Legend has it that there was an argument one evening over a red-headed woman. Shots were fired, and the redhead and a fast talking New Orleans roughneck headed north on the old causeway. Neither they nor their gold Hudson were ever seen again. But they left behind a man on the floor... and possibly a ghost! Over the years many strange occurrences have been reported by customers as well as employees. Chairs move. Doors slam. Lights blink on and off. Voices in conversation have been heard long after the last customer departed. One old-timer used to order two beers every time he came in. He said the second one on the bar was for the ghost!

In 1962 the flamboyant entrepreneur and amateur magician Colonel Larry Platt bought the little bar and added a dining room. He called it the Spanish Kitchen, and from the start, it was the "in" place to go on the North Beach. Popular for good food, fun, and a gathering place for friends and visitors, the Spanish Kitchen tradition continues today as Blackbeard's on the Beach. Next to the clean beaches of Corpus Christi Bay, the *Lexington*, and the Texas State Aquarium, Blackbeard's is proud to be part of the new North Beach . . . fun, lively, and the place to be!

And while some do, and some don't, believe in ghosts, we at Blackbeard's still leave a beer on the old bar in memory of that summer of '55.

Now, this story on the menu was so fascinating to me, that it just naturally called for some extra sleuthing. I talked on the telephone at length with Paula Bonillas, Steve's wife, who was kind enough to put me in touch with Colonel Platt, who now resides in Pleasanton, south of San Antonio. Incidentally, the "Colonel" is an honorary title, bestowed on the gentleman as an "Honorary Colonel of Texas" by then-Governor Alan Shivers.

A conversation with Colonel Platt seemed to refute much of the legend printed on the Blackbeard's menu. He revealed that the bar and restaurant he opened in 1962 was an entirely different building from the earlier structure. He said when he bought the lot, the building that was there was so run down, he had it completely demolished and built his place of concrete block where the other building had once stood. He did not mention that he had any feelings that the building might have been haunted during the time he ran the business there, nor did he put much credence on the "red-headed woman" story. He did say that he had one theory why the place might be haunted now, however.

The Platts owned a motel . . . they were called tourist courts back then, that was adjacent to the Spanish Kitchen. It was called Stewart's Courts, the Colonel told me. There were about sixteen separate little cabins, with a parking space by each one, and the place was usually well occupied. Platt recalled one man, a fellow in his mid-forties, who had a job over at Ingleside at the Reynolds Plant and actually resided at the motel. He would come into the Spanish Kitchen night after night, sit down at the bar, and proceed to down a few beers. He was a strange character, according to Colonel Platt. He always carried a hunting rifle with him, and he loved to play the jukebox. Platt said he would play the same song over and over until he would have to ask the man to lay off for a while so the other customers could have a turn at playing their selections. The tune he played over and over again was "As Time Goes By." The man had revealed he was very depressed over the fact he was newly separated from his wife. Platt said he guessed the man was even more despondent than anyone had suspected, because one night after downing a couple of beers and playing "his song" on the jukebox, he walked out of the restaurant, entered his little cabin, put his rifle in his mouth, and pulled the trigger. Colonel Platt said if there's any kind of "spirit" around, it certainly could be that of the man who so tragically ended his life. Maybe he is just returning to listen to the jukebox and down a few beers at the bar.

Whoever the "spirit" may be, Steve Bonillas firmly believes that Blackbeard's is haunted. He told me lots of times they feel cold spots in the place. Chairs have been known to move around when the place is closed for the night, and the door, which is very heavy, has blown open when no wind was blowing, and it sometimes has even blown open when a high wind was blowing against it! Felipe Villanueva, one of the cooks at Blackbeard's, once saw the salt and pepper shakers jump up and fly across a table! Bonilla, Villanueva, and Dennis Marshal, another cook, all have witnessed the door opening when no one was around, and all three men strongly believe something they don't understand is causing strange things to happen periodically at Blackbeard's.

For whatever reason "it" comes around, we're glad "it" stays away from the kitchen. The Mexican food we ate at Blackbeard's sure was good, and we wouldn't want anything to change that!

The "Great Blue Ghost"
Has Ghosts of Her Own!

After serving her country for nearly fifty years (1943-1991), the great aircraft carrier U.S.S. *Lexington* (CV16) has come to a permanent safe harbor, at the port city of Corpus Christi on the Texas Gulf Coast. As a naval museum, under the custodial care of the Corpus Christi Convention and Visitors Bureau and many devoted and dedicated volunteers, she will be visited and suitably honored for many years to come.

During World War II, the *Lexington* was often referred to as the Great Blue Ghost, a name bestowed upon her by Tokyo Rose, who gained notoriety during the war for her propaganda broadcasts to Allied troops. Painted in Measure II "Sea Blue," the ship blended well with the azure seas she sailed. Hit once by a torpedo in December of 1943 and severely damaged by a kamikaze attack in December 1944, the Japanese reported her sunk at least four times. But after repairs and restoration, she came back each time to contribute greatly to the U.S. war effort in the Pacific theater. The valiant ship received the Presidential Unit Citation: "For extraordinary heroism in action against enemy Japanese forces in the air, ashore, and afloat in the Pacific War Area from September 18, 1943, to August 15, 1945." The "Lady Lex" earned battle stars and awards for operations in the Gilbert Islands, Asia-Pacific raids, Lyte, Luzon, and Iwo Jima, as well as the Third Fleet operations against Japan. She was everywhere, and anywhere, she was needed, with her crew of 2,500 men and 250 officers and her hangar bays capable of handling at least forty aircraft ready to strike.

The huge ship with its 910-foot flight deck (so large that 1,000 automobiles could be comfortably parked upon it!) has been "home" to literally thousands of seamen and aircraft crews over its fifty-year history. There were many casualties during her years of service, including nine men killed and thirty-five wounded after being torpedoed, and forty-seven men killed and one hundred twenty-seven injured after the 1944 kamikaze attack. There were probably many other deaths as well, from illness, fever, and various accidents on board ship.

Today the ship is no longer sailing; she is no longer the launching pad for countless naval aircraft. She is no longer painted blue, either. When she was given a streamlined island structure and a new mast, and her deck was angled to accommodate the coming of the jet age, she was also given a new paint job. Today she is "haze gray."

From 1962 until November of 1991 she served as a training carrier, based at Pensacola, Florida. From her first training operation in 1963 until her decommissioning in 1991, an average of 1,500 pilots were carrier qualified on her each year.

Now, men are known to love their ships. That's probably why they have always referred to them as being of the feminine gender. A ship always seems to be called a "she." As for the "Lady Lex," there are some men whose spirits have never left the ship they served and loved so well. They still remain in the staterooms, briefing rooms, decks, passageways, and sick bays of their ship. Therein lies a story, or several stories, in fact.

Soon after my husband and I visited the *Lexington* in February of 1993, I spoke with a friend about having seen the great ship. This gentleman, Sam Nesmith, is a well-known military historian, and he also possesses great psychic powers. After I mentioned my visit, he told me

The U.S.S. *Lexington* after modifications to superstructure and deck, 1960s

that he and his wife, Nancy, had recently visited the ship as well, and he said he felt the ship had a number of "resident spirits," earthbound to the ship and either unable, or unwilling, to leave. He said he especially felt a deep sense of pain and sadness in the dark corridor near a first-aid station, and in the "fo'c'sle" area, near the anchor, he also noted a very strong "presence." But it was in the Pilot's Ready Room Number One that he felt an overwhelming presence. It literally filled the room! Sam had brought a camera, with very high-speed film. He took a direct shot into the room. When the film came back from being developed, there, very visible, was a pilot, seen from the shoulders up. Very discernible was a collar and a head with a World War II era pilot's helmet and goggles. The face appeared to be "skull-like," according to Nesmith, who strongly believes it was the spirit of a pilot who did not make it back after a sortie, and is still struggling to return for his debriefing.

As we were planning another trip to Corpus Christi in August 1993, I decided to try and contact someone connected with the Lexington Museum to see if anyone there had experienced any unusual encounters of a supernatural nature. A telephone call to the curator's office brought me in contact with Derek Neitzel, assistant to the curator and the resident graphic artist at the ship museum. He didn't laugh when I asked him "Could there possibly be a ghost on the *Lexington*?" Instead, we made an appointment to meet on the ship on Friday, August 13.

I met Derek, a very personable young man, at 10 a.m., and we spent the next two and a half hours in conversation as he showed me some places on the ship not on the regular tourist route. He also told me about some of his personal experiences, as well as those of his coworkers. He showed me a short videotape made by a local television studio, that included an interview with Derek speaking about some of his experiences with "spirits" as he took the TV crew over various parts of the ship, where he later took me. He said one of the first experiences he had was at twelve noon on a Saturday, when he was working alone in his office. This was very soon after he had come to work on the ship. He heard, in a passageway near his office, the loudest banging and rattling imaginable! He traced it to the metal door to the ship's former radio station, WLEX. The door was actually shaking and vibrating. Derek said, "Hello," to which there was no response, and no letting up. Then he went to find the "D.C." (damage control) personnel. This is the name used on the ship for the firemen, paramedics, and security staff people. When the man arrived, there was no one there, of course, and no way to explain the vibrating, banging door. Incidentally, the door, which Derek pointed out to me, is a very heavy metal sliding door which is secured by a sliding metal bar.

We discussed various "happenings" that Derek recalled during the months he has worked on the ship. One night stands out above all the others. It was the night of February 13-14, 1993, and the "spirits" were really active all night long! In fact, there was no holding them back! Derek gave me a Xerox copy of the ship's log with the hourly reports noted by the "D.C." personnel as they signed in at all hours of the night while making their rounds. Derek said he had been there in his office, working, most of the evening. Since so much activity was taking place, he just stayed on throughout the entire night.

As various members of the Damage Control staff made their entries in the log, it became apparent this was a most unusual night, and a very wet one as well.

Some of the entries noted included the following:

0010: Water still coming down in Hangar #1, due to problem in C.O.'s room above.

0155: Smoke detector 02-126-1 malfunction. Checked out. All ok, reset system.

0300: Made routine round of all tour areas. Found two areas with water running into sinks in C.C. Admiral's quarters. One sink full of water. Unknown why water running. Still can hear water running in pipes in bridge area.

0345: Found sink in Admiral's quarters with water running, sink full, water on floor, this seems very strange why fresh water left running.

0400: Made rounds of pier area. Unable to go to fo'c'sle area due to fresh wax.

0410: Wayne notified about water running. He advised D.C. to secure all water running in heads (toilets).

0530: Made rounds of bridge and flight deck. Raised flag.

0630: Made rounds of pier, opened gate, water leak in hangar stopped.

And so it went. Derek attached his own personal notes to the D.C. log for the night of February 13-14 as follows:

In addition to those incidents reported in the D.C. Log by Richard Longoria who was scheduled at the time, Wayne, with D.C., was there with Wayne Fellers of Ship's operations at the Admiral's galley at about 9:20 on the night of the 13th. I overheard a radio report of water running in the Admiral's galley which was locked and sealed at the bottom with screws. It has a two-part door.

I ran up to help, in that I might be able to find a key since I have access to the locksmith's shop. I was told to bring either a key or a crowbar. I was gone approximately 7 to 10 minutes. When I returned, the group of Wayne F., and his son, Wayne with D.C., and Art Smith, the ship's electrician, had already pried the door open. I came down to the hangar deck and caught up with Wayne to ask what the cause of the water running was. I was told that a water faucet had been turned on. I know for a fact (for I was there) that I witnessed Pete Valentine (the ship's locksmith) lock the door a number of weeks previously and I had installed the screws on the back side. This was just a day before we opened this tour line. I also know Pete was the only one who had a key. One final note: I was in the next compartment aft (the admiral's stateroom) at 6:00 the same evening working on lashing ropes for the stanchions in the same room and I would have heard it had it been occurring at that time.

And then on February 17, Derek notes:

Addendum. Today I talked to D.C. "Shane" who was on duty during that night (February 13) He reported that two of the sinks were behind locked doors and one instance was the shower being on in the captain's sea-cabin on the 06 level. This was accounting for the water running sounds which he and Richard Longoria traced to the sea cabin. All in all, it was four sinks total, plus the shower and a faucet in the galley. D.N. 2-17-93.

Derek, in discussing this strange night, said that some of the faucets that were running hadn't been turned on in a long while, and he added they were so stuck and tight that it would have taken a strong man with a wrench to turn them on. Yet there they were, running freely, and in compartments behind firmly locked doors! He said the whole week centered around February 14 was "very active" and he referred to it as "hell week."

Derek went on to tell how the swivel chair that the bookkeeper uses often would swivel and squeak when she wasn't even there. This chair is in the photocopy office.

A man named Wayne, on the Damage Control staff, has a son whose name is John. This young man told his father that he had a very strange experience on the ship. He suddenly felt terrified for no particular reason. Then, he heard a distinct voice speaking to him, saying, "You'd sure hate to be here when them planes were taking off." The voice was very clear, and there was no mistaking what it said. John has never forgotten this incident.

Numerous times Derek has experienced the sensation of being followed down various passageways. He hears the sound of heavy military type shoes following along behind him. When they come to the coamings (raised door openings in the passageways) they do not break cadence as they should. He has also been followed by the same heavy treads as he comes out of the "head" (restroom) near the officer's dining room. These footsteps have followed him for some distance.

Another time, as he was disassembling a table in order to move it from the galley where it was located to the passageway outside, Derek could hear footsteps. There were no lights on in the passageway, but he had a flashlight. The steps were going from aft to forward. He asked, "Who is it?" but of course, there was no answer.

Derek took me on a tour over many areas that are off limits to visiting tourists. I felt the presence of "something" in several areas, sort of a feeling of loneliness and emptiness. The place that drew the most shivers in me was the former brig where there were a number of small, dark, barred cells. However, my host said that there had never been any reports of any ghostly happenings around that area.

Derek told me many of the ship's staff members have discussed their own experiences with an "unexplainable presence" on the huge vessel. One of the volunteers, John Dau, told Derek he had served on the carrier in the 1960s, and he knew then there were ghosts on the ship even while it was still on active duty.

One of the janitorial staff working there on contract, Jimmy Caldwell, told Derek he actually saw a medical corpsman in the sick bay about 5 a.m. one morning. He saw the figure just briefly, and then it totally disappeared.

Although Derek, who spends lots of hours on the ship at night in the print shop or doing artwork, is not fearful of the resident spirits, he says that they are at times very "disturbing." Finally, after one particularly exasperating night, he asked them to "Just lay off...just quit bothering me and trying to frighten me. I can't do my job as well with you disturbing me." He said he believes they are really intelligent entities, and they understood him, because he has had a relatively peaceful time of it since he made that request!

I might add a postscript to this story:

A very recent visit with Derek aboard the *Lexington* revealed the spirits are still active. Two security guards have reported hearing voices when no one is around on several occasions. Derek, who is convinced that these otherworldly seamen will never leave the *Lexington*, is not worried about any more disturbances. He's moving soon to West Africa.

The U.S.S. *Lexington* during World War II in the Pacific. Note the original superstructure and flight deck.

The Disappearing Nun

There have been a lot of hitchhiker ghost stories told down through the years. The most frequently told ones usually involve a dark and rainy night, a lost and distraught young woman who is found wandering beside the road, and a kindly motorist who gives her a lift. Then suddenly she vanishes before her destination is reached, leaving a very disturbed motorist to ponder what might have happened to her.

There's a story that was told for years down around Corpus Christi that might be called a variation of the old disappearing hitchhiker stories. I first read the story in an article entitled "Ghosts of the Coastal Bend" by Jane Ammeson of Corpus Christi, which appeared in the October 1983 edition of *Texas Highways Magazine*.

It seems during World War II a bus load of sailors was traveling from Houston to Corpus Christi. At a small town bus stop, a Catholic nun carrying a suitcase got on the bus. Soon after she sat down she started to talk to some of the sailors seated near her. She was very interested in them and told them she thought the war might end soon. After traveling some distance, the tired sailors were dozing and the bus became silent. Just before they reached Corpus, someone realized the little nun was gone. But she couldn't be! The bus had made no stops! A thorough search revealed neither the nun nor her suitcase.

As soon as the bus arrived in Corpus Christi the driver and a couple of the sailors went out to the convent that the nun had mentioned. They asked one of the sisters there if the missing nun had arrived there. The sister told them they weren't expecting anyone to arrive, but she would be glad to show them some photos of the convent's sisters to see if any was recognizable as the missing nun.

The driver and the sailors all selected one photograph, saying "There's no doubt. That's the nun who talked with us and then disappeared."

The sisters at the convent were stunned. "It can't be. That sister has been dead for several years," they said.

The Circle of Flames

Along with the story about the missing nun, Jane Ammeson wrote in the October 1983 issue of *Texas Highways Magazine* in her article entitled "Ghosts of the Coastal Bend" about a strange occurrence that took place in Corpus Christi many years ago.

There was a county judge who was highly respected named Judge Walter Timon. Once when he was visiting in the home of his father on Mesquite Street in Corpus Christi, he was startled to suddenly look up and see the apparition of a man, standing by the fireside. What made the figure so strange was that a circle of flames surrounded the figure's waist. As the startled judge watched, flames engulfed the entire apparition. Then, just as suddenly as they had begun, the flames started to recede, and then the figure disappeared as well, leaving the puzzled judge standing alone in the room.

Other people have also seen the same apparition. Mrs. Millie Sullivan Timon saw it on midnight, November 2, 1909. She was alone, as her husband was away selling some cattle from the Bayou Ranch where they lived, on the Nueces River. At first she thought the figure she saw was that of her husband. Then, realizing it was not, she watched in absolute terror as flames started to encircle the man. She was speechless! She finally found the breath to murmur, "Lord, have mercy on his soul," before the flames and the figure both disappeared.

Ammeson wrote that the apparition appeared once more at the Bayou Ranch house. This time a friend who was taking care of the Timons' children while they were out of town saw the figure.

Later on, the Bayou Ranch burned down. Was it because of the ghostly figure? Who was he, and why did he come? To this day, no one has been able to find out.

CHAPTER 5

The Ghosts of Galveston

Galveston Island

Galveston Island was first explored by Europeans, who found it to be frequented by Karankawa Indians. Pirate Jean Lafitte established a settlement there in 1817 which he called Campeche. Galveston Island was so named for Bernardo de Galvez, Viceroy of Mexico, and the city was first called Galvez-town. Lafitte was, in 1819, president of the Galveston Republic. The interesting island city has a lot of "firsts" to its credit: it had the first Catholic convent in Texas, the first telegraph station, the first brewery, and the first medical college! And while the disastrous storm of 1900 completely inundated the island, drowning between 5,000 and 7,000 people and destroying countless homes, today a vast 10-mile-long seawall protects the city, and has proved its worth many times during heavy storms. Galveston is truly a city that would not die! There are spirits in the grand old city that are content to stay there, too!

Strange Spirits at the Williams House

At 3601 Bernardo de Galvez Street in Galveston, there's a charming old house in the midst of one of the city's most historic neighborhoods. This was the home that Samuel May Williams, an early Texas pioneer, built for his family in 1839, just three years after Texas won her independence from Mexico.

Williams had served as secretary to Stephen F. Austin and had helped to finance the Texas Revolution. As the first banker in Texas, he had often foreclosed on people's property. According to an article by Stephen Long which ran in the October 29, 1993, edition of the *Houston Chronicle*, Williams would never have won any popularity contests. In fact, according to Long, who quoted Shirley Holmer, who

Mr. Mario Cecacci, next-door neighbor to Williams house (which is in background)

works for the Galveston Historical Foundation, Williams was reputed to have been the "most hated man in Texas."

Maybe that's why strange vibes have stuck with the old house! It seems "Little Sam," Williams' son, died of an unknown illness when he was just 10 years old. And apparently a slave once tried to kill Williams' wife, Sarah, by lacing her food with finely ground glass! Fortunately, the glass was discovered in time. The guilty servant was locked up in a room below the kitchen as punishment.

Today the house is open to the public for viewing. It is a project of the Galveston Historical Society. An unusual, and very effective, audio-visual program lets the visitor listen in on "conversations" with the Williams family members and their friends. One can almost sense Samuel Williams relaxing in his favorite chair while his young daughter, Caddy, plays the piano in the old parlor!

Upstairs were the children's bedrooms, those of young Sam and his sister, Caddy. The former director of the Williams House Museum, Kathleen Hink, told me she had had no personal encounters or experiences of a supernatural nature while she served as museum director, but according to Long's article, she had told him as she worked there late one evening, a lamp in the downstairs hallway was turned on. She turned it off, and then the lamp started rattling "ninety to nothing."

We recently enjoyed a visit with Mr. Mario P. Ceccaci, Jr., who has lived next door to the Williams house since 1951. He told us that a docent who once worked there told him about the visit of a lady who claimed to be a psychic. She had just entered the house and paid her admission to tour the building, when she suddenly said she couldn't go on the tour. She had felt Mr. Williams' presence so strongly that nothing could persuade her to go past the front door!

Ceccaci said the house had belonged to a Tucker family for about ninety years. After Mrs. Tucker died in 1952, the house remained closed up for many years and rapidly deteriorated. Many Tucker antiques were still inside, and Mr. Ceccaci said he would periodically go into the house and check to see if everything was all right. On one of his checkups he noticed that a fire had recently burnt in a previously empty fireplace. Embers and ashes still remained. To his knowledge, no one had entered the building recently. A careful check failed to show any signs of a forced entry. He knew he was the only person who had access to the house. He firmly believes there was a ghostly visitor who had enjoyed a warm fire on a cold night!

Numerous visitors from various places have reported feeling a strong presence, and a coldness on the second floor landing just outside the children's bedrooms. No one has reported a sighting, but the strong feeling that something is there still pervades.

It's pretty much a sure thing that at least one of the Williams family has remained in spirit, just to make sure everything is in order, over 150 years later. After all, time stands still for a ghost!

Miss Bettie's Still in Charge
at Ashton Villa

In September of 1992, my husband, Roy, and I were the guests of the East Texas Tourism Association on a familiarization tour of Southeast Texas communities. Included in our jam-packed itinerary was Galveston Island. The representatives of the Galveston Convention and Visitors Bureau pulled out all the stops to show our group a wonderful overview of the historic landmarks of that great city on the Gulf of Mexico.

Our group was treated to an elegant progressive dinner. After the salad course, which we enjoyed at the beautiful Moody mansion, we moved on to Ashton Villa, where the main entree was served. This magnificent mansion, a project of the Galveston Historical Foundation, is located at 2328 Broadway. The splendid villa was built by James Moreau Brown in 1859. Brown, a hardware magnate, was one of Texas' leading businessmen, and his home became a meeting place of the great and near-great from across the land. While no mention was made of Mrs. Brown, we were told that his colorful daughter, Rebecca, generally known as "Miss Bettie," served as his hostess and presided over the household for many years. And therein lies a story. . . .

After our group had dined in a large reception room, we were given a tour of the beautiful residence. As I wandered through one of the upstairs bedrooms, I felt something . . . a little shiver, perhaps just a feeling as I looked around. Then I walked down the broad staircase and strolled into the main parlor known as the Gold Room. I felt some presence was with me as I walked. Then, as I moved towards a beautiful antique piano, the hair stood up on my arms and a real shiver went right through me. I stopped, walked out of the room, and sought out one of the Galveston hostesses. I asked her if she knew whether or not Ashton Villa was haunted. She said, "Well . . . there are stories." I couldn't get much more from her as it was time for our group to move on to still another landmark, the Old Opera House, where we were served our dessert course.

Having felt something, some special energy in the Gold Room, I was most anxious to pursue the subject further. Finally, some time later, I obtained some printed material from Galveston's famous Rosenberg Library. Casey Edward Greene, the Assistant Archivist, sent me copies of articles from the files in the library that substantiate that I had, indeed, almost had a "close encounter" with "Miss Bettie" Brown.

In the days when the Browns entertained in their grand mansion, guests were often shown into the formal reception room, or salon. There, elegant Victorian galas and musical recitals were held. "Miss Bettie," who never married, would have been quite at home in today's liberal society. She was way ahead of her own day; a liberated woman before the term "woman's lib" existed! An accomplished and multi-talented artist, she traveled, alone and unchaperoned, all over Europe. She smoked a pipe, and was said to have urged at least one of her male admirers to drink champagne from her golden slipper! "Miss Bettie" was definitely an individualist and possessed a very strong personality.

Ashton Villa, at 2328 Broadway in Galveston

An article from Galveston County's *In Between* (the October 1978 issue, featuring Galveston County's ghosts) stated that the furnishings of the Gold Room at Ashton Villa were true reflections of the lifestyle of Rebecca Brown. Many of her most treasured possessions are shown displayed in a small alcove. There are costumes, fans, an Egyptian mummy's head, and a diamond-studded cat's head she purchased in Paris. Two of her original paintings also hang in the room. One depicts a demure Victorian lass on a swing; the other portrays two rotund cherubs, one of whom boasts the wings of a butterfly!

In the adjacent dining room there is a photo on display which shows a servant standing in a doorway. But what sets the picture apart from the ordinary is that to the left of the mantel pictured in the photograph, the image of another man's face is plainly visible. Could it possibly be a ghost?

Then, there's that magnificent piano . . . the same instrument I stopped near when the feeling of a presence overtook me. The story from *In Between* stated that a caretaker who had lived in the carriage house adjacent to the villa vividly recalled a night when he was awakened from a sound sleep about 3:30 a.m. by the sounds of a piano playing. Because there had been some attempted break-ins, he decided to go check the villa. As he entered, he heard the music emanating from the elegant Gold Room. As he came into the room he was startled to see the faint image of a woman in nineteenth century clothing seated at the piano bench. In just a moment, both she and the music which was playing faded completely away. The caretaker was quoted as saying that he turned on every light in the building and stayed awake for the remainder of the night!

Steven Long, a newswriter for the Houston *Chronicle*, wrote an interesting feature for the October 29, 1993, edition of that paper. The article, which was titled, "Haunted Houses," stated that Lucie Testa, weekend manager at the villa since 1988, had experienced several strange happenings there. On February 18, 1991, the alarm system went off, for no particular reason, three different times. Then, as Testa prepared to close the house for the day, she noticed the ceiling fan at the top of the staircase had come on. She climbed the stairs to turn it off, only to find it running again when she arrived the next morning! She noted that Miss Bettie Brown had been born on February 18, 1855! Extrovert that she was, maybe she just wanted to make sure somebody remembered her birthday!

Testa also told about feeling a ghostly presence in Miss Bettie's former day room. At the end of the single bed there is an ornate chest that she purchased on a trip to the Middle East. The key was lost many years ago. Sometimes the chest is locked. Other times it is unlocked. There is no explanation whatsoever for this.

Long's article in the *Chronicle* also related that a volunteer who came to work at the villa during the "Dickens Christmas on the Strand" weekend reported seeing a lady standing at the top of the grand staircase. She was wearing a beautiful turquoise blue dress. He reported seeing her to Testa, but there had been no one in the house wearing that color on that day. Turquoise was known to have been Miss Bettie Brown's very favorite color!

When I made a recent telephone call to Ashton Villa, one of the docents to whom I spoke confided that there was one upstairs bedroom in which there is a bed that never stays properly made up. No matter how many times a day the staff members straighten the spread and smooth out the wrinkles, it always appears rumpled and wrinkled. She said this was in Miss Bettie's bed-sitting room. I wondered if it was the room in which I had first felt that strange otherworldly presence.

One might make a final conclusion about the Ashton Villa and all the strange, unexplainable things that have occurred there over the years. The former mistress of the household is still around, at least in spirit, and she's just keeping everybody aware of the fact that she is still very much in charge!

A Welcome to The Oaks

One of Galveston's most charming historic homes is known as The Oaks. The magnificent peach-colored plantation-style wooden house with its plethora of galleries is surrounded by great, spreading oak trees. It is the island's oldest surviving house.

The Greek Revival structure was built in 1838 by Augusta Allen, founder of Houston. It was later sold to Michel Menard, a founder of Galveston, and is most often referred to as "The Menard Residence."

I learned from Virginia (Mrs. Merle E.) Eisenhour, a Galveston historian, that her ancestor Edwin Ketchum purchased the property in 1880 from the divorced wife of Michel Menard's son. The house stayed in Ketchum's family for ninety-seven years. Currently The Oaks is unoccupied. When we were in Galveston in February 1994, a crew was working at restoring the lovely old mansion. It will be restored to its former grandeur.

Mrs. Eisenhour said her family moved into the ancestral home in 1941, when she was a teenager. She said she was very lonely at first, as there was nothing to do and she had no friends in Galveston. One rainy, gloomy evening, she was sitting at the top of the stairs with her pet dog. She said the animal began to growl and bark and became extremely agitated. He was gazing downward, towards the front entry hall and doorway. Virginia cast her eyes downward, and was astounded to see reflected in the light from the hallway chandelier the image of the head and shoulders of a young woman, which began to form in a pool of light on the front door. She was clearly visible. Her hair, which was straight, was pulled severely back from her face, arranged into a bun. A brooch or cameo was at the neckline of her gown. The image was not full-length, just the portion above the waist. Virginia ran to get her mother, and she also saw the woman's image quite clearly.

Although they looked for the image the next night, and other nights to come, the face of the young woman never again appeared to them. But dating from that appearance, things started to turn around for the young Virginia. Invitations began to arrive, the family started to meet a lot of people, and soon they had a real sense of belonging in Galveston!

Later, Mrs. Eisenhour said, she learned that former slaves had told some of her ancestors that when Colonel and Mrs. Menard lived there, they had two adopted daughters, Helen and Clara. The story told by the slaves was that one of the girls had tripped and fallen down the front stairs, breaking her neck. Whether this was true, Mrs. Eisenhour has not been able to document. However, it is definitely known that Clara died young. Perhaps it was she who appeared to Virginia so many years ago, a beautiful ever-young spirit come to welcome her to her new home at The Oaks and into Galveston society!

The Oaks

Sarah, the Friendly Spirit

The October 31, 1990 edition of the *Galveston Daily News* carried an interesting story written by Bob Whitey. It was about the Virginia Point Inn, and Sarah, the friendly live-in ghost!

A telephone conversation with Eleanor Catlow, the owner, verified what Bob Whitey had written was true. Sarah Hawley and her husband were the first owners of the house, and Catlow feels certain it is her spirit which returns, not to frighten, just to look after her old homestead. And although there have been many incidents of windows closing, doors opening, footsteps heard on floorboards, and rocking chairs rocking of their own accord, Mrs. Catlow has never felt frightened or intimidated.

Mrs. Catlow and her husband bought the house six years after he retired. It was the first house they looked at, and seemed like home immediately. They looked no further. Mrs. Catlow has since turned the place into a bed and breakfast inn, and of late, she said "Sarah" has not made her presence known.

Many of the Catlow's guests have reported strange experiences. One relative who came to the inn to be married reported a presence in her room the night before her wedding. She said she heard the rustling of a wedding gown, and she also reported a rocking chair rocked, while a door opened repeatedly all through the night. She said she knew something was in the room with her.

A couple who stayed at the inn reported two pictures falling to the floor the night they stayed there. It seems those folks had relatives who did not get along well with the Hawley family. Catlow added, "The chain wasn't broken or bent . . . the pictures just crashed to the floor." They had never fallen previously and haven't fallen since. It just had to have something to do with Sarah not wanting that particular couple to stay there!

Still another guest claimed he was invited downstairs during the night for an otherworldly conversation. Supposedly the man was awakened about 2 a.m. by a spirit voice which asked him to come downstairs and "visit with me awhile." The man said it was a "good feeling." He said he had a wonderful visit with the spirit and then calmly went back upstairs to bed!

We recently learned that the inn has been sold. We wonder if Sarah will take kindly to the new owners.

Virginia Point Inn

The Boarding House on Avenue K

Galveston Island has many haunted places. One of them was the subject of a Halloween newspaper article on October 31, 1989. The *Galveston Daily News* article was researched and written by Sonja Garza.

My interest piqued, I tried to contact the owner mentioned in the write-up, Barbara Stanford. Finally, I located a distant cousin of Stanford's who told me she had sold the house and moved to California some time ago. She believed the deserted house might be owned by the city of Galveston.

The *News* article stated that the old house at 23rd Street and Avenue K is slowly decaying and the paint is flaking off the wood.

The 90-year-old mansion was a former boarding house. There are some twenty-seven rooms within its three stories.

Linda Groh, a married daughter of Ms. Stanford, was quoted as saying she had "vivid memories of unexplained footsteps, eerie laughter, and nightmarish visions." She slept on the second floor. Every night about midnight for an entire summer, she would hear tapping on the floor above her, almost like people tap dancing. She also heard distant laughter and faint music playing. This happened sometimes when she was alone. The third floor always gave her the creeps.

Jessie Glasgow, Barbara Stanford's son, had his own experiences to relate. He told about how chairs stored in a room on the third floor would move around by themselves. "One day I'd go to the room and they would be stacked on top of one another. A few days later, they'd be off in the corner," he said.

Amy Wagner, a Galveston resident who once attended a party in the old former boarding house, said one boy at the party got so frightened by something he saw while he was in the house, he jumped out of a second story window. Luckily, a tree broke his fall.

Joseph Witwer, who owns the property next door to the old house, says he knows for a fact that several people died in the boarding house over the years. "An old seaman and others have died of natural causes there, but nothing of a violent nature," he said.

The article quoted Olivia Meyer, spokeswoman for the Galveston Historical Foundation, as saying the most current records kept on the house are dated 1912. Meyer believes the home might have been built about 1905 in another city and moved to Galveston about six years later.

Garza stated in her article that Mrs. Stanford was no longer bothered by the ghosts. She had had a spiritualist come and check the place out, and she had determined that there were probably two spirits there, one male, and one female. Stanford was quoted as saying, "The medium told me in order to get rid of the spirits, I'd have to leave also because they were emotionally attached to me. I plan on staying."

What made Barbara Stanford change her mind and move on? Did the "attached" resident spirits go away, or did they follow her to California? Or are they still hanging around the old house?

During a recent visit to Galveston we learned the building has been purchased by Mr. David Goodbar, the owner of a beautifully restored mansion in the same block in what is known as Galveston's "Silk

Former boarding house at 23rd Street and Avenue K

Stocking" district. Restoration and remodeling of the building was to be completed early in the summer of 1994. It is being leased to numerous antique and art dealers who will display their goods in a boutique-like atmosphere. The many rooms that make up the boarding house lend themselves well to such an endeavor. According to Mr. Goodbar the house was built as, and always was, a boarding house for roomers. The genial owner didn't hesitate to admit the old building is reputed to be among Galveston's most haunted habitats!

The Ghost of Fire Station Number Six

According to Galveston County's *In Between* issue of October 1978, Old Fire Station Number Six at 3712 Broadway had a ghost!

Captain Jack was a fireman, and he served for over twenty years at the oldest fire station on Galveston Island.

Although he died over forty years ago, it is said that for many years he still would often be heard climbing the stairs which led up to the firemen's sleeping quarters. It always sounded like a fireman in full fire fighting regalia. His ghost didn't like anyone to sleep on the cot by the south window, because that was his spot. Rookies who made the mistake of using Jack's old cot often were rudely awakened. One fire fighter reported that his blankets and sheets were pulled away by an unseen force while he slept!

No longer a fire station because the old building could not accommodate today's larger trucks, the building has for the past three years has been the home of Alford Air Conditioning Company, Inc. Donna Briones, the office manager, shared some of her experiences and impressions with us. Shortly after the old station became the home of the air conditioning business, Donna started to notice unusual occurrences. For instance, on several occasions she has sensed the strong, almost overpowering fragrance of a man's cologne or after-shave lotion as she sits in her first floor front office, or at the top of the stairs just off the bathroom and shower room that once served the men stationed at Fire Station Number Six.

One morning when Donna was in the building very early, prior to opening time, she stretched out on the couch upstairs to catch a short catnap. As she was just about to drift off to sleep she heard music. It was faint at first, and a little "static-y." She couldn't tell what the piece was, but it was definitely music. She looked all around. There was no radio in the room. She thought maybe a car might be parked outside the building with the car radio turned up loud, but when she checked she found no car outside. Then she went back upstairs. She heard the music again, "rather scratchy and muffled, like a well-worn record being played on an old victrola." She never was able to trace the source of the music.

One morning as she sat in the office, Donna heard heavy footsteps descending the stairs just outside the office. She thought it must be her stepfather, who owns the business. When the office door did not open immediately, as she had expected, she wondered why. She opened the door and looked out into the open section of the building which used to house the fire trucks. She also glanced outside, and found her stepfather's van was not even parked alongside the building. She was completely alone in the building!

Because of so many unexplained noises and happenings, Donna has become quite interested in the history of the old building that once housed the firemen. She has turned up the rosters of various captains and their companies who served there over the years. Several records dating back to the early 1920s revealed one captain who served there for a long time was listed as "Captain A.J. O'Mara." We wonder, could the "J" possibly have stood for "Jack?"

We are glad the old building is still there, providing a restful haven for the spirit of an old fireman who served his community so faithfully for so long.

Is the Captain Still There?

They called him "Captain Mott." Born near Alexandria, Louisiana, on June 21, 1837, Marcus Fulton Mott moved with his family to Galveston in 1845. He grew up on the island and later became a successful lawyer in the firm of Bellinger, Jack, and Mott. During the Civil War, Mott was a colonel in the Confederate forces. Later, the honorary title of "Captain" was bestowed on him by the Galveston Artillery Club, and that's what he liked to be called.

Captain Mott built a lovely, big Victorian home for his family in 1884. The address is 1121 Tremont. It was purchased by Tommy Witwer in 1943, and today, the lower floor is used for businesses, while the current occupant, Joseph C. Witwer, one of Tommy's sons, lives in the upstairs portion of the building.

Former home of "Captain" Mott, at 1121 Tremont in Galveston

According to Tommy Witwer, who was quoted in an article in *Eagle Images*, October 1980, the first indication the place might be haunted came when his daughter reported hearing voices in the attic. Years later, Witwer's granddaughter reported that the "Captain" had come into her room and spoken to her. A conversation I had with Witwer's son Joseph indicated that the spirit most often appeared to youngsters. He said more than one child had seen the "Captain," and that he had also seen the spirit when he was about twelve years old. He said it rarely appeared to adults, but he did vividly recall seeing the ghost when he was a youngster.

Some very strange incidents occurred when a young man named John Implemence moved into the household as a tenant. Soon after his arrival, he was lying on his bed one day when he distinctly heard a voice tell him to "get out of here." His mattress then lifted, and he was thrown into the air and across the room! In the next few days, pictures flew off the walls and the furniture moved about. After these incidents, John invited some of his friends over to visit him in his room, and they began to hold Ouija board sessions. When Implemence questioned the "Ouija spirit" about what it meant to do to him, it said something about coming after him with "a wet rope." That night, as he was preparing to go to bed, Implemence heard a voice which seemed to come from the attic. He opened the door and walked up the steep steps. When he reached the top, a great heaviness seemed to overcome him. An unseen force seemed to hold him. He felt as if he were actually tied to the newel post, and he was unable to move from 2 a.m. until daybreak when he was suddenly and inexplicably released.

Later, during another session with the Ouija board, it was asked why it had decided to haunt Implemence. It replied, "because he loves himself." It also added that Implemence bore a strong resemblance to Mott's son, whose portrait was up in the attic of the house.

Implemence found the portrait, which revealed the son to be a stocky, blonde-haired young man. Strangely, Witwer, the owner of the house, said there was nothing but an empty frame when he bought the house, and the picture just suddenly appeared there. Mysterious, to say the very least!

Now, John Implemence was a Navy veteran who had won seven service medals in Vietnam, and he was not a person who was easily upset or frightened. But, he certainly was "impressed" by many events which took place during the time he resided in the old house. He said that one Ouija session finally revealed that there had been three undiscovered murders involving the house. Three young women were murdered, and according to the "Captain," his son, Abey, was the culprit. The board slowly spelled out A-B-E-Y, which was the name of Marcus Mott's son. (At the time of the Ouija sessions, Implemence and his friends said they did not know the name of the former owner, Mott, or any of his family.)

When questioned further, the Ouija board said the bodies had been thrown into a nearby well. A cistern, in which rainwater was stored, was located, but it was too shallow to throw bodies into. However, there may still be a long-covered-over, and therefore, undiscovered, well on the property. During this session, which mentioned the well, the spirit said it would haunt the house until the bodies were located.

After John Implemence moved to Dallas, the incidents of strange noises, unusual occurrences, etc. seemed to slow down. But Neil Witwer, Tommy's son, who has lived there since childhood, said his first wife, Cathy, had heard noises like pacing back and forth coming from the attic, and she had also seen the image of a man in a mirror that left the impression with her it was the "Captain." Then Neil's four-year-old daughter started talking to her parents about the "Captain," also.

There have been no recent manifestations in the house, which must be a great relief to the current occupants.

Captain Marcus Mott died in 1906 as the result of injuries he suffered in a fall from a streetcar. He is believed to have succumbed in his house.

The Ghost Who Left His Walking Cane

When Althea Wade and her husband, C.P., moved into their "new-old" home in the 1300 block of Sealy Street in Galveston, they had no idea they'd soon be sharing their new address with an otherworldly resident! It was soon made apparent to them, because they began to hear strange noises every night soon after retiring. Althea described them as "a drag, a plop, and a drag, and a plop." Deciding that they just might have some rambunctious rats in the attic, they set a trap. When C.P. went up to check the trap, he found a beautiful gold-headed walking cane lying on a pile of books. The cane bore the inscription, "J.D. Skinner, Nov. 6, 1895."

William Skinner, the son of J.D., had built the house in 1895. Strangely, when the Wades moved in, C.P. said, they'd gone over every inch of the house, including the attic, and there had been absolutely nothing there. They decided they had to have a ghost, and he must have left the cane there as a sort of housewarming gift because he liked the Wades!

Besides hearing strange noises, there were other unexplainable occurrences. Once, when C.P. was out of the house with the two older boys and Althea was home alone with their three youngest children, one of the tots wandered out into the parlor. She came back into the room where her mother and siblings were watching TV and asked Althea, "Mama, who is that man going up the stairs?" Althea asked her daughter, who was only about three years old, if the man she saw was tall like her daddy, or not-so-tall like her grandfather. The child replied he was "not-so-tall, like Grandpa, and he had on a long, white coat."

When C.P. and the boys came home, they all searched the house, but no one was there. They didn't really expect to find anyone, however.

Once, a visitor to the house was pushed from behind as she stood on the stair landing. She fell down the stairs but was not injured.

During the entire twenty years the Wades lived on Sealy Street, they were never afraid. In fact, they felt very comfortable with "George," the name they affectionately called their star boarder.

The Haunted Portrait

Mrs. Catherine Polk makes her home in La Marque, a small city on the Texas coast just north of the causeway leading to Galveston Island. This charming, friendly lady warmly welcomed my husband and me into her large, two-story Tudor English house, where we enjoyed a nice morning visit and a lively discussion concerning the other "occupant" of her spacious home.

The ghost is that of Elvie Bertha Weller, Catherine's great-aunt, who died at the age of fifteen in 1904. Elvie's spirit has long clung to a portrait made of her when she was about 13 years old.

Elvie was born in the small town of Sublime, Texas, on August 24, 1889. She was one of five daughters in the loving, close-knit Weller family. When she was very young the family moved to Brownsville. All the girls except Elvie were sent off to various convents and private schools in Brownsville and San Antonio. Elvie, always very sweet and rather shy, was apparently the family pet, according to Catherine Polk. Her parents elected to have her remain at home, receiving her education under the tutelage of the family governess. Musically talented, she played both the piano and organ, and by the time she was 12 years old, she played the organ for services at her church. She was also the only Weller daughter whose portrait was made. Catherine is not sure if it is a good watercolor or an old photograph which was hand-colored, as was the custom in those days prior to the invention of color film. I personally believe it is a photograph because of the sepia tones of Elvie's face.

Young Elvie was very highly esteemed in the city of Brownsville. The summer of 1904, when she was 14, she became very ill with Bright's disease, a then-fatal kidney ailment. The Brownsville city officials became very concerned. It was an extremely hot and humid summer, and the windows of the young girl's bedroom had to be left open to allow ventilation to flow through the house. The city sent out wagonloads of sawdust to be spread in the street in front of the Weller home to muffle the sounds of horses and carriages passing by, which might disturb her rest.

As Elvie's condition worsened, and the family realized she would not last much longer, the entire Weller family, except for one absent sister, gathered at her bedside. Just before she died, only two weeks after her fifteenth birthday, Elvie exclaimed to her assembled family, "Look! don't you see them? The angels! They're so beautiful, and they have come for me!"

Nancy Polk, Catherine's oldest daughter, who lives in Houston, shared the death notice announcing Elvie's passing, which ran in the Brownsville paper. It stated:

> Dead in this city, last night at twelve o'clock, Elvie Bertha Weller, born at Sublime, Texas, August 24, 1889, aged fifteen years and thirteen days. The friends and acquaintances of the deceased and of the family, are respectfully invited to attend the funeral from the family residence, corner of Levee and Eighth Streets, this afternoon at three o'clock. Brownsville, Texas, September 7, 1904.

In those days, news must have traveled very slowly. Nancy has in her possession a copy of the eulogy which ran in the Cuero, Texas, newspaper, on December 18, 1904, some three months after Elvie's death. Cuero is in DeWitt County, which borders Lavaca County, where the tiny town of Sublime, Elvie's birthplace, is located. Supposedly named by early German settlers to the area, Sublime bears the name of a town in Germany. According to Fred Tarpley's *1001 Texas Place Names*, Sublime had a population of seventy-five people on June 14, 1875.

The Cuero paper may have been quoting from the Brownsville paper, or the article may have been composed by a Cuero staff writer. The words formed a beautiful tribute to the young girl:

> It is best. Too beautiful and too pure for this world's sin and sorrow, Elvie Bertha Weller closed her eyes in death in Brownsville, Texas, September 6, 1904. Of rare physical beauty, with a mind exceptionally bright, combined with a gentle, loving disposition, she readily won the love of those she met. Though a sufferer for many months without the

knowledge of those who loved her best, she patiently bore her sufferings, only saying, "she did not feel well." A fair flower of only fifteen summers, God, the Father, took it back to bloom only once more in the great celestial garden.

Calmly calling each loved one, she bade them "kiss her goodbye." And then, with faltering lips came the words, "Mama, I have seen God; I have prayed to Him and He said, 'Elvie, I have forgiven all your sins. Come home and rest.'" To her, death was only "the gentle nurse, whose goodnight kiss precludes one's entrance into bliss."

"Oh," she said, "the other world is so beautiful." And love borne on a faith in Christ, she prayed that she might be spared to see an absent sister.

Oh, my friends, what sublime faith and trust in one so young. She asked that "Nearer, My God to Thee" and "The Haven of Rest" be sung at her funeral. So they laid her down to rest, far from her childhood home, on stranger soil.

The dead and the beautiful rest but her soul has entered into immortal life.

Oh, dear ones, all be comforted; such a beautiful death is full of the Balm of Gilead. Although with bruised and breaking heart, with sable garb and silent tread, you bare her senseless dust to rest. You say she is dead, ah, no, she has but dropped her robe of clay to put her shining garments on. She has not wandered far away. She is not dead, or gone, and when the trumpets sound and the dead be raised, incorruptible, not changed, but glorified, Elvie, bright with the beauty and celestial glory of an immortal grace shall meet the poor broken-hearted mother, with the same face that you have loved and cherished, divinely fair.

Whom God loves, He chastens, and when His finger touching our loved ones into sleep that takes them from us, He whispers into our aching hearts, "let not your hearts be troubled; in my Father's house are many mansions." Cuero, Texas, December 18, 1904.

Elvie's grief-stricken mother kept the portrait of her deceased daughter in her bedroom. Catherine recalls, as a youngster, she would go and gaze up at the picture of the young girl, admiring the sweet faced

image, which was gowned in a
white dress with a white rose
caught at the neckline. She told her
great-grandmother that she would
love to have Elvie's portrait someday. She was very disappointed
when Mrs. Weller left the picture
to her youngest daughter, Kather-
ine Lenora, whom Catherine Polk
called "Aunt Kate."

When Catherine visited her
great-aunt Kate in Brownsville,
back about 1960, Kate asked her if
there was anything among her ef-
fects that Catherine might like to
have at her death. Without a moment's hesitation, Catherine said
she would like to have Elvie's por-

Portrait of Elvie Bertha Weller

trait. Kate gave it to Catherine right then and there, saying that her
grandson, who was living with her at the time, had removed it from
where it hung in his bedroom because it "gave him the creeps."
Catherine took the portrait back to her home in Harlingen where she
was then living with her Air Force husband and children.

As the years went by, Catherine and her family noticed little things
that were a bit peculiar, but at first they did not attach any significance
to them happening around the portrait. The events have become much
more pronounced since Catherine bought the big old family home in La
Marque from her parents, some years back. The Tudor house on an acre
lot, shaded by giant oaks, is furnished with lovely family antiques,
many of which once graced the childhood home of Elvie and her siblings. And then, of course, her portrait is there, hanging on the wall at
the first landing of the staircase leading up to the second floor. Her spirit
seems to be there, as well, its bailiwick centering around the staircase,
the upstairs and downstairs halls, the entryway, the dining room, and
the butler's pantry.

Many times, by day or night, definite sounds of footsteps are heard
on the wooden stairs. Catherine said the first time her daughter Nancy
heard the footsteps she was alone in the house. She was so frightened
that she telephoned her mother, who was at a meeting, to please come

home at once, as she thought an intruder was somewhere hiding in the house!

When all her children were still living at home, at night they sometimes saw what they thought was the shadowy form of a woman descending the stairs. There is a big window at the landing, and the walls of the house by the staircase are painted white, so a dark, shadowy form would be easy to see. At first the children thought it was their mother, but when they tiptoed to her bedroom, they found her fast asleep!

A few years ago, when Nancy was spending the night at her mother's home, she heard what she described as a "whispering" noise, and then she saw the dark form of a woman descending the stairs. She thought it was her mother, Catherine, taking one of her cats outside. Not really sleepy, she decided to get up and go have a visit with her mother. She was certainly surprised to find that it was not Catherine she had seen, or heard whispering, on the stairs. Her mother was sound asleep in her bedroom!

Nancy told me when she was just a small child, about 7 or 8 years old, she had a very frightening experience which she has never forgotten. The family was living in Florida at the time. One night Nancy was restless and couldn't sleep. She got out of bed and went into the living room and lay down on the couch with the family pet, a big dog named Homer. She gazed up at the portrait of Elvie, which was hanging over the mantel. Imagine her shock as she saw the chest heaving up and down, as if the portrait were breathing, and then the lips started moving, as if she were speaking to Nancy. Nancy was so terrified she ran back to her bedroom, dragging the dog with her to sleep with her the rest of the night! She said it was a long time before she told her mother, as she was afraid no one would believe her, but she is convinced to this day that what she saw that night was real and neither a dream nor a figment of her imagination.

Catherine, who today lives alone in the big house, says she isn't afraid of Elvie, and indeed, rather enjoys having her spirit around. She does find it a bit annoying when the ghost plays childish pranks, probably to gain attention. We must remember, Elvie was barely 15 when she died, and she had led an extremely sheltered life, in Victorian days, so she really was very much a child at the time she passed away.

To illustrate what Elvie's spirit will do to gain attention, Catherine said she often removes her red earrings when she talks on the telephone. When she takes them off, they usually disappear right away. They will always reappear a few days later, generally in the middle of the dining room table or in the butler's pantry. Also, her favorite sewing scissors frequently quit their usual spot in Catherine's sewing box, which is kept in the pantry. Sometimes they are gone for weeks at a time. Then they always reappear in the box after their sabbatical with Elvie.

Catherine showed us a dear little china tea set that belonged to Elvie. The saucers are in the shapes of faces of cats and dogs. It is displayed on an antique whatnot stand. Catherine often hears the clinking of the china dishes as Elvie rearranges the pieces of one of her beloved former possessions. After hearing this, Catherine often catches a brief glimpse of the bottom of a long white skirt flying up the stairs! She has never seen the full figure of Elvie. But Nancy has!

About two years ago, when she was visiting her mother, Nancy decided the carpet in the front entry hall needed vacuuming. She was busily at work when she chanced to glance upwards. There, in the upstairs hall, peering over the stair railing was a full-length figure of a young girl, smiling down at her. The face gazing at Nancy looked exactly like the face of the portrait, except she was smiling. The hair, which in the portrait is arranged in corkscrew curls, was brushed out loosely about the shoulders. The apparition wore a white gown which looked to be a peignoir or granny gown, instead of the lace-edged blouse of the portrait. Nancy stood staring at the figure for several seconds, utterly in shock at what she saw. She finally looked down at the floor. When she glanced up again, the figure had totally disappeared!

The figure Nancy saw was probably how Elvie looked at the time of her death. Her hair would not have been so carefully arranged in long curls during a long spell of sickness, and she would have probably been wearing a long nightgown, also. Nancy confessed that seeing Elvie so plainly was pretty frightening.

We had such a lovely visit with Catherine that we were sorry we could not have spent more time with her. Catherine is head of the English department at the high school in La Marque. She is very contented there in her lovely big home with a trio of friendly cats, lots of friends, and frequent visits from her children, all grown up now. And of course, there is the sweet, playful spirit of Elvie to keep her company!

CHAPTER 6

Houston…A Haunting City

Hauntings in Houston

The largest city in the Southwest and the fourth largest in the nation, Houston, Texas, is a great metropolis. Named for General Sam Houston, whose army on April 21, 1836, defeated the Mexican army under General Lopez Antonio de Santa Anna, Houston began as a small riverboat landing founded by the Allen brothers in August of 1836. At the time of the battle between the Texan and Mexican forces, no town had yet grown up around the Buffalo Bayou where the battle was fought.

Today, Houston ranks among the top three seaports in the nation in total tonnage. It is connected to the Gulf of Mexico by a 50-mile-long ship channel. It is also the home of Johnson Space Center. It is a city whose main industries include petroleum, steel, cotton, and ship building.

As Texas' largest city, it would come as no surprise to find that Houston is home to a plethora of ghosts. These errant spirits have singled Houston out as a fine place to do their nocturnal roaming, and show no signs of moving elsewhere!

I am deeply indebted to the staff at the Houston Public Library (which, incidentally, is haunted) for assisting me in my research in the area, and to several property owners and building occupants who have kindly shared their personal experiences with me.

Uneasy Nights in Lovett Hall

The June 1985 issue of *Houston City Magazine* ran a great collection of ghost stories concerning Houston's spirit world inhabitants. One of special interest concerned Rice University's Lovett Hall. Pat Ivy, who is now a dispatcher for the Rice University Police but who at the time was a night custodian, told about some of her unusual and unexplainable experiences. While she swept the darkened halls of the empty building at night, in the third-floor classrooms the sounds of typewriters clicking away could be heard plainly. The only thing wrong with this was there were no night classes in the building, and the typewriter classrooms were no longer located on the third floor!

There had once been classrooms up on the third floor of the old administration building, but at the time Pat worked there, the rooms were no longer used for classes.

When Pat would be up there around 9:30 p.m. she would hear people yelling "help!" and there would often be the sounds of women crying up on the fourth floor. Other custodians reported they had also heard the same sounds.

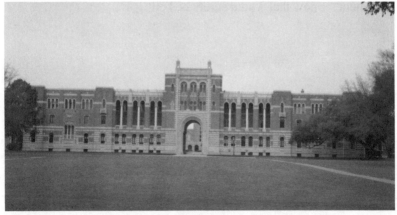

Lovett Hall at Rice University in Houston

Once, as she cleaned the building, she heard a noise on the stairway. When she turned to look, she saw a tall, white figure looking back at her. It was still standing there as she went to call her supervisor, John McRee. When he arrived, he watched as the tall figure turned and grabbed a chair at the end of the stairway. "It came down the stairway, picked up the chair, and threw it at Mr. McRee," said Ivy. Then the startled McRee threw it back at the apparition, and in turn, the ghost picked it up and tossed it back again! McRee and Ivy called in some other officers, but by the time they arrived, the ghost, or whatever it was, had disappeared.

Ivy also stated that another night while she was working, sweeping the landing at the third floor elevator area, she heard a man's voice. It was coming from behind her. The voice plainly said "Get the hell out of here!" she recalls. She said she stood there sort of stunned for a moment, then when the voice repeated the same warning, she got out of there fast! Although she called her supervisor to investigate, nothing ever turned up.

Mary Montana, who was working there at the time the article appeared in the magazine, said she also heard the same voices, so the hauntings persist in the old building.

Incidentally, the upper floors of Lovett Hall now house the departments of philosophy and religion . . . perhaps the proper routes that lead to knowledge of what goes on in other dimensions. One graduate student wondered if this is what happens when one fails the finals . . . and then commented, "to forever walk the halls of the Rice philosophy department . . . now that would surely be hell!"

The Sounds of Strings

A very interesting article appeared in the *Houston Post* on October 28, 1984, that stated there's a resident "spirit" at the Julie Ideson Building at the Houston Public Library. The building, which is located at 500 McKinney Street, was constructed in 1926. It housed the public library until a newer, more modern structure was built to replace it in 1976. The Ideson Building is still open to the public, and today it houses the Texas and local history departments, "special collections," archives, and manuscripts.

For ten years, from the day it was built until the day he died in 1936, the same janitor lovingly tended the building, polishing the tables and dusting the books on the shelves. Mr. Cramer lived a quiet, solitary life with his pet shepherd dog, Pete, in a small apartment in the basement. When the last employees and library researchers went home each day, Mr. Cramer would spend his leisure time tending his plants or playing his violin. It is said that he would stroll the halls and rotunda playing his favorite melodies by the hour. Ten years after he came to the library, Mr. Cramer died quietly in his little room in the basement. Although his mortal remains were taken away for burial, there are many who say his spirit has never left the building he loved and tended so carefully.

You see, library employees have long claimed they still hear eerie strains of violin music wafting through the old building. Hattie Johnson, who came to work at the building in 1946, said they would usually hear the music on cloudy, dreary days. The music would play for the longest time. Johnson said they all got used to hearing it. Some skeptics said the sounds were caused by the wind, but they had to toss that theory aside, because the music played mostly when there was no wind blowing at all!

Although Mr. Cramer was known to be a quiet, mild-mannered man, solitary and unassuming, whose life centered around his job, his dog Pete, his plants, and his music, his ghostly presence still seems to upset a lot of people. Johnson said the place spooks her. "The whole building is frightening," she maintains. "You always feel like someone is watching you."

A custodian who used to work the predawn shift, coming to work before daybreak to open up the library for the day, said he used to carry a broomstick with him for protection. The man, whose name is Scott Gould, said "It's just plain weird over there. I really don't know if I believe in ghosts but it is just plain weird in that building." Gould no longer works that shift, but he hasn't changed his mind about an unknown spirit living in the old building.

The June 1985 issue of the *Houston City Magazine* stated that Louise Franklin is one of only a few people around who still recalls Mr. Cramer and his music. She recalled the way he once tended a little seedling sprung from an acorn of a tree that had died on the grounds when the library was first built. When it had grown strong enough to transplant, he planted the seedling on the west side of the library entrance. Today, its lovely broad limbs shade the whole lawn. Miss Franklin says, "It's a beautiful tree . . . Mr. Cramer's tree."

The *Houston Post* article mentioned that one of the areas Mr. Cramer liked to roam, in life, as well as in death, is now the Texas and local history room of the library building. How fascinating to this writer! I just checked the return address on the large manila envelope containing research material for this book, sent to me from Houston. You guessed it! The return address is: "Texas Room, Houston Public Library, 500 McKinney, Houston, Texas." Wow!

The Montrose Ghost

On Barnard Street, in the inner city section of Montrose in Houston, there's a little house that was once haunted. Maybe it still is. But the owner, whom we will call "Clay," isn't particularly frightened. When he first found the place, he didn't know it was haunted. He just liked it and felt drawn to it. According to an article in the *Houston City Magazine*, June 1985 issue, he found out it was haunted from the Realtor on the very day he closed the deal. Clay said he had felt "something sort of different" that made him a trifle uneasy at times, and sometimes caused goosesbumps to rise, but he was really startled to find the little gingerbread house he felt so drawn to had actually been the scene of a vicious murder!

The previous owner had been a quiet, elderly gentleman named Mr. Cowen. He kept the lawn manicured and the house neat and tidy. The neighbors never had any trouble from the pleasant, rather private Mr. Cowen.

The old gentleman had befriended a young man who often visited him at the house. One night the two had a heated argument, and the young man took a knife to Mr. Cowen, leaving him in a gory pool of blood on the tiled kitchen floor. For months after Mr. Cowen's body had been removed, the little house sat empty and forlorn. The lawn Cowen had loved to tend soon became overgrown with weeds.

Clay was shocked at the story, but he still wanted the house enough to go ahead and close the deal. Soon after he settled in, he started to notice strange things about the house. When they would visit him, his friends complained about cold spots and that they felt they were being watched. His dog howled mournfully whenever he came into the kitchen where Cowen's murder had taken place. Numerous times objects moved around on their own. For some reason, none of this really bothered Clay that much.

Then a friend from England came to stay over the weekend. He slept in the living room on the couch. He was awakened by something blowing in his ear. He woke Clay to tell him he was uneasy. Clay made light of it and told his friend to go back to sleep. Soon, the friend was back to report that a ghost was walking on his bed, and he wasn't about to stay there any longer! Clay said he wasn't actually surprised, as he had felt a presence in the house, too, and so he did believe what his houseguest had to say.

Clay believes that Mr. Cowen was a kindly man who loved his home. He's a "caretaker" kind of ghost, who just wants to keep an eye on things and make his watchful presence known. Clay has no trouble accepting his presence because he is sure Mr. Cowen would approve of the care that Clay is taking of the house he loved so much.

The Strange Old Pagan Church House

In an old section of the city of Houston known as Montrose, at 903 Welch Street, there's an old house that was built about seventy-eight years ago. The big, two-story dwelling is constructed of wood, with a sweeping circular porch and a matching second-story veranda. They used to say it was haunted.

Back in the late 1960s, the era of the flower children, the house was rented to a "Reverend" Jim Palmer, a former postal worker and the organizer of what he called the "First Pagan Church of Houston." Nobody knows much about the inner workings of the strange cult, but it is said that Palmer taught what he called the "mental, occult, and hypnotic arts." His followers held nightly sessions in the "church." Many classes were held while the members were completely in the nude, and they studied such subjects as psychic phenomena, sex, yoga, and karate. The cultists placed huge papier-mache Greek figures on the front porch, and nude pictures were plastered all over both the interior and exterior of the house. A sign in the front yard read, much to the horror of the neighbors, "Stand up for sex. Lay down for love. The joys of heaven are not all above."

George Brown, who has lived within three blocks of the old house for many years, recalls the sentiments of Palmer's neighbors. "Nobody liked it," he said. "I even went by there as a kid and shot out some windows with a slingshot. They had these nudist colony magazine pages glued to the outside of the house. Back in those days, this neighborhood had more older-type people who really didn't appreciate that. People were kind of scared of them." Brown was interviewed for an article that ran in the Sunday, October 25, 1981 issue of the *Houston Chronicle Magazine.*

It was said in the wee hours, the horrible screams of animals being sacrificed would be heard coming from back rooms as followers of the strange "religion" chanted. The Palmers' teenage daughter was nicknamed "the Ghost" by the neighbors, because of her pasty-white complexion and glazed, spaced-out look.

In 1974 an attorney named Thomas L. Whitcomb evicted Palmer and his family from the property. Whitcomb was buying up a whole block on Welch Street for renovation and wanted to start work on the "church" house.

Shortly after the eviction, weird things began to happen at the house. A young man that Whitcomb hired to clean up and work on the place related some really strange occurrences. He didn't want his name used, so we will call him "Jay," just as the writer in the *Chronicle* article referred to him. He related how another young man, a friend of his who had come to help him with the monumental task of cleaning up, was hit on the arm while walking down the stairs. He called out to Jay that something had hit him. The two men just quit working and went home that day. Then, another time, a couple of Native Americans who were hired to help walked off the job, saying they were thoroughly spooked.

For about three weeks while the cleanup job was going on, Jay lived in the house, staying in a room on the second floor. He had strange nightmares while there, something he had never experienced before. He says the people in his dreams were so bizarre that he feels he was being persecuted in his dreams. He finally moved out, partly because of the weird dreams, and also because of the noises he heard. There was the constant creaking and groaning of the old house. There was also the continual scurrying of rats. It all combined to give him a general uneasy feeling.

One acquaintance of Jay's decided that he wanted to spend a night in the place. The man, whom Jay described as someone prone to emotional difficulties anyway, spent his first night trying to "invoke the devil," Jay said. It's unclear as to what happened that night, but the man elected not to return. The very next night he stayed in another house in the neighborhood and set fire to that structure. "He was a little bit on the loose side, anyway," Jay said. "By word of mouth, I heard he ended up in a mental institution."

Since Jay had seen a popular movie of that era called the *Exorcist*, he suggested to Whitcomb it might be a good idea to have this place exorcised. Whitcomb went to see Rev. Francis E. Monaghan, vice president of St. Thomas University. The Father agreed to come over, and "bless" the old house. It wasn't a formal exorcism; he just sprinkled some holy water and said some prayers, but it must have done some good!

We are delighted to report the former pagan church has gone through a real transformation since the article appeared in the *Chronicle*. A recent (February 1994) visit to the Montrose area revealed a cheerful, yellow-painted house, with white and turquoise trim. Its well-kept yard is surrounded by a sturdy wrought-iron fence. Gone are the graffiti, the ugly door-side statues, the lewd slogans. It is just another charming old turn-of-the-century corner house on a quiet street. The neighbors must be relieved!

903 Welch Street, Houston, Texas

The Newport Story

If you saw the film *Poltergeist*, you will recall that a family bought
a lovely "dream home," but ended up having to leave the house with
all their belongings behind, fleeing as fast as they could, just to get
away. . . .

The house, which had been built over an old unmarked cemetery,
had become the dwelling place of satanic spirits and poltergeists. This
film could have been based on a true story. The upper-class Newport
subdivision on Lake Houston has been almost abandoned. Many former residents left after strange and eerie events began to take place in
the area soon after they took possession of their lovely new homes. You
see, these weren't ordinary garden variety ghosts! One family, Ben and
Jean Williams, wrote of the terrors they experienced in a book entitled
Black Hope Horror (Morrow Publishing Company). One of their
daughters went insane, and another died of a heart attack after warning
her mother not to dig in the backyard. All told, four members of the
ill-fated family died of cancer within six years of their moving into the
house, which they finally abandoned.

There were eight families in the neighborhood that moved away,
after reporting such strange occurrences as garage doors opening and
closing themselves, television sets turning on in the middle of the night,
strong winds blowing through their houses, and huge, rectangular sink
holes suddenly appearing in their yards, while snakes were seen de-
vouring birds!

The families learned that the Purcell Corporation had constructed
the homes in the subdivision over an old Negro graveyard, once known
as Black Hope Cemetery. The unmarked graves, long overgrown by a
tangle of weeds, were not visible, and the builders apparently did not
intentionally or knowingly build the custom-made homes over the
cemetery.

One couple, Sam and Judy Haney, sued the Purcell Corporation for
damages they claimed to have suffered in the form of "mental an-

guish," but they did not succeed in winning their case. The Haneys discovered a grave containing the remains of two corpses in September of 1983 while digging for a swimming pool. Strangely enough, a stranger who noticed they were building the pool warned them a cemetery might be at that location! According to an article in the August 27, 1987 edition of the *Houston Chronicle*, the disinterred remains were left at the Harris County medical examiner's office for about six weeks, when the Haneys asked for and received permission to rebury them in a small casket which they had built for the purpose. The bodies stayed buried in their backyard until 1986 when the Purcell Corporation received a court order to move them away from the area. Testimony showed that as many as sixty poor people had been buried in unmarked graves in the unconsecrated area, a sort of "potter's field," many years ago. The Haneys believe that the bodies in their yard were those of former slaves who worked at the nearby old McKinney estate.

Although the Haneys did not win their court case against the Purcell Corporation (the jury found that the Haneys should have known about the cemetery being there in 1981, and they didn't file the lawsuit until 1984, meaning the lawsuit would be barred by a two-year statute of limitation), they said they still felt they had scored a victory. They said the major reason they brought suit was to gain recognition for the cemetery. Judy Haney said of her obligation to the dead, "These are people that were born slaves and that were lost for a long time. I think that's really sad."

The Haneys went on to say that when they first disinterred the remains, many unexplainable occurrences took place in their home. Shoes mysteriously disappeared and then reappeared, side by side, in the opened grave site! Their television set came on at night at least twice, and although they never saw or talked to any "spirits," they were sure that although unseen, they were definitely there!

The *Black Hope Horror* book, which details the experiences endured by the Williams and Haney families, is worth reading. But be forewarned. It is not a good bedtime story.

More Spirits Than Ale at the Ale House

From time to time, the "spirits" at the Ale House, at 2425 W. Alabama, are mentioned in one publication or another. The popular drinking establishment was mentioned in an article delving into Houston's supernatural side in the June 1985 issue of *Houston City Magazine*. The writer, Laura Perkins, stated that the beautiful house, built in the English Manor style, was once a "speakeasy" during Prohibition days. She quoted the manager at that time, Mike Holliday, as saying that the woman who had lived there operated an illicit drinking establishment on the middle floor, the customers coming and going by a fire escape. They were said to have paid well for their libations, and thus the woman kept her estate intact.

She is reported to have passed away in her bedroom on the third floor. The house was sold to business interests, and there have apparently been several owners. Odd occurrences have continued to plague the old building. "The old owners," said Holliday, "used to put a chair out on the top porch during business hours so she would leave the customers alone. Their maintenance man was the only one I ever knew who saw her. He refused to stay here after dark."

Today the third floor bedroom is decorated like an English pub, with a bar and dart boards, a favorite English pub sport. Employees claim that after they lock up at night the lights upstairs will turn themselves back on. Musical equipment rearranges itself, and when customers speak lightly of the legend of the ghostly former owner, glasses have been known to break in their hands!

Several waitresses claim the top floor emits an intense sadness when the customers are all gone. Two of the girls recalled becoming so overwhelmed by the feeling, that upon ascending the stairway, they began to tremble and broke into sobs that ceased only when the customers began to arrive for "happy hour."

It has been suggested that the old owner's spirit may be comforted by a bar full of young people laughing, dancing, and drinking together.

According to another article which ran in the *Houston Chronicle* on October 31, 1991, during a radio interview with the manager of the Ale House, an unexplainable voice was heard echoing in the background. A young woman was heard distinctly to cry, "Let me out! let me out!"

The manager at that time, Angela Jenkins, said, "The place is overrun with ghosts. There are times when you feel like someone is looking at you. You'll hear noises like a party is going on when there's no one in the place. Mugs will be swinging and chairs creaking."

Once, Jenkins said, the air conditioner turned on even though it wasn't plugged in. Jenkins says the Ale House is home to both a good and a bad spirit. The first, a former maid, plays with the light switches and musicians' equipment. The latter, who some believe may be an irate sea captain, throws lighted candles and smashes glasses.

A telephone conversation with genial Tim Case, who identified himself as the night manager of the Ale House (as of August 1993) revealed the ghost, or ghosts, hasn't departed. Case has been at the place for several years and says he is often alone at night in the dark at the place more than anyone else, and he certainly didn't deny that there is a spirit still roaming the Ale House. He made no mention of maids

The Ale House, 2425 W. Alabama in Houston

or sea captains, but went straight to the point that the former owner ran a "speakeasy and a house of prostitution" at the address. She is still there, at least in spirit, and she makes it a point to let her presence be known, as if to say, "I'm here and I'm still in charge." Case said he had intended to do some extensive research on the building for some time, to find out the name of the woman who ran the speakeasy and the names of subsequent owners to see what kind of experiences they might have had, but he just had not had the time to get around to it. Such research should surely net some interesting stories!

Case said there are instances every now and then when doors open just after they have been locked, lights will turn on by themselves, and glasses will fly off racks or shelves for no logical reason. Sometimes keys and other objects "misplace themselves." Recently, Case said he had questioned another employee named Nat, why he had not turned the third floor lights out.

Nat told Case that he certainly had turned off the lights. They both went back up to the room on the third floor reputed to have been the former owner's bedroom. This is where the dart boards are now. The lights above all three dart boards were turned on, and even more unusual, all three boards had been rotated about fifteen degrees on the wall from their customary positions! This happened just minutes after Nat had checked everything and turned out the lights before coming downstairs.

Case also mentioned that he had noticed that same aura of sadness that was mentioned in the *Houston City Magazine* article. It sometimes pervades the whole third floor. He believes the original owner must have experienced great sorrow in leaving the place she loved, or else, another theory we might inject . . . perhaps she regretted the nefarious activities that took place in the house under her management. For whatever reason, her spirit is still hanging out at the Ale House, and it doesn't appear she plans to leave anytime soon!

A Few "Mini" Ghost Tales

In researching for this book, I ran into a few very interesting but very brief accountings of Houston hauntings, that I wasn't able to explore any farther than what I originally found in news articles and clippings. There wasn't enough to go by to do much farther investigation, but they were so intriguing, I thought I would share what little I could find out:

* There's one old Houston neighborhood near a little Catholic church where a cemetery is located. An occult shop is located in the area, and the owner of that place of business was quoted in a *Houston Post* article of October 28, 1984 as saying people in the neighborhood had spotted white ectoplasms near the church. Other people reported a "mysterious ghost-like figure" in the neighborhood. Some described it as a "white amorphous blob" while others said it looked like a woman in white. They have reported seeing the filmy spirit inside the priest's church, near a grocery store across the street from the church, and in an empty warehouse a few blocks away.

* On Durham Street, an elderly Mexican woman has abandoned her home completely because of an infestation of what she calls "lechusas," large birds with human heads. In Mexican mythology, the lechusa will bring doom to a household.

* In Spring Branch, a young couple expect to take a $30,000 loss on their home because "spirits" keep driving potential buyers away.

* In Pasadena, a family has long listened to the song of what they say is the ghost of an Indian maiden singing for her lover in their backyard.

* There are those who say a ghost lurks at the Alley Theatre, 615 Texas, where longtime managing director Iris Siff was robbed and strangled with a telephone cord outside her office in the middle of a January night in 1982. A security guard was convicted of the heinous crime.

Spring's Haunted Saloon

Spring, Texas, is a small city a few miles north of Houston on Interstate Highway 45. The Harris County town was founded by German immigrants in 1840. But it wasn't until the early 1900s that the little town began to flourish. When the Great Northern Railroad came to town, a real building boom took place. Seven saloons and a number of small hotels sprang up, practically overnight, to accommodate the railroad workers and the travelers the rails would carry on this Galveston-Houston-Palestine line.

Jane and Carl Wunsche were children of some of the German immigrants who first settled Spring. Two of their sons, Charlie and Dell, who were former railroad men, acquired a piece of property near the railroad depot in what today is called Old Town Spring. Along with another brother, William, or "Willie," as he was called, they constructed a two-storied frame structure on the property. It was the very first two-storied building in Spring!

The new establishment, which opened for business in 1902, was named The Wunsche Bros. Saloon and Hotel. The main purpose of the new business was to accommodate railroad employees on overnight stopovers.

The town prospered, and so did the Wunsche brothers, until 1923, when Houston and Great Northern (now known as the Missouri Pacific) moved the Spring railyard to Houston. By 1926 most of the little town's wooden buildings had been torn down, the lumber salvaged for barn construction and firewood. Somehow the Wunsche establishment survived. The saloon was the last one to close in Harris County when Prohibition hit.

In 1949 a lady named Viola Burke leased the building, renaming it the Spring Cafe. She was known for her delicious homemade hamburgers which the railroad workers passing through town delighted in ordering. In fact, word of her wonderful burgers spread far and wide, and soon the cafe had the reputation of having the best hamburgers anywhere in the country! When Viola died in 1976, her daughter, Irma Ansley, inherited the business and continued making the famous hamburgers.

In fact, the entire shopping village of Old Town Spring traces its origins back to the famous hamburgers! Back in the 1970s, just getting one of the burgers required a long wait, because all were made to order. Sensing a good opportunity, an enterprising couple opened a gift shop for cafe customers to shop and browse in while they waited for a table. Slowly, more and more houses and buildings were converted into shops, until quite a variety of gifts, crafts, antiques, and works of art were made available to the cafe patrons.

As Old Town began to flourish, the little cafe that helped to bring about its birth was going downhill. Finally, the building, now quite dilapidated, was sold in 1982 to an enterprising couple, Brenda and Scott Mitchell. The old building was carefully restored by Scott, a Woodlands builder, and his wife. Today, the building, which bears a Texas Historic Landmark plaque, is a popular restaurant. Staying

Wunsche Bros. Cafe and Saloon, Spring, Texas

in tune with its pioneer heritage, the Mitchells call the place, The Wunsche Bros. Cafe and Saloon. (It's no longer a hotel, so don't plan an overnight stay!) From the looks of the menu, and a delightful cookbook entitled *The Wunsche Bros. Cafe Cookbook* written by owner Brenda Greene Mitchell and offered for sale at the cafe, there are plenty of good viands available at Wunsche Bros. including the famous made-to-order hamburgers.

In addition to great food, there's also a ghost! Well, maybe more than one; the owners aren't really sure. Telephone interviews with Brenda Mitchell, who now resides in Austin; her current manager, Sherry Sinini; and former employees Alma Lemm and Ilona Langlinais all indicate that Charlie (they're pretty sure that he's the "haunting brother") still comes around to check up on things at the place.

Lemm, a cook who retired a few years ago, is now in her 70s. She loved working for the Mitchells and it was only on doctor's orders that she finally hung up her apron. She said in about 1988 (she recalled it was in the fall of the year) she had a real shock when she went to the linen closet to get a hand towel and heard the unmistakable sound of a man's voice. "It was sort of mumbling. I couldn't understand the words he said but I definitely did hear a voice," she said. She was so startled that she shut the closet door and scurried to the kitchen to tell a fellow worker what she'd heard. She says now she wishes she had had the presence of mind to ask it what it wanted. This was the first time she heard a voice, but there were a lot of unexplained occurrences all during the time she worked at the cafe.

Lemm said she and Gladys Barton, another employee, were in the habit of having a cup of coffee together early in the morning to kind of "get going." The tables in the cafe had candles on them that were lit each evening for the dinner hour. They were always extinguished when the last patron had departed. But on Saturday mornings, Lemm and Barton kept finding one candle lit when they opened up the restaurant. Each Saturday the lit candle would be on a table closer and closer to where they customarily sat for their morning coffee visit. When the candle finally "arrived" one Saturday and was glowing on their table, it never came again. There is no possible explanation except that Charlie finally had a silent Saturday morning visit with them!

Back in 1989 and 1990 the ghost was more active than he is now. Lemm said every time a new manager came in there would be quite a bit of unexplained activity. (This is not unusual. Ghosts dislike change, and until Charlie was reasonably sure the managers were doing things that met with his approval, he would naturally have become more agitated.) Sometimes when she came in very early, about 5 a.m., Lemm said, the chairs would "rattle and move about quite a bit."

When she first went to work at the cafe, an upstairs room in the section that had been part of the old hotel was rented out to a young man who was an artist, according to Lemm. One morning when he came downstairs, he asked the cooks if they knew something strange was going on. They told him, yes, indeed they did.

Soon after this, a former waitress with whom I also spoke, Ilona Langlinais, actually saw the ghost! The young artist who lived upstairs was able to draw a sketch of him from her very accurate description. Langlinais said one October day in 1984, around 9 a.m., she was in the upstairs section, which in those days was used as a dining area to accommodate the overflow from downstairs. She had just made a fresh pot of coffee and was carrying it down the hallway. Langlinais was very startled when she glanced into a room off the hallway and saw an elderly man seated at a table. Although he had his back to her, she could see he had longish white hair, worn over the collar, and he had on a tall-crowned black hat and a black suit. He was sitting sort of hunched over at the table, and to her he looked dejected, just from the way he was sitting. Langlinais said a feeling of great sadness suddenly came over her as she saw him there. She thought a cup of coffee might be just what he needed, so she asked, "Would you like a hot cup of coffee?" As she spoke, she said, a gust of wind hit her with a tremendous "whoosh!" and at the same instant, the man she had seen so plainly literally vanished in front of her eyes!

After she spoke to the figure, whom she feels might have been the spirit of one of the Wunsche brothers, she said she never again felt or heard anything strange at the restaurant. She believes the spirit left . . . at least during the rest of the time she worked there. She was glad, because she said seeing the figure, then having it disappear so suddenly, definitely gave her a good case of the "heebie jeebies."

Several waitresses reported that salt and pepper shakers and sugar packets used to be scattered all about the tables and on the floor when they would open up in the mornings. And pictures on the walls of members of the Wunsche family would often be crooked as if intentionally rearranged. No other pictures were ever touched, just the Wunsche likenesses.

Owner Brenda Mitchell says she has never seen or heard the ghost, but she believes in the veracity of her employees and therefore acknowledges the existence of a ghost at her restaurant. The place is very busy these days, with the restaurant operating on the ground floor and a successful gourmet food mail order business operating out of the former hotel rooms on the upper floor.

Why don't you drop by the Wunsche Bros. Cafe and Saloon next time you're in Spring? You might not run into Charlie, but the home-made hamburgers are worth the trip anyway!

CHAPTER 7

Ghosts of the Golden Triangle

The Golden Triangle Area

The three cities that form the Golden Triangle are in the far south-eastern corner of the state of Texas. The stories in this chapter are about the area around the cities which comprise the triangle: Port Arthur, Orange, and Beaumont.

Port Arthur was first called Aurora when it was founded as a small settlement in 1840. The city, which is located on the northwest shore of Sabine Lake, nine miles from the Gulf of Mexico, was named after Arthur E. Stillwell, a Kansas City financier who was instrumental in bringing a railroad to the town site and thus assured its success. The area claims it "oils the world," because nearly a million barrels of crude oil are refined in the area daily.

Orange, the easternmost city on the Sabine, is right at the Louisiana boundary. It was established in 1836, the year Texas won her independence from Mexico. It was named by early French and Spanish explorers who found large groves of wild oranges growing along the banks of the Sabine. Today it is a deep water port terminal 42 miles inland at the junction of Sabine and Neches rivers and the Gulf Intracoastal Waterway.

Beaumont is the northernmost city of the triangle. It was established as a fur trading post in the early 1800s by French and Spanish explorers. It is believed to have been named for its slight northeast elevation, called Beau Mont in French. The town site was laid out in the 1830s, but it came of age in 1901 with the discovery of the first oil well gusher at Spindletop. The small village became a city of over 30,000 in less than a month!

MYSTERIOUS NIGHTS
Docia Williams

There are happenings so mysterious
That they fill our hearts with fright;
There are rivers flowing, and lights a'glowing
And spirits that walk in the night.

There are "things" that we as mortals
Just cannot understand
About the restless spirits
That haunt this ancient land.

Oh, would that we might help them
Find their way to peaceful dreams,
Beneath the spreading live oaks,
That shade the crystal streams.

Then we might freely travel
And never fear the sight,
Of these souls, so lost and lonely,
That wander in the night.

Spirits at the Sabine Pass Lighthouse

The Sabine Pass Lighthouse, built in 1857, served as a beacon to passing ships for many years, up until about the time of World War II, in fact. Now it's deserted, and the elements are slowly taking over. Some say it's still "occupied" with something, or someone, from another time.

According to an article that appeared in the *Port Arthur News* on October 29, 1992, "The lighthouse always has had a ghostly appearance, dating back to the 1930s when the captain of a tanker complained the lighthouse could not be distinguished in the early morning fog. In 1932 the tower was repainted with black and white horizontal bands ten feet apart."

It's said that a caretaker back in the early 1950s asked to be removed from his job. This was after he saw the specter of a man wearing a black suit with bold brass buttons and a cap that looked like the uniform of a former lighthouse keeper. It was presumed this was the apparition of a former keeper of the light.

Then, a daughter of a former keeper said she once saw a huge "thing" with round, red, glowing eyes. It was covered with fur! She presumed it might be an evil "swamp monster" who didn't want people intruding upon his swamp area. And the president of the Port Arthur Historical Society, Sam Monroe, said he believed the ghost that inhabits the house is the figure of a soldier killed during the famous Battle of Sabine Pass. Monroe expressed the belief that the spirit is both harmless and benevolent.

By the various descriptions, one would have to presume the old monument is inhabited by more than one spirit or ghost. There have been few sightings in recent times, since no one lives at the lighthouse anymore. Some people want the house restored, while others wish to tear it down. The ownership has actually moved from Texas to Louisiana. Parts of the huge light that once served as a beacon to ships sailing off the coast are now in storage, waiting to someday be displayed in the Museum of the Gulf Coast.

Today the old lighthouse sits forlorn and alone on its tiny wind-swept spit of land. The big windows that once housed the life-saving light look like empty eyes gazing sadly out to sea. The once bold black stripes have almost disappeared.

Such a shame that this historical monument to another time should be left standing deserted and forlorn; not even a very good home for a ghost!

Joe Lee Never Left Nederland

When I first began this book project, I sent out letters to numerous South Texas newspapers in the coastal area, hopeful they would run an article about my project and that people who had a "ghostly encounter" to share would contact me about their personal experiences.

I was not disappointed. Many people who had previously kept secret their encounters with the supernatural did contact me. I believe they were relieved to at last talk about what they had experienced, having found someone who would believe them and not question either their veracity or their sanity.

One such person is Anne Malinowsky Blackwell, of Nederland, a small town midway between Port Arthur and Beaumont. We have been in contact by mail and telephone for the past year. Her story is most interesting, and heretofore, unknown and unpublished.

Ms. Blackwell stated in her first letter to me, dated March 5, 1993, "Your letter caught my attention because six years ago I bought a house in Nederland that was built around 1922. I knew nothing about its history nor did I believe in ghosts prior to living here. After several years of strange occurrences that were totally inexplicable, I have accepted the fact that there is a ghost in my house. In fact, when I finally met a descendant of the man that built the house my first question to her was 'Who died in this house?' 'My grandfather,' she replied, 'on New Year's Eve on the stroke of midnight.'"

In another letter, in which Ms. Blackwell enclosed a photo of her home, she stated, "I've also included background information on me so you'll know I'm not a lunatic (at least not yet!). Actually, I'm the least suitable person I know of to be haunted. Certainly, if you find this of interest, you have my permission to use my Ghost Story, and my name if you wish. Maybe, with some exposure, we can find someone who appreciates him. I certainly don't!"

Nederland house built around 1922 by Joe Lee at 1616 Elgin Street

Anne Malinowsky Blackwell is indeed a fascinating and accomplished lady. The personal photograph she enclosed in one of her letters also shows her to be as beautiful as she is "brainy." In fact, her brunette good looks would certainly border on "extremely glamorous" in finding words to describe her appearance. The owner of Maco Construction Company, Blackwell was the first female contractor in Southeast Texas, the first female to be licensed as a civil contractor by the state of Louisiana, first female contractor to perform underground construction for United States Environmental Protection Agency projects, and the first female contractor to be utilized on United States Department of Energy projects. Well qualified as an independent construction consultant, she has testified in numerous cases in state and federal courts and has been sought by a variety of federal agencies, senate committees, and the EPA which have incorporated many of her suggestions in their regulations. She is a member of Sigma Lamda Chi, the National Construction Honors Society, the Southeast Texas' Women's Hall of Fame, received the Jefferson Award for Public Service, Avon's Women of Enterprise Award, Female Entrepreneur of the Year, and holds membership in the National Association of Female Executives. Her honors, accomplishments, and educational background fill two single-spaced typewritten pages!

This lady, to use her own words, is definitely "no lunatic." And therefore her story is to be believed, just as she wrote it to me, in her own words:

I heard about the house in Nederland months before I ever saw it. I had lived in Beaumont or Port Arthur for most of my life and for the past seven years had resided in Louisiana. I had made frequent trips back to Southeast Texas, where I also had a business.

In 1986, I realized it was time to move back to Texas. Since I owned a second home, a townhouse, in Port Arthur, I didn't really need another house, but became intrigued by the house in Nederland that two of my employees frequently discussed between them. This house, I heard, had formerly been a run-down shack that someone had bought and spent several years remodeling. Now it was for sale. The more I heard about the house, the more I realized it sounded "like me." Finally, I asked for directions, and found it. It was exactly right for me. Not large . . . two bedrooms when I bought it (one's now my home office), a small formal living room, and a very large, open kitchen-den area with lots of windows giving an almost "beach house" effect.

It sat on two lots that were covered with huge live oak and pecan trees. The old, quiet neighborhood suited me very well. I live alone and like my privacy. There was even a dog pen for my beloved "Beaux," who I had acquired in Louisiana earlier that year. I bought the house at 1616 Elgin and moved in that October of 1986.

I knew little about the house's history beyond the prior owners, a young couple who only lived there three or four years before divorcing. It had been built around 1922 by a man named Joe Lee. It was empty for many years prior to being remodeled in the early 1980s. There's not much more I know about its history now, except that Joe Lee died here of a heart attack on a long-ago New Year's Eve, just at the stroke of midnight. He was survived by a wife, who was, according to his granddaughter, a "witch" (what kind, I don't know, and I don't even know what became of her). But somewhere between learning that Joe Lee built the house and that Joe Lee died in this house, I have come to believe that Joe Lee has not ever left this house.

For the first year and a half that we lived here, Beaux and I were quite content in our home. My only complaint was a shortage of closet space in my bedroom. It finally occurred to me by taking out the folding door closet that ran along the bedroom's east wall (the wall between the bedroom and the kitchen) and building a walk-in closet off the north wall (the back of the house) I could increase the size of my bedroom and my closet space. Since I am a contractor, it was a simple matter of bringing my carpentry crew in and lining them up.

First, we built the addition onto, but not yet accessible to, the bedroom. Then we took down the wall of folding closet doors and finished the former closet's interior. After a week or so of work, we were ready to cut a doorway through the north bedroom wall into the new closet. The carpenters pulled my bed out to the middle of the room in preparation, with Beaux's dog bed a few feet away from the right side, as usual. That night, actually about 2 a.m., I was jarred out of a deep sleep by a violent shaking of my bed. Beaux and I jumped up at the same time. For a minute we just stood there, stunned. I fully expected a "boom!" The last time I'd experienced such a tremor was during my childhood when the Texas City refineries blew up! There was no sound to follow. Beaux laid back down. I stayed up, looking out the windows for the glow of a fire from one of the Port Arthur refineries. There was nothing but darkness outside.

The next few days I asked everyone I encountered if they had felt any sort of tremor that night. No one had. Meanwhile, the carpenters finished the doorway and moved the bed to the east wall. We looked over the bed, the floor, and even under the house for any clue to what had caused the bed to shake. There was simply nothing to explain the event. After a week or two, I decided it was just some sort of a freak one-time occurrence.

And then it happened again . . . and again . . . and again! Just about every week, and sometimes twice a week, the bed would suddenly start shaking violently for five to fifteen or so seconds. I literally tore the house apart trying to find a reason, any reason. There was none. Eventually I realized that it wasn't the house shaking, for never did glass rattle or pictures shift during these occurrences. I started sleeping (when I slept at all) with one eye open and the lights on. But I never saw a thing. Beaux, after the first time or two, slept through the rest, just a few feet away, undisturbed. Not me! After four months, I was a wreck. The bed-shakings were now occurring two to three times a week, happening most often right after I fell asleep, no matter what time of night. I continued to explore every possibility with no results. Finally, I simply left the house for two weeks.

When I came back, things eased up somewhat. The bed-shakings now were only happening two or three times a month, then once, or twice. By fall of 1989 I had acquired a second dog, a female named Char, and it seemed as though the bed-shakings lessened in frequency when she started sleeping at the foot of my bed, under a bench I have there.

After a few months of relative peace, a new and terrifying event took place. I was in bed watching TV. The lights were on and both dogs were asleep in different corners of the room. Suddenly, something hit the side of the bed, eight times in succession. It was like a giant fist hit the side of my mattress! I had time to sit straight up and clearly look in all directions while the bed jumped from the invisible blows. There was absolutely nothing to see. That was sometime in 1990. The bed wasn't "touched" by unseen hands again. But I was.

One night about a year after the eight "bed-thumps" I was lying crossways across the bed on my stomach, reading. Suddenly, someone tapped me on the shoulder... hard! I leapt up in absolute terror prepared to face an intruder. I was even more terrified to see no one there.

Last year, I was again in bed, reading, wide awake. I was sitting, my back against the pillows and my hair had fallen over my forehead, almost in my eyes. Gently, very gently, something lifted my hair off my forehead and brushed it back into place. I froze for a second and when I finally got the courage to lift my eyes I saw, for just about two or three seconds, a faint, white mist. That is the only time I have seen anything.

Occasionally there is a loud thump or crash that I can't explain. Then, again, there are those I can explain.

The most awesome event took place in the living room. The previous owners had installed brass wall sconces with glass chimneys on each side of the fireplace. I had inspected these very closely to see if they could be moved, but found that they were each held by two sturdy screws through the sheetrock into the solid wood wall behind. One day, the dogs and I were outside when I heard an enormous crash in the house. I ran inside to find one of the sconces on the floor, with glass everywhere. I couldn't believe my eyes. There was no way it could have simply come out of the wall. I looked at the wall. If the sconce had fallen downward, the bottom hole through the sheetrock should have been elongated by the screw pulling loose. But it was the top hole that was elongated, upward! The sconce had been pulled upward, and out, by some tremendous force!

Then there was the night I came home to find no hot water at any faucet in the house. But when I checked my gas water heater it was running fine. I called several people, including a plumber, and no one could give me any possible reason. After making arrangements for the plumber to come out the next morning, I shut the hot water heater completely off, figuring something had to be wrong with it. Two hours later, I went to the kitchen to fill a pot to heat water to wash up in, and the instant I turned the faucet on, hot water came out! The plumber found nothing wrong. There was no possible explanation!

The most recent incident happened only a week or two ago. [Note: This would have been in March 1993.] The dogs and I (I'm up to three now) were in the den one evening when I heard a crash in the bedroom. I ran in to find a heavy, nearly solid crystal perfume bottle smashed on the carpeted floor. This bottle had been on a tray on my dresser surrounded by a dozen or so smaller, more fragile perfume bottles. But all the other bottles still sat undisturbed. I cannot possibly explain how one bottle in the middle had fallen, or how such a sturdy bottle could shatter on . . . thick carpet. Actually, I can't explain any of this.

Char, my female dog, now weighs fifty pounds, about the same as Beaux. She sometimes wakes me up in the morning by jumping up on my bed. And a fifty-pound dog jumping on my bed does not shake it with near the force of the unexplained bed shakings.

While the dogs don't appear to sense anything, there have been many times one of them, usually Beaux, has suddenly yelped, jumped, and slunk away to hide in a corner and look at me with hurt eyes, just as if to say, "Why did you hit me?"

The bed-shakings seemed to have stopped about the time that Joe Lee's granddaughter visited. When I told her about all my incidents she did not seem at all surprised. She simply nodded and said "Paw-paw's still here. You need to tell him to either behave himself or leave." I did. And at least I can get a decent night's sleep now.

The only pattern I have been able to think of is that the events have happened, or at least started, after men were in my house. The bed-shakings started while the carpenters were here; the wall sconce crashed the day after a party, the perfume bottle fell after a young man had dog-sat for me for a week.

As I said, I don't "believe in" spirits. I don't talk about this often because people often act like they expect me to try to convince them there are such things. I've found it's not a matter of believing or convincing. It's simply a matter of realizing and finally accepting the fact that Joe Lee (or someone else) lives with me at 1616 Elgin in some form or another. I don't like it, and I don't want it. But, whoever, or whatever, it is here.

Is the Spirit Still Around?

Debbie Sandifer read in the *Beaumont Enterprise* that I was seeking ghost stories. She telephoned me right away with her story!

During the two years, from 1971-1973, that Debbie and her husband, Jim, rented a small four-room house in Nederland, so many unexplainable things happened there they are convinced they played host to a poltergeist!

As is typical of many homes in the coastal area, this small dwelling was built up on piers. From the first night the Sandifers resided there, strange manifestations began. There was a small dining area, no larger than 4 by 6 feet, off the kitchen. As the Sandifers and another couple sat around the table chatting after dinner the first night they spent there, they noticed a small copper pipe which was located on the floor start to move up and down, coming up about one to 1 to 1 1/2 inches from the floor level. It was the type of tubing that would have been used for an icemaker, only their refrigerator had no icemaker. Astounded, they decided there must be an animal under the house, and it had caused the pipe to be pushed up through the floor. They went outside, taking their big German shepherd dog, King, with them. King showed no interest in the area under the house from which the pipe had emerged, and a good look under the house turned up nothing. The two couples went back inside, and several times during the evening the small pipe would move up and down in the floor!

Debbie told me during their two years of living in the house "things moved around a lot." A neighbor who lived across the street was bodily pushed through his open patio door, also. This neighbor believed at times the Sandifers' ghost visited his house as well!

The gas heater the Sandifers used to warm the house during chilly weather would sometimes turn itself off at the wall after it had just been lit. When they questioned their landlady, the Sandifers said she was very reluctant to discuss the possibility that the house might be haunted, even though the neighbors assured Debbie that previous tenants had also experienced peculiar things at the house and the landlady was well aware of it.

When the Sandifers took a trip to Lubbock, in West Texas, they arranged for Jim's parents to have a house key so they could come in and feed and water King while they were away. Debbie left a note of instructions on the kitchen counter as to what to feed the dog. When they returned from their trip, they were astounded to find this note firmly glued to the kitchen cabinet with a "white, milky-looking substance," some of which had trickled down the cabinet. When Debbie questioned her mother-in-law about why she had pasted the note on the cabinet, she was so shocked to hear this that she came right over to Debbie's house to see for herself how the note got stuck to the cabinet!

Once, to surprise her husband, Debbie purchased a small model automobile kit. Since it was like the car they owned, she thought he would enjoy having the model. Her sister was with her when she bought it, and both ladies agreed the kit was well wrapped and sealed up, all parts intact, at the time of purchase. When her husband got home that night, Debbie asked him if he had seen her surprise. He had not, so she went to where she had left it and was shocked to find the package all unwrapped!

In a similar vein, Debbie said she liked to sew and often had projects going. Once when she had worked all day on a dress, she laid the finished product out to show her husband when he came home from work that night. She had it all finished except for sewing on the buttons, so she just placed them where they would go on the dress. Then she left the house and drove to pick Jim up from work. As soon as they got home, she took him to show off the fruits of her day's labor . . . only to find the new dress she had so carefully laid out was "all rumpled and wrinkled, and the buttons all scattered about everywhere."

Several times Debbie saw what she believed was a dark, shadowy form in the hallway, but she never found anything there upon checking closely. She got to the point where she was even afraid to sleep on her stomach because "it" might come up behind her. She said once when her sister spent the night with them, she asked Jim, Debbie's husband, ·why he kept calling "Debbie . . . Debbie" all night. He said he had slept soundly, and never once called out to Debbie. In fact, Debbie said he never did call her by her name at all, preferring the more affectionate term of "Honey" when he spoke to her.

Once when the Sandifers were having a plumbing problem, Jim went out in the backyard and dug up a portion of the sewage pipes. He had just uncoupled the pipes when a tremendous gush of water came through the pipe! Someone, or something, had obviously flushed the commode, and Jim knew there was no one in the house at the time. He rushed inside in time to hear the commode still running!

On other occasions, Debbie said she heard the clothes dryer running. She would go in to check it, and it would immediately shut off. It was never warm inside, as it should have been, after running.

As disturbance followed disturbance and the sleepless nights began to add up, Debbie finally discussed their problem with the parish priest. She said she went into great detail. The priest did not laugh at her or question her veracity, but he did tell her since the spirit had been only "mischievous" and had done nothing really evil, he believed it would be best to let well enough alone and not tamper with the status quo. From questioning a number of people who were familiar with such manifestations, Debbie said she and Jim came to the conclusion that the spirit they shared their home with may have been that of a child or young person, because it did only mischievous things, not really cruel ones. But child-spirit or no, Debbie said she was more than relieved when they at last decided to purchase a home in Port Neches and moved from the haunted property.

I also talked with a former neighbor of the Sandifers who is a contractor and did some renovations to the place after the Sandifers moved out. He reported he would turn off all the lights in the evenings when his work was done and lock up the place. When he would arrive the next day, he would find them all turned on! He also said that the phone company had come in and installed a new telephone. He did not know how they got in, because he had the only key to the house and he kept it locked up except when he was on the property! He said one hot summer day, he was working in a back bedroom. He was very uncomfortable and asked his wife to go to the store to buy him some cold beer. A short time later the front door opened, and he heard footsteps in the hall. He put down his hammer and walked out of the room, fully expecting to see his wife and a cold six-pack! Imagine his disappointment . . . and utter shock . . . when he realized his wife had not yet returned from her errand and he was completely alone in the house.

Debbie showed us the little house on a recent trip we made to Nederland. We wonder if the playful spirit is still there.

The Ghost of Christy Hardin

Not right in the Golden Triangle but just slightly to the west of Beaumont lies Liberty County. Liberty is one of the oldest settlements in Texas, named for an earlier Spanish settlement called Libertad. The old town was already settled prior to the Texas Revolution, and after the Battle of San Jacinto, the compound that held the captured Mexican troops of the defeated General Santa Anna was located in Liberty. Later, in 1840, General Sam Houston, first president of the Republic of Texas, maintained his law office in Liberty.

Kevin Ladd, Director of the Wallisville Heritage Park in Wallisville, Texas, sent me this account of a prominent early Liberty County family and its ghost:

During the 1820s and 1830s, a young man by the name of Franklin Hardin grew to prominence and position in Liberty. He organized a group of locals during the Texas Revolution and led them onto the field at San Jacinto in 1836. Hardin and his wife, Cynthia O'Brien, built an impressive home in Liberty, in what is now the 1800 block of Sam Houston Avenue. They called their home Seven Pines, and it was there that they raised a family of truly extraordinary children.

Christopher O'Brien ("Christy") Hardin was their youngest son. Born in 1842, he went off to the Civil War and then settled back home after the war. One day in the winter of 1866, Christy and one of his black servants went out hunting. The servant caught some movement in the brush, and presuming it to be a deer, fired a shot. Tragically, Christy Hardin was dead, at the age of twenty-four years.

The black servants often looked out in the evenings to see Christy's ghost standing restlessly by the front gate of the property. Aunt Harriet Evans would often say, "I saw Christy's ghost again last night, down by the gate. He can't rest." The old house has long since disappeared, and a modern new cultural center stands on that same property, given to the city by members of the Hardin family. Those who work there think Christy Hardin's ghost is still there.

The Cove Light

When I contacted Kevin Ladd, Director of the Wallisville Heritage Park, he was kind enough to send me the following story about an interesting "ghost light" over in western Chambers County:

> One of the most unusual ghost light stories we have ever heard dates back several decades to the little town of Cove, in western Chambers County. This mysterious light first appeared at the home of Luther and Elizabeth Wilburn during the 1860s, while the family lived several miles further south in what is today Beach City. The Wilburns moved to Cove about 1870, and the light apparently followed them there. The light revealed itself in a lot where the family kept a mare penned up. It certainly scared the mare, which jumped the fence and tore off into the safety of the darkness!
>
> The light continued to appear periodically up until the time of Luther Wilburn's death in 1882. His widow moved off to Tarkington Prairie in Liberty County. The light followed the family there and did not return again to Cove until Elizabeth died in 1918, at which time it seemed to "adopt" one of their sons and appeared to him from time to time up until his death in 1939. The light was last documented to have been seen in Cove during the 1970s.

The Ghost of Turtle Bayou

Another story sent to me by Kevin Ladd, Director of the Wallisville Heritage Park in Wallisville, is interesting to me for more than one reason. For one thing, I am interested in the history of that part of the state, and I had not previously known of Turtle Bayou. Secondly, I found the ghost in Ladd's story very closely correlates with two stories you will read in the final chapter. Perhaps the Turtle Bayou story serves that part of Texas as a good folk-legend, just as "La Llorona" is well known among the Hispanic families of far South Texas and "Sara Jane" is known around Port Neches. That they all carry a similar central theme is a fact I found extremely fascinating.

Turtle Bayou is a narrow stream that connects with Turtle Bay (now Lake Anahuac) a few miles from the old town of Wallisville. It rambles on north into Liberty County and plays out near Moss Bluff. It figures prominently in the early history of the Texas Revolution. After local residents, aided by colonists from Liberty and Brazoria, marched upon the Mexican fort at Anahuac in 1832 and freed William Barret Travis and Patrick C. Jack, they retreated to Turtle Bayou and drafted a set of resolutions that were the first written complaints lodged by Texans against their Mexican overlords.

In later years, a couple of kinsmen, Robert D. White and Monroe White, operated general merchandise stores on opposite sides of the bayou. A shipyard and a couple of sawmills operated there for a while. A small but thriving community developed at Turtle Bayou during the late 1800s and early 1900s.

One day many years ago, a lady by the name of Exie Green drowned her child in Turtle Bayou. For years and years afterward, folks could occasionally hear the cries of the mother, mourning for her lost child and her own actions. When conditions are just right, and the moon is full, you can often hear her still.

The Mysterious House at Browndell

An article that ran in the Jasper, Texas, *News Boy* just before Halloween in late October 1993 interested me enough to do some investigating. It was written by Diane Cox, managing editor of the paper, and was sent to me by my sister-in-law, Juanita Williams, who lives in Jasper.

On a recent trip to visit in that interesting and pretty old town, I managed to meet with Diane, and she took me to see her house, which she wrote about in her story.

The old Browndell Community, some 13 miles north of Jasper, was once a well-established mill town, consisting of 143 buildings. There were houses for the mill workers, a post office, general store, depot, and various other buildings. The town was built by the Kirby Lumber Company. In 1903 they built a large house for the mill manager and his family. The sawmill eventually burned down and was rebuilt. The mill burned a second time, and this time the company did not rebuild. The community rapidly dissolved as workers had to move elsewhere to seek other employment. Today only the mill manager's house remains, although a sign on the highway still states it's the "Browndell Community."

The old house, which originally consisted of two large rooms located on either side of an open gallery, or "dog trot," has changed hands, and appearance, numerous times in its long and rather colorful history.

The Walker family purchased the place in 1928. It was used, over the years, for various purposes: as a residence, a rental property, a hotel, a rooming house, and even for a time, standing unoccupied, was used as a place to store hay! The house finally underwent extensive remodeling and restoration in 1965.

Today, the rambling structure sports a new tin roof, which has replaced the original. The "dog trot" has been sealed in, becoming a long and spacious central entry hall. A large kitchen, a laundry room, and a bathroom were also added during the restoration period, as was a large carport at the side of the house.

Diane Cox, who is the present owner, is a very interesting story-teller and a talented artist as well. The old house is filled with her paintings, mostly beautiful landscapes and still lifes. Cox says many people in the Jasper area lived in, or visited, the old house at one time or another, and it was the scene of many memorable, and sometimes turbulent, events. She feels there is a lot of "energy" attached to the house and the land where it is situated.

By 1974, Claude and Sybil Walker were the owners of the place. They also owned and operated the Browndell Liquor Store on Highway 96. It probably did very well, because Jasper, the nearest town of any size, was "dry." According to Mrs. Cox, Claude Walker came home one Saturday night with the day's receipts in his pocket. As he climbed the steps from the carport and entered the house through the laundry room, an assailant (or perhaps more than one) awaited him in the dark laundry room, armed with one of Walkers' shotguns taken from the house. Walker was apparently first struck with the butt of his own shot-gun, then brutally shot several times with the weapon. His wife, Sybil, arrived home a little later and was shocked to find her husband lying mortally wounded in a pool of blood on the floor. (Police reports later noted it took every sheet they could find in the house to mop up the blood.) Although Mr. Walker was still alive when the ambulance

Mill manager's house built in old Browndell Community by Kirby Lumber Company in 1903

arrived, he died en route to the hospital. Even today, twenty years later, one of the square white acoustical tiles on the ceiling bears deep brown stains, bloodstains, dating from the night of the murder. Mrs. Cox did not offer any explanation why she had not replaced the gruesome reminder of the tragedy.

The police later discovered Walker's wallet lying on the Highway 96 right-of-way, where it had been tossed aside after being emptied by the perpetrators of the crime. Several firearms were also missing from the Walker house. The killer, or killers, have never been brought to justice, and the unsolved crime still remains on the Jasper County criminal records. The murderer must have known Claude Walker and his custom of carrying large sums of money late at night as he made his way home from the liquor store. Because the house was in a remote area and the people in the area all knew their neighbors, the Walkers probably left their house unlocked. This would have made it very easy for the assailant to enter the place prior to Walker's arrival.

Soon after her husband's brutal murder, Sybil Walker decided to sell the property. Fearing another attack, she was terrified to remain alone in the rambling country place. The Coxes, who came to Jasper from Alabama, purchased the house and the sixteen adjoining acres from her.

Diane Cox vividly recalls the first Halloween night she spent alone in the old house. It was 1976. Her three teenage children were in town attending a football game, her husband was away on business, and she was all alone. She made herself a cup of hot cocoa and sat in her kitchen, trying not to think too much about the heinous murder that had taken place in the laundry room adjacent to the kitchen where she now sat.

Just to make sure all was well, she timidly peeked into the room. As she stated in the article which first touched off my interest in the house, "The hair stood up on my arms, just recalling what had happened in that room. Although I was terribly frightened, there was nothing there, and I breathed a sigh of relief."

Then Diane heard a ghostly wail . . . an "Oooooooh" sound that really got her imagination going. She first thought it might be her three youngsters just trying to give her a good Halloween scare! The sound was repeated several times. Finally, when the young people arrived home she accused them of standing outside and making weird noises to frighten her. They assured her they had just that minute arrived home, and to back up that claim, they all heard the same mournful moan as they stood together in the living room!

Several times during the next few weeks the sound was heard again, always at night. Cox became increasingly nervous whenever she was in the house alone.

Then, about three weeks after the strange noises began, Mrs. Walker, from whom the Coxes had purchased the house, called Diane to say she hoped that she wasn't afraid, but their old "yeller dog" kept running back to his old home. Anytime the hound would hear a train whistle or a siren off in the distance, he'd start to howl. Mrs. Walker said she'd gone to bring him back home several times in the daytime, when the Coxes were all away, but she still had trouble keeping him home at night. This explained the "Oooooooh" sound that had slowly been driving Diane up the walls for nearly a month!

At least that problem was solved. But Diane says there are other strange things that keep happening in the old house. The children are all grown and gone now. Mr. Cox has passed away, and Diane lives there all alone, except for two very large dogs that I'd hate to tangle with.

Diane says there are several "cold spots" in the living room, with a "magnetic place" in the air, that makes the hair stand up on her arms and the skin prickle. Lights go on and off at will, and then there are the "voices" which are heard, engaged in nocturnal conversations in various parts of the house.

Several years ago, Diane decided to have what she called a seance to try and learn more about the house in which she lives alone. A gentleman named Ray Nevels from the nearby community of Brookeland whom she variously described as an herbalist, an Indian shaman or healer, and a hypnotist, was invited to come and help her make contact with the spirit world. Besides Diane, her mother and stepfather and a lady friend were present. The hypnotist succeeded in placing Diane into a hypnotic trance. While "out," she said she distinctly saw a young woman who looked to be in her early 30s standing in the kitchen in front of an old wood stove, which is no longer there. She wore a long dress with an apron. Diane said the dress was in a geometric type print that was very popular back in the 1920s. The woman also had a hair style that dated to that era. Diane said she recalled the apron had a bib front and was safety-pinned to the bodice of the dress she wore. A toddler, no more than about two years old, and still in diapers, was hanging on to her skirts. The woman was stirring something up in a big mixing bowl, and Diane distinctly felt that she was making a birthday cake! Diane also had the name, "Rini," come to her while in the trance-like state.

Then, Diane said, she suddenly felt she was in the laundry room and had "become" the victim of the Walker crime. She said she "saw" and "felt" the awful murder that had taken place there. She said she could actually feel the bullets as they entered her body! And she experienced a terrible fear, just as Mr. Walker must have felt, on that last night in his life. She said she then snapped out of the trance, but the memories of that evening still remain very fresh in her mind.

A couple of years after the seance, or psychic experience, Diane met a lady whose husband's grandmother had once lived in the house. She described her vision to her and also asked her if the name "Rini" meant anything to any of her family. The woman's husband said, "Why, Rini was a close friend of my grandmother's," but he had not heard her name mentioned in many years!

Diane said she also once had a distinct vision of a group of men, probably sawmill workers, engaged in an animated conversation on the back porch of the house. (The porch is no longer there. It was altered to make room for a bathroom.) It must have been a hot evening, as the men were shirtless, wearing just their customary work overalls.

To this day, Diane says, often when she is reading in her front living room she suddenly hears a lively conversation "like a party going on," in the kitchen, or when she's in the kitchen, the same sounds emanate from the living room! She does not find these "otherworldly" conversations particularly frightening. By now she seems to take them for granted.

There are two big dogs that live with Diane. They won't go into the central hallway (which used to be the open "dog trot") after dark. And her brother absolutely refuses to remain in the house at all after the sun goes down. Diane herself admits she always reaches around the corner and flips on the light switch before entering a darkened room. However, she is not particularly uncomfortable about living alone in the mysterious old house. She says she's trying to take good care of the place, and she calls herself a "caretaker." She has the theory that "they" don't threaten "caretakers."

It's an interesting house. And Diane Cox is a very interesting lady . . . and pretty brave, too, in my opinion.

Where the Ghost Car Used to Run

Dan and Pat Chance bought a beautiful piece of property about six miles from the quiet Southeast Texas town of Jasper in 1973. The wooded plot of 268 acres abounds in lovely pine and hardwood trees. Their house, a comfortable red brick dwelling, sits on a gentle rise off a rutted dirt road that runs off Highway 63 West. A quiet running little creek follows the road that runs through the acreage.

Pat Chance graciously showed me around the place the November Saturday morning I came to call. The tour included a look at a small family plot type of cemetery not very far from the house. The plot, overgrown somewhat with native vegetation, is only about 12 feet square, and is surrounded by an old wire fence. The gravestones of Alan Bishop, who was buried there in 1874, and his wife, Dorcas, are there, and Pat said she believes other Bishops, including stillborn infant twins, rest there as well. She said she's been told that when the Bishop family came west from Georgia in a covered wagon caravan in 1849, they brought some hickory nuts with them for the children to eat on the long journey. When they arrived at their new homestead, there were only five of the nuts left, and they planted them on their new property. At least one of the hickory trees that sprang from that planting over 100 years ago has survived to shade the little family burial plot!

The land stayed in the Bishop family for many years. One of the descendants of the original settlers who later lived on the land was the colorful "Beaver" Bishop, sheriff of Jasper County. But more about him later.

Dan and Pat Chance purchased the property from the old Hancock estate, the land having gone out of the Bishop family some years before. After they purchased it, they lived for a time in a small house off the dirt road at the back of their property. Today the house stands on a little high spot up above the creek, which occasionally floods. The house is deserted, surrounded by high grass, and is slowly being taken over by the elements.

But in 1973 it was a fairly comfortable little house. One summer day soon after they moved in, Dan said he came home at noon, and after having a bite of lunch, he decided to take a short nap before returning to his office in Jasper. It was a very hot day, so he undressed and lay down on the bed, clad only in his undershorts. He was alone in the house that afternoon. Before he was able to fall asleep, he heard a car approaching. He said it had the unmistakable sound of an old "flat-head" engine. It pulled up and stopped, and he heard the car door slam. He hastily got up and pulled on his trousers, and went to the door to see who his unexpected caller might be. Imagine his surprise to find no car was there! There was no way it could have driven off without him hearing or seeing it. The dirt road there in front of the house is very narrow and there is no place it could have turned around. He was so astonished that he didn't mention the strange event to anyone, including Pat, for a very long time!

Later, Dan learned that the same car sounds had been heard by a number of people who had once lived on the property. The little house was fully three-quarters of a mile off Highway 63 West. Because the dirt road was so narrow, no one could drive off without being seen or heard. The sounds of what they called "the ghost car" had puzzled and unnerved many people over a long period of time.

Once a young friend of the Chances' son came over to visit the family on a Saturday afternoon. He went off in the nearby woods behind the house to hunt. Soon he heard the sounds of a car engine coming right at him, and there wasn't even a road where he was walking! Then, the car stopped and the car door slammed. There was no car anywhere in sight, of course. Chance said the young man fairly flew out of those woods!

Now, back to Sheriff "Beaver" Bishop. Just a few hundred yards from the Chance home there are some small bits of the foundation of the sheriff's old home, which burned many years ago. There is so little left of the cement slab portion of the old foundation, if Pat Chance hadn't pointed it out to me, I would have missed seeing it. Pat said the former sheriff was a very colorful, sometimes controversial, character from all she had heard. We must remember that the days when he was sheriff, from 1918 to 1928, were very turbulent times. He was the chief lawman in a county where stills were in almost every ravine and every thick grove of trees. In spite of prohibition, moonshiners were every-where, and it was rumored that some of the very best, the "creme de la creme," of illicit whiskey was brewed in Jasper County. Chance said there were a lot of stories she had heard that centered around Sheriff Bishop, but what is truth and what is legend she couldn't say.

Nida Marshall, a former Jasper public librarian and newspaper-woman, has recently written an informative history of Jasper in her book, *The Jasper Journal*, published in 1993 by the Nortex Press in Austin. The story she wrote about Beaver Bishop is very interesting. Beaver, whose real name is thought to have been Andrew Jackson Bishop (no one has come forward who has actually ever seen his real name in print) was born in 1886. His parents were John Allen Bishop and Cooper Reese Bishop. Beaver was the great-grandson of the original Jasper County settler, Alan Bishop. Beaver was a big man, well over 6 feet tall, and he weighed over 200 pounds. He always wore a Stetson hat, which added a few more inches to his stature! His formidable appearance, plus the fact he carried a gun he knew how to use, made him a figure to be reckoned with! The 1920s were a tough time to be a lawman, but Beaver managed to pretty much rule Jasper County for a decade during those wild and woolly days. It was rumored that he had several notches on his gun!

Beaver grew up in Jasper, and went to schools there, and by the time he was 16 he had worked for several local lumber companies. In

Deserted old home on Dan Chance's farm

1910, when he was only 24, he was appointed a deputy sheriff. Then in 1918, at the age of 32, he was elected sheriff and served ten years. He married Dessie Mae Stephenson, and in 1916 their son, Jack, was born.

Bishop made lots of raids on local stills and many a moonshiner was put out of business during his administration. The sheriff had made more than a few enemies by the time he went out of office.

According to Marshall's book, the former sheriff was wounded in an "affray" in 1930. It seems the misunderstanding arose over some of Bishop's hogs. Two brothers, whom he suspected of stealing his hogs, were caught up in the "north quarters" selling fresh pork off the back of a wagon. Bishop looked into the wagon and saw his mark on the hog's ears. To quote Nida Marshall, "Hog stealing was then an unpardonable crime resulting in stiff penitentiary sentences. Owners branded their individual marks in the ears of the hogs for identification. The law required that the ears of butchered hogs be left intact when they were brought to market."

When Bishop drew their attention to the fact he knew they'd taken his hogs, one of the brothers took the long butcher knife he was using to slice the pork and drew it across Bishop's midsection, wounding him. The former law officer drew his side arm and shot and killed the man.

The Chances believe the sounds of the car (or it might have been a small truck) that they used to hear might have been the sheriff's vehicle, looking for moonshiners.

But the sounds of the "ghost car" are not the only strange things that the Chances have witnessed over the years on the former Bishop property.

For a time, the Chances lived in a mobile home they brought in to their property after they vacated the house which was their first home. One night a nephew spent the night with them. In the night the young man took suddenly ill. As he came out of the bathroom, he glimpsed a woman at the end of the hallway. She was wearing a pink housecoat, and he only saw her from the back. He presumed that it was his aunt, Pat Chance. The next morning he apologized for waking her up in the middle of the night. Pat told him she hadn't awakened at all; in fact, she had slept soundly all night long! When he described the figure he had seen, she assured him she didn't even own a pink housecoat!

In the same vein, several men driving down Highway 63 West once reported having seen several women, clad in housecoats or robes, walking along the side of the road. When they stopped to see why the ladies were out at night dressed in that fashion, the women literally disappeared in front of their eyes. They were never seen again! A theory is that maybe some of the ladies occupied one of the several houses that were scattered about the property at one time. Maybe they were former "ladies of the night" that the sheriff had arrested, and they were out to find him and take revenge. Who knows?

After she showed me the location of Sheriff Bishop's old house, Pat Chance remarked she had heard that a lady who later lived in the house after the sheriff's death reported seeing so many "ghosts and spirits" that she finally suffered a nervous breakdown and ended up confined to a mental institution. Pat Chance said she believed the house burned down thirty or forty years ago. There's really nothing left of it, so the fire must have done a thorough job.

In 1946, when he was 60 years old, the giant of a man who had survived lots of close calls was killed. The death of Sheriff Bishop was listed as a hunting accident, and it was said a friend of his shot him by mistake, taking him for a deer. Mrs. Chance said a lot of people believed he was murdered. She said she had heard that a man was later arrested and sent to prison for the crime, and he died while in confinement. The Chances were told that on the night the sheriff died, the bells in the tower of the old courthouse in Jasper rang, but they were not rung by human hands! Whether they were mournfully tolling or cheerfully pealing would have to depend on what side of the law those who heard them might have been . . . .

It's been quite a number of years now since the sheriff's old flathead engine car has been heard on the dirt roads of the former Bishop place, and no one has seen any housecoat-clad spectral females for a long time either. Things seem pretty peaceful and quiet these days out on the Chance property, and that's the way Pat and Dan like it.

Jasper's Old Haunted House

Although it no longer exists, there once was a haunted house in the town of Jasper, and stories about it still abound. In her new book, *The Jasper Journal*, Nida Marshall writes about the big house that was built in the late 1840s or early 1850s by Bill Maund, one of the founders of Jasper's First Baptist Church.

The clapboard house stood on the highest point of land overlooking the little town. It had tall windows and high, airy ceilings. Its two front parlors were used as school rooms, and private classes were held there. This was prior to the establishment of a public school system in the area. Mrs. Harriet Merritt, a widowed schoolteacher, rented the house. Several students boarded at the house with Mrs. Merritt and her young daughter, Lacy.

In 1866, when Jasper was just recovering from the awful losses suffered during the Civil War, a terribly tragedy struck the big house up on the hill.

Lacy Merritt was a beautiful and popular young woman of about twenty-one years of age at the time. Many young men had come calling, and she had had numerous proposals of marriage. But only one young man interested her in the slightest. Unfortunately, he did not return her affections. One evening, she stood talking with him on the front porch of the house. Heartbroken by his lack of romantic feelings towards her, she suddenly pulled out a pistol and mortally wounded herself.

This was a thoroughly shocking event in the small town where no woman had ever committed suicide. Her youth and beauty made the event even sadder, and her death was the talk of the town for a very long time.

According to Marshall's account, a minister from Milam in Sabine County wrote a letter to the *Texas Baptist Herald* on October 3, 1866, that discussed the tragedy. The man, who signed his name only as "Paul," wrote:

A sad occurrence had transpired at Jasper three days previous to the sitting of the court. A young lady named "Merritt," either tired of the burden of life, or goaded by life's ills into a state of frenzy, deliberately shot herself! The causes that led to this dreadful act of suicide, are known only to the Great Judge of All. But as far as outward demonstrations can evidence, there appeared to be a combination of causes. A young man... romance novel reading... love... love slighted... hopes blighted... then despair... madness... and the awful leap into eternity... self condemned and self murdered!

Paul expressed his feelings of self-revulsion "too revolting to contemplate," unless it could serve as "an awful warning to youth and maidens" about trifling with each other's affections. Pointing out the evils of novel reading, he advocated reading instead "more of the truths of inspiration" which would offer comfort "in every extremity of life's trials."

Soon after the death of her daughter, Harriet Merritt closed her little school and left town. The owner of the house had difficulty renting it out to anyone. People would lease it, move in, and very rapidly move out again. Each short-term resident reported hearing strange sounds, such as voices heard in the night, footsteps, and other unexplainable noises, leading them all to believe that the place was haunted.

In time no one would live there at all. The house sat vacant, rapidly deteriorating. Marshall stated, "In truth it looked like we think a haunted house is supposed to look. On the road leading up to the old cemetery north of town, its forbidding appearance by the very nature of its weatherbeaten boards, sagging shutters, and gaping windows was heightened by a surrounding of mammoth old pin oak trees, moss-hung and mistletoe infested. Night travelers gave it an especially wide berth."

Finally, a former schoolteacher, L.D. Scarborough, attracted by the low price at which the owner offered the place up for sale, bought the house. He moved his family in, and the ghosts, to whom Scarborough had declared the house "off-limits," moved out. Scarborough's daughter, "Miss Sadie," became a schoolteacher and educated many a Jasper student in her nearly fifty-year teaching career. She loved to talk about the old haunted house she had once lived in.

The house was torn down in 1923, and after her marriage "Miss Sadie" built another house on the very same spot. That location is now 731 North Main Street.

Strange, isn't it? Schoolteachers seemed to be the only people who lived any length of time at that location.

CHAPTER 8

Legends Worth
Telling Again

STRANGE UNEXPLAINED THINGS
Docia Williams

When you read these legends, it might be they'll make
You shiver with fear; you'll quiver and quake;
For they're legends of things we cannot explain
As weird and as mystic as legerdemain.
Strange, unexplained things that go "bump in the night,"
Creatures, with features, that elucidate fright!
Like Llorona, who dwells in the rivers and streams,
Luring her victims with sorrowful screams.
And that great glowing orb that lights up the trail
Where once ran a train on a long silver rail...
And horsemen that ride in the dark of the night
Headless, and soundless, a most dreadful sight!
There's the woman who roams to Ben Bolt and back,
They say she was hanged in her garments of black;
When the moon rises full and the night's deathly still
And shadows fall over the forest and hill,
There are "things" out there lurking we don't comprehend...
Their stories are here. Just read them, my friend.

Legends Worth Telling Again

According to Webster's Ninth New Collegiate Dictionary, one definition of the word, "legend," is "a story coming down from the past, especially one popularly regarded as historical although not verifiable."

This chapter includes "legends," stories that have been around South Texas a long time. Some go back over a hundred years. They have been told by different people in different versions, yet all are recognizable.

Did you ever play the old parlor game of "gossip," where the players would sit in a circle, and one person would whisper a short "episode" to the next person, who would repeat it to the next, and so on, until it reached the last player? This player would have to repeat what was told to him. Many times, the "story" was almost unrecognizable from that which began with player number one!

Legends are a little that way, especially if they were not written down and were handed down through the generations by word of mouth. That is why we often find more than one version, or "spin-off" of a story.

Just about all the stories in this chapter are well-known, loved legends about the dark side of South Texas . . . the ghostly side. To delete them from a collection of ghost stories would do them a terrible injustice, and that is why they appear in this, the final chapter of *Ghosts Along the Texas Coast.*

La Llorona

From the depths of the river, the sad mournful cry
Of La Llorona is heard, to those who pass by,
But no one can save her, forever she's there,
Luring her victims, her sorrows to share.
She's dressed all in white, a temptress so pretty,
And that's what she wants; your trust and your pity.
Keep your children away from the rivers and streams;
Don't let them be lured by her sorrowful screams.
She's waiting to claim your child for her own . . .
So hurry away . . . leave La Llorona alone!

"La Llorona," which means "weeping woman," is as well known to Hispanic communities in South Texas as the "boogeyman" is to Anglo cultures. And just as symphonic works often feature variations on a theme, this story appears in many variations, as it has passed down by word of mouth for generations. To write a ghost story book . . . any ghost story book, about this part of the country and not include La Llorona would be unpardonable!

In spite of the variations of the story and the strange twists and turns it might take, there seems to always be an overlying theme, a lesson in morality and safety that is still used to advantage by many Hispanic mothers to teach their offspring to follow the straight and narrow pathway!

The story goes way back in time. Before Hernando Cortes and his band of Spanish conquistadors arrived, the Aztec Indians in Mexico are said to have heard the nightly, ghostly screams of "Cihuacoatl," a pre-Columbian earth goddess who ruled both childbirth and death. Her cries of "My children, we must flee," echo through the stone canyons of Tenochtitlan. Some years later, her warnings came to fruition with the arrival of Cortes and his men. Aiding him in his conquest of the Aztecs was "La Malinche" (which meant "the tongue"), his beautiful

Indian interpreter and mistress whose role of translator helped bring about the downfall of her own people. Many years later, Cortes announced to Malinche that he would return to Spain without her, but he would take their son with him. She pierced her heart and that of her little son's with an obsidian knife. Today, many Hispanics, some of whom are of Aztec descent, believe "La Malinche" and "La Llorona" are one and the same woman.

Legends concerning the weeping woman seem to be most prevalent in far South Texas, although she is also well known in New Mexico and other parts of the Southwest. John Igo, respected in San Antonio as a poet, writer, and educator, told me he has long been fascinated with stories of La Llorona and shared some of the versions with me. He said the stories go back almost 300 years.

One of the versions of La Llorona's background says she was a young woman married in a big cathedral in Mexico. She wore a beautiful white wedding gown. She promised that she would give her firstborn son to the church to become a priest. However, when she had children, she decided this was not what she wanted for her offspring, so she went back on her word, and her firstborn son was not delivered up into the priesthood. As a consequence, her house caught fire, the children all burned up, and she herself was burned and deformed, her face taking on the characteristics of a donkey, or horse. She is doomed to wander the earth searching for her children. Her searches seem to center around creeks and rivers. Women are said to have seen her, but men mostly just hear her plaintive cries for help. Some men have drowned trying to reach her. A dim figure in white has been seen near creeks by many people, according to Mr. Igo. He said in San Antonio, people living near the confluence of Alazon Creek and Martinez Creek have reported hearing her cries. She is said to call out "Mi hijo! Mi hijo!" ("my son! my son!") from a river or stream. Those who heed her calls and venture to rescue her are often drowned in the attempt. Those who have survived are said to have seen "something white" floating on top of the water. For some reason, she is seen, and heard, most often on foggy or rainy nights.

Mr. Igo said the Texas Folklore Society has done a great deal of research into the legends of La Llorona, and I searched out *Legendary Ladies of Texas*, a publication of the Texas Folklore Society XLIII in cooperation with the Texas Foundation for Women's Resources, where

I enjoyed reading much interesting material in a chapter written by John O. West, entitled "The Weeping Woman."

There was another version of La Llorona's story in the October 1983 edition of *Texas Highways Magazine*. The author, Jane Simon Ammeson, is a Corpus Christi psychologist. This is what she had to say:

Stories of beautiful women who have been wronged are many. Supposedly, their ghosts walk at night, searching for justice. La Llorona, the Weeping Woman, can be seen walking along several Texas rivers. She is the ghost of Luisa, a beautiful peasant girl who was courted by the wealthy, aristocratic Don Muno Montes Claro. When his family refused to allow him to marry Luisa, Don Muno bought her a little house. For six years he lived a "double life," spending his days tending his estates and family business and his nights with Luisa. They had three children and were happy, until one evening Don Muno didn't come to the little house.

Luisa waited that night and many more before summoning up the courage to walk to the big mansion where Don Muno lived. She begged to see Don Muno, but a servant told her it was impossible. Don Muno was getting married to a wealthy woman of his own class. Luisa ran from the house, but not before seeing her lover and his new wife as they made their way from the church. In a frenzy, she rushed home and murdered her children, throwing their bodies into the river.

She was taken to jail and died there, crazed, calling for the little ones she had killed. On the day she died, Don Muno, in his fancy house with his new wife, mysteriously died also.

Some say that Luisa was freed from jail after killing her children and she lived a carefree and abandoned life (instead of dying in jail). When she died, and went to heaven, Saint Peter asked her where her children were. Shamefaced, she looked away from him. Her children were in the river, she replied, so Saint Peter sent her back to search, endlessly, for her lost little ones. Even now, people warn their children to stay away from the river because "La Llorona" may be there, just waiting to drag them under, sending them to the same fate she sent her own offspring.

Another version of the La Llorona story as told around Laredo from *La Voz Latina de Kuno*, the April 1991 edition, says that in the barrio in an area called the "devil's corner" a very poor woman lived. She and her three little children lived in a miserable hovel that seemed to hang on a cliff overlooking the river. Her husband spent most of his time and money in bars over across the Rio Grande in Nuevo Laredo. The poor lady washed and ironed for people, and sometimes she was even forced to beg for money to feed her children. She herself ate very little. She didn't want much for herself, but it broke her heart to see her little ones suffer.

She kept hoping her husband would come back and help them. He finally did come back, but only to tell her that he had found a new woman and would not be coming back to her or the children he had fathered.

Her heartache was too much to bear. She looked at the peaceful Rio Grande flowing below her little shack. Poor little angels... her children would be so much better off in heaven where they would never go hungry again. She dropped them into the river, and then smiled for the first time in months as they disappeared into the depths of the river. She could just see them all three with a shiny halo already, up in heaven where God would surround them with love. She went to bed happy and fell asleep.

The next morning, the terrible realization of what she had done hit her. She missed her little ones. Life was nothing without them, and so she threw herself into the river and drowned as they had done.

Many people attest to the fact that when the moon is full one can hear the moans and cries of the woman, searching along the river for her lost children.

A San Antonio friend, Jerry Salazar, who is on the staff at the *San Antonio Express News*, said as a small boy growing up in Laredo he knows that he once saw La Llorona. She was standing on the opposite bank of the river from where Jerry stood with a group of children. "She had on a long white gown. She had masses of dark, long hair and appeared to be very beautiful. She kept reaching out her arms to us, beckoning us to enter the river and cross over to her." Jerry said the children all had the good sense to turn and run home as fast as their legs could carry them!

Another version of the legend which is prevalent down near La Bahia, outside of Goliad, was printed in the *Texan Express*, October 31, 1984 edition. The story by Sandra Judith Rodriguez, stated:

Don Ramiro de Cortez, a noble soldier of high rank fell in love with Dona Luisa de Gonzala and their courtship resulted in her having a baby out of wedlock. In facing her embarrassment she swore she had rather see her baby dead than in the hands of her former lover. When he sent word he was coming to claim his child she replied that the baby would be ready to go. He knocked on the door and Dona Luisa welcomed him, taking him to the crib where the baby lay. "There is your son," she said, "which I would rather see dead than in your hands." He removed his sword from his scabbard and uncovered the veil of the crib. He was shocked by the sight he saw, his baby son all covered with blood.

Don Ramiro immediately called his soldiers to gather wood and to bring a large wooden stake to burn Dona Luisa. It was customary to burn witches and criminals at the stake at that time. As Dona Luisa was burning, everyone watching saw, to their amazement, that Dona Luisa was loosened from her bonds and flew off in the embers and wind of the fire; dressed in a long white tunic, with her long, beautiful hair flowing behind her. She was crying, a very sad noise, as she was crying not for her pain, but for her dead baby. Legend has it that she is still crying and flying along the rivers, looking for her baby son.

Henry Wolff, Jr., who is a columnist for the *Victoria Advocate*, sent me an article he wrote about La Llorona for the Tuesday, November 10, 1992 edition of his paper. He states:

Jim Leos, Jr., saw the ghostly figure while working at night in the old fortress of La Bahia at Goliad as a security guard. Leos described voices of crying children coming from an unmarked grave, with a woman in a white layered wedding dress materializing in front of the grave near the presidio chapel, only later to drift off towards and over the back wall toward the old cemetery behind the presidio.

Crying babies and a woman in white fits the description of La Llorona, and while she usually is said to appear along river banks, the old presidio and its unmarked graves are just a short distance uphill from the nearby San Antonio River.

La Llorona is a popular ghost story in Mexican folklore, and especially in South Texas where the woman in white is said to have appeared along virtually every river. In Victoria, she is sometimes called the Ghost of the Guadalupe, and while I have never actually met anyone who has seen her, I am familiar with many stories of La Llorona and how she comes to the riverbanks to cry over her lost children.

I don't know why La Llorona would be at La Bahia, but there is a lot of similarity in Leos' description and everything that's ever been said about La Llorona. I've also heard others speak of hearing babies cry deep in the night at La Bahia, and several years ago in visiting with Victor and Joe Martinez, I heard the story of how an older brother once encountered the lady in white near the presidio.

That was back around the mid-1930s, when the Civilian Conservation Corps was building the Goliad Auditorium across the river, near the reconstructed Mission Espiritu Santos in Goliad State Park, and the brother had been singing with CCC workers who often gathered at night to entertain themselves around an open fire.

The moon was shining pretty that night, they said, when their brother came to a big dip beside a creek called Sparrow Hollow on his way home. There she stood with her long hair, and all dressed in white.

The following night, Joe Martinez went with his brother to where the apparition had appeared, and at the same spot they heard what sounded like a big rock rolling down the steep bank of the creek, but didn't see the lady in white again, or ever afterwards.

Wolff said he didn't know if Jim Leos actually saw La Llorona, or just a look-alike.

Wolff also brought forth the theory that the story has been handed down for generations by mothers bent on keeping their children from playing too close to rivers and streams, and then pointed out that a researcher at Texas A&M University, Ed Walraven, has tried to modernize the old legend by attempting to document sightings of La Llorona at city dumps! Wolff agrees with Walraven that it is a good thing to keep children away from city dumps since they are also dangerous places to play. Walraven says the ghostly figure has been sighted at least twice in landfills!

And so it goes. There are stories of the crying lady, La Llorona, all over the Southwest. She's been seen crying out from the palm tree shaded resacas of Brownsville, and she's been heard weeping from the banks of the Nueces. She is often mentioned as having been around the San Antonio River as it flows south to empty into the Guadalupe just before it reaches the Gulf of Mexico. She is everywhere, because she is very real to the people who believe in her.

On dark nights, people who have heard the stories since early childhood say that goose bumps still rise on their necks and their skin crawls. They believe that La Llorona wants to get even with those who are happy, and that is why men, the cause of her sorrows, are often driven mad by the very sight of her in the night. You see, she is very beautiful, until she is observed closely. Some say her face is totally blank. Nothing is there at all. Others say she has the long, distorted face of a donkey, or a horse. She wears long, flowing gowns of white, and her long shiny silver fingernails resemble glistening knives in the moonlight.

Whether she actually exists, or whether she is a figment of many vivid, overworked imaginations, La Llorona is very much a part of South Texas folklore. And her legend teaches several good lessons to those who would heed them: "It is best not to mix with those of an entirely different social or cultural class." And to mothers: "Don't be cruel to your children or you will live to regret it." And to the children themselves: "Stay close by your mothers. Don't go near the water."

The Ghostly Lady in Black

Numerous writers have related the story of the ghostly lady in black who has been seen by many people as she wanders the area where Highway 281 crosses Highway 141 between the small towns of Ben Bolt and Premont, down in far South Texas. Dr. Juan Sauvageau, former professor at Texas A&I in Kingsville, wrote an interesting book of Texas legends, titled *Stories that Must Not Die* (Pan American Publishing Company), and high on his list of "keepers" is the story of the mysterious lady in black. He cites the strange experience of four men who were driving to work at the Exxon refinery in the middle of the night. Suddenly, a woman, dressed in black, appeared from nowhere and stood right in the pathway of their car. They couldn't avoid hitting her. According to Sauvageau's account, "There was no thud, no bump, but the passengers of the car were sure the lady had been killed." A thorough search turned up nothing. The men even called the sheriff, and when the lawman and his deputies arrived, not one single sign of the woman, whom all four men swore they had seen, could be found.

Dr. Sauvageau questioned an elderly rancher in the area about the appearance of the strange apparition, and he knew exactly who she was and why she was out there on that lonely stretch of road.

According to the old gentleman, the lady, always clothed in black, is the ghost of the lovely Dona Leonora Rodriguez de Ramos, who lived, and died, many years ago.

The story goes that Leonora, one of Mexico's most beautiful young women, married an influential man named Don Raul Ramos, a wealthy landowner. This was way back when the Rio Grande Valley was then known as a part of the Spanish province of Nuevo Santander.

Soon after the wedding, Don Raul was called away on important business and had to travel far away, back to Spain, leaving his lovely young bride back on his ranch in Texas.

Upon his return, some six months after his departure, he found his young wife was six months pregnant. At first he was overjoyed, but his joy soon turned to unbridled rage when he was told that the baby was not his, and that his wife had been unfaithful to him. The teller of such an unfounded story was the daughter of a neighbor who had hoped she would be the choice of Don Raul and was enraged when he chose to wed another. In her jealousy, she told this terrible lie to Don Raul, who was known to have a terrible temper. So enraged was the rancher, that he ordered two of his most trusted ranch hands to take his young wife, who had been clothed all in black, out on a day's ride to the north of his estate. There she was to be hanged until dead. This was at the approximate spot where Highways 281 and 141 cross today.

Although Leonora protested her innocence and pled with her executioners to spare her, the ghastly orders were carried out by the vaqueros, who were afraid of going against the wishes of their employer. Before she died, Leonora swore she was innocent, and said she would return, so that all who saw her would know an innocent woman had been sentenced to death.

At the same time the vaqueros were riding north, escorting the lovely Leonora to her death, Don Raul rode south. Just about the time his wife and the unborn child she carried were put to death, he must have had a terrible feeling of guilt. Because when the vaqueros got back to the ranch, they learned that Don Raul had put a bullet through his brain. His ghost has never been seen around. But lovely Leonora continues to carry out her promise to appear, and reappear, over, and over again. Dressed in the long black gown in which she died, she comes once more to proclaim her innocence.

The Girl in the Pink Dress

There are several versions of this story around. It's such a haunting tale, it deserves to be told again. Dr. Juan Sauvageau wrote about it in his *Stories that Must Not Die*, and I also saw it in a copy of the *Corpus Christi Caller-Times* (October 31, 1992) written by staff writer Scott Williams.

The story goes back to 1950 when a young man named Manuel got into his pickup truck to drive up to Benavides for a Saturday night dance. As he drove, the lights of his truck picked up a pretty young girl in a pink dress standing by the roadside. He stopped and asked if she needed a lift. She told him, yes, she wanted to go to a dance. He told her he was on his way to a fiesta and she was more than welcome to come along.

The girl told Manuel her name was Maria, and that she didn't know many people in those parts because she had been away for the past ten years.

Manuel had a great time at the party. He couldn't get over his good luck in finding such a pretty date. And could Maria dance! Now, she had a little trouble following the new "cumbia," but he'd never seen anybody polka like Maria! She was just great; as light as a feather on her feet!

The band stopped playing around midnight. Manuel and Maria were sorry to see the evening end, they'd had such a great time dancing together. As they went out to get into Manuel's pickup, he noticed that Maria was shivering, so he took off his jacket and placed it around her slender shoulders.

When they got to the place where Manuel had picked her up, Maria asked that he let her out. He hated to do this, as the night was very dark and he saw no lights in the vicinity. She assured him it was where she wanted out, and he told her to keep the coat he had loaned her. He would come and get it the next day. (A great excuse to see the pretty girl again!)

The next morning Manuel drove out to the place where he had picked up Maria the night before. Off about a quarter of a mile, down a dirt road, he saw a small white house. He drove up, got out of his truck, and went to the screen door and knocked. A woman came to the door in response to his knock. Manuel asked if he could see Maria. The lady turned deathly pale . . . "My Maria died ten years ago," she said.

Manuel assured her that he had seen Maria and danced with her the whole evening before. He told the woman Maria had on a pink dress, and that she just loved to dance, especially the polka. The woman told him that Maria had been buried in a pink dress, and that yes, indeed, she had been a wonderful dancer, but she had been tragically killed in an accident ten years before.

Manuel found this very hard to believe. He told the woman he had even loaned his jacket to Maria when the evening had turned a little chilly, and that he had told her he would come back later to get it.

"If you'll just come with me, young man, I will show you my Maria's grave. She is buried in our little family cemetery over there by the road."

They walked to the little family graveyard. There was a grave marker with the inscription, "Maria Lozano. 1920-1940. RIP."

On the grave, neatly folded, was Manuel's jacket.

The Romantic Story of
Princess Kisselpoo

Note: I first read this story in a brief article in the *Port Arthur Times*, October 28, 1992. Since then, I have come across numerous versions in several publications. It's a charming legend.

Around Lake Sabine, close by the Louisiana border, a legend of star-crossed Indian lovers has been told for many a year. It's the story of little Princess Kisselpoo, whose name meant "full moon," and her lover, Running Bear.

It's usually late at night, when all is calm and quiet on the big lake, and the full moon is shining its beams across the still waters, forming a glittery pathway, that you're apt to see them. There, on the silvery, shimmering waters, a canoe bearing a young Indian couple can be seen, slowly drifting along the moonlit waterway.

The Attacapa Indians used to live in a little village close by the lake. There they hunted, and fished, and lived their daily peaceful lives. The chief of the tribe had a lovely only daughter, who had been named Kisselpoo because she was born when the moon was at its fullest, and the tribal leaders believed she would be under the protection of the moon goddess.

When Kisselpoo was 15 years old, tales of her beauty and charm had spread among other tribes, far and wide. Many young braves came to woo the fair-skinned, almond-eyed beauty. Her father and his tribal leaders finally singled out a man to be her husband. He was much older than the chief himself, and already had many wives. But he was powerful, ruling over much land to the north of the Attacapa territory. Arrangements were set in motion for the nuptials. It didn't matter that little Kisselpoo did not love the man.

The arrangements for the wedding festivities were far advanced when a young stranger, a brave named Running Bear, appeared in the village. He lived "seven sleeps" away, towards the west. Tall, straight, and handsome, he brought gifts of stones bluer than the sky (these must have been turquoise, much valued among Western tribes) to show Kisselpoo of his interest in her. She fell in love immediately with the handsome young man, but she could not back out of her betrothal to the elderly chief whom her father and his council had chosen. So it was with a heavy heart she waited in her father's lodge for her hand-maidens to come and accompany her to the lodge of her husband-to-be.

As she waited in her father's lodge, she heard Running Bear's voice softly calling her name. She crept out of the lodge and with him she fled to the big lake where his canoe lay waiting. They swiftly took to the waters. The princess was missed almost immediately, and the chief from the north, along with some leaders and medicine men from her own tribe, followed close behind the young lovers. Kisselpoo's father had had a strange, mystic dream in which the moon goddess had appeared to him, urging him to relent and let his daughter marry the young Indian from the west, so he did not join those who were in pursuit of Kisselpoo.

The Attacapa medicine men called up the wrath of their gods and soon a terrible storm came up, causing great waves to form upon the lake. The little canoe could not bear up under the turbulence and soon was upset. Kisselpoo and Running Bear were last seen being swept away on the turbulent waters. Only the shimmering water glistening in the light of the full moon was to be seen . . . .

When the moon goddess, the guardian of Kisselpoo, learned what had happened, she called upon her kinsman, the tropical storm god, and he swept down with a furious hurricane, causing the waters of the lake to sweep over and destroy the Attacapan village. For a long time after the storm, the lake waters became murky with silt and there were very few fish. The shore birds that used to nest around the lake disappeared, and the shores of the lake were stained and ugly.

Finally, many years later, the moon goddess has loosened the curse that almost destroyed the lake, and today the beauty of Lake Sabine has been restored. Fine sand again covers the lake floor, and tall cypress trees grow along its banks. Schools of fish have returned to make their homes in the lake and waterfowl and shore birds nest in the reeds along the banks once more.

To those who have the power to see such things, on the nights of a full moon, a little canoe can be seen, riding a trail of moonbeams across the still and peaceful waters of Lake Sabine, according to the legend.

According to an article which was printed in the *Port Arthur News* on October 27, 1984, entitled "Love Legend Lives for Kisselpoo," by staff writer Regina Segovia, there are those who live around Lake Sabine who have seen the canoe and its occupants on more than one occasion.

It seems there was to be a big Halloween party at the home of pretty young Tammy Theriot. Her father was a schoolteacher, and he very clearly preferred that she date Roger Landry, who came from a wealthy family, to young Buddy Boudreaux, whose dad was just an old Cajun country boy who worked over at one of the refineries. Buddy was just plain crazy over Tammy, but he knew he wouldn't be welcome at the Halloween party she was having that night... at least her father wouldn't be glad to see him. So Buddy talked his cousin Kevin into going fishing on the lake that evening. He just didn't have the nerve to show up at Tammy's party, knowing how her dad felt about him.

His cousin Kevin didn't really want to go out on the lake that night. It was cold, wet, and misty. But Buddy talked him into getting his dad's boat out and the boys headed out into the lake. As they started out, they suddenly heard a sad and mournful cry. A deep voice was heard as the full moon appeared from its covering of grey clouds. The voice said, "Kisselpoo."

Buddy asked Kevin if he had heard the voice, but he could already tell by the startled expression on his cousin's face that he had, indeed, heard the voice. They could see each other clearly as the moon had come out full now, and cast its light upon the waters. At the same moment, they both saw a canoe, with a huge man standing in it with his giant arms crossed over his chest. Seated in the canoe and looking up at the man was the most beautiful woman the boys had ever seen.

The couple were bathed in a golden light, and the girl, whose hair was jet black, wore beads and feathers, and looked to be in an authentic Indian costume. The brave was dressed in fur pelts.

Buddy told Kevin, "Don't take your eyes off them for a minute. I brought my camera, and I have to get a picture or nobody will believe that we saw them."

At just that moment the wind picked up and the water started getting choppy. The boat swung around, and they lost sight of the canoe. By the time Buddy got his camera out of its waterproof case, the moon had slipped behind the clouds, leaving them in the darkness. But they could hear the sobs of a young girl, crying as if her heart would break.

According to the article, "They cranked the motor on and could still hear the sound of the cry. They slowly moved in its direction. They were scared to death, but even so it could be the cry of someone who needed help. The boat began to buck, and they picked up speed. Suddenly there was a thud and everything in the boat was flying around. Kevin was looking at small bubbles and sinking. "I'm underwater," he thought, and then panic gripped him.

"Buddy managed to grab a life jacket and he held it with one hand and swam to save his cousin. He grabbed for Kevin's hand and felt the strong palm of something he knew was not his cousin. It was the Indian!

" 'Your friend will live,' the Indian said, his voice thundering so loud it hurt Kevin's ears. "But what is life without love. And I, who have given a century of sadness for love as a brave who fought a tribe and the gods for my Kisselpoo, say this: Love is for the heart and not for those who use it to gain land or wealth. You are a coward to run from the challenge of the heart.

"Then the Indian silently but forcefully pulled Buddy under the water. 'I'm dead,' he thought. 'This is it. This is death . . . dark, wet, and cold holding onto some big red man's hand. Who would have thought . . . .' "

Before he could gather his thoughts, Buddy saw before him a village of huts with fires burning . . . and he heard singing . . . yet he knew he was underwater . . . how strange . . . .

He heard the voice of a woman speaking, but he could see nothing but the Indian village. He tried to swim, but the big hand of the Indian brave pushed him back down. The woman's voice was telling all about the betrothal of the lovely Kisselpoo to the old Indian chief. Buddy saw the beautiful Indian princess, who was surrounded by women who were combing oil into her long black hair and rubbing her feet with flower petals. He knew she was sad. Then the woman's voice he had heard told all about how the princess was betrothed to an old man, even though she loved a handsome young brave. The voice continued to tell Buddy all that had happened, including the princess' escape from the village, and the way the canoe had been upset by the storms. All the time Buddy felt he must be dead . . . maybe even in hell . . . maybe he was even a ghost by now!

Then, suddenly, Buddy's head bobbed up from the water, and Kevin, who was still spitting and cursing, pulled him into the boat.

"Did that all really happen?" was all Buddy could say. Kevin had climbed back into the boat, and was sitting there sorrowfully thinking how could he tell everybody Buddy had drowned. Just as he had begun to accept that Buddy was really gone, up he popped from the water, and Kevin was very angry with him, thinking he had played a Halloween trick on him. As for Buddy, "He was as silent and as white as the underbelly on a fish."

When they got back to Buddy's uncle's house, it was clear the old man had a few drinks under his belt. Even so, he could tell by the way the boys were acting that something was wrong. "You two boys got some gumption going out on the lake on Halloween night with the Indians out there and all," he said. "What?" the boys both asked, in unison. Buddy thought maybe his uncle had pulled a fast one on them so he told his uncle what had happened.

Their uncle, his grizzled beard working and his eyes glittering with excitement, said he believed the story the boys told him. When he was 17, he saw the Indian once, he said. And then he told them the legend. Buddy had never heard the story before, but he had seen it re-enacted before his very eyes. His uncle missed a few things, but Buddy didn't say anything. It was close enough.

According to the *News* account, Buddy Boudreaux cleaned up and hustled himself on over to Tammy Theriot's Halloween party after all. He decided to take the big Indian's advice and keep an eye on his own little "Kisselpoo." Whether her daddy liked him or not, Buddy decided that he'd give old Roger Landry a real run for his money!

The Legend of the Indian Maidens

This old legend came to me through the generosity of Yolanda Gonzalez, librarian at the Arnulfo L. Oliveira Memorial Library at the University of Texas at Brownsville. It appeared in an anthology of stories entitled *Studies in Brownsville History* edited by Milo Kearney. The story was told by Felipe Lozano to some of his grandchildren at the beach in 1964, and was recorded by Peter Gawenda.

It seems that many centuries ago this part of the country belonged to a fierce tribe of very tall Indians whose hunting grounds reached from Tampico all the way up to Corpus Christi across to San Antonio and Laredo and back into Mexico. They were feared because of their size, and of their ability to throw a spear more than four hundred yards. Sometimes they are said to have been cannibals who ate the hearts of their enemies, but this is not proven. [Author's note: This sounds like the Karankawa tribe.] There is an old story, though, that has been told for a long time.

The young Indian male had to prove his bravery to his young bride before he was permitted to take her with him. At times this proof of bravery cost the young lad his life. The young bride had to follow her groom to insure that he would be permitted into the eternal hunting grounds. As it was believed that the hunting grounds started beyond the sea, the young maiden was taken in a boat to Padre Island and was permitted to keep her loincloth, a small bowl with water and one cob of corn. The boat then went back to the mainland. The marriage marks for the Indian maiden were one black streak across the forehead and two white streaks on the cheeks. The girl would first sing her wedding song and then perform the customary death ceremony. Then she would get up and very slowly walk into the sea. When only her head was still above the water the face would look almost like a sea gull. But the maidens had to keep on walking until they were completely under water, and it is said that the gods of these Indians would allow the soul of the maiden to return to earth as a sea gull.

Hardly any traces or artifacts are found that have been left by these Indians. But if it's true that the souls of Indian maidens return as sea gulls, many young Indian lads lost their lives before their wedding ceremonies!

When Padre Island was not yet covered with concrete and still had sand dunes, every once in a while one could hear the marriage song in the soft winds at night or the death cries coming from the water, and Felipe insisted that sometimes you could even see the image of one of the maidens kneeling on the beach.

The Legend of El Muerto

There are several really hair-raising legends that have been around South Texas for many long years. They concern headless horsemen. One of the best known stories is that of the "dead man" or "El Muerto" as he is most often called. I first read of him in a column written by Henry Wolff, Jr., columnist for the *Victoria Advocate*. He had interviewed Marilyn Underwood, an English instructor at Victoria College. Underwood was brought up in San Patricio, and she had first heard the grisly tale from her father, Woodrow Hicks, Sr.

Later on I came across other versions of the story, in newspapers, in the late Ed Syers' book *Ghost Stories of Texas*, and from several individuals who had heard the story at one time or another. It's the sort of tale you *don't* tell little children before tucking them into bed for the night!

It seems a man known only as Vidal roamed South Texas earning his questionable livelihood by stealing and selling cattle. Then, as now, cattle rustling wasn't exactly an acceptable occupation. Vidal had stolen some livestock from a man named Creed Taylor, a rancher who lived "up river, in the hill country" according to Wolff. Taylor got a party of horsemen together to track down the thief. One of the group was a frontiersman who had earned the reputation of being a pretty tough man to come up against. His name was "Bigfoot" Wallace. A pioneer Texas Ranger, he was a tough lawman, fast with a gun. You just didn't want to tangle with "Bigfoot."

The posse caught up with Vidal and justice was swiftly carried out. Wallace had the hapless man beheaded, and with the help of the other men of the posse, he lashed the dead outlaw to his saddle, which was placed on the back of a wild mustang. His hands were tied to the pommel and his feet to the stirrups, so he would ride sitting up straight. His head, still wearing its big sombrero, was lashed by means of a rawhide thong to the saddle horn. The terrified horse was turned loose to wander the countryside, unable to get rid of his grisly burden.

Wild to start with, afraid of men, and now living with the stench of a decaying corpse on his back, the mustang carried his burden far from civilized areas. Even so, an occasional lone rider or cowpoke would spot the headless rider. Many, terrified at what they saw, shot at the mounted rider. Many knew they had hit him, and why he still remained astride the horse was a real mystery to them.

Probably some innocent riders were shot at, also, since stories of the ghost rider spread far and wide and spooked a lot of cowboys into shooting almost anything they saw from a distance and could not distinguish.

Finally, the mustang was spotted drinking at a water hole called the Bull Head. He was roped and captured as he drank. Still strapped to his back was the sun-dried corpse of Vidal, riddled with scores of bullet holes, his skull still covered by his big sombrero. The body was cut off the mustang and buried in a hastily dug, unmarked grave somewhere out on the prairie near Ben Bolt. The mustang was turned loose at last, freed of his terrible burden.

That should have ended it. But there are those who say that "El Muerto" is still out there. He can be seen on clear moonlit nights, clinging to his mount, his sombreroed head swinging back and forth like a pendulum from the thong tied to the saddle horn.

In Syers' story, he said one tale around old San Patricio mentions there also is a headless horseman who was a wealthy Kentuckian murdered and beheaded for his money. Another version told is like the Wolff story . . . only it was a horse thief instead of a cattle rustler that was beheaded, and is said to be the ghostly rider.

No doubt, there are more headless horsemen around, if only we had the time to really get out and hunt for them.

The Headless Rider at
Dead Man's Lagoon

According to several accountings, this must be a true story. It has been handed down for a number of years. It's the gruesome account of a headless horseman that's been scaring folks over in Duval County for a long time.

In a write-up in the *Corpus Christi Caller-Times*, October 31, 1992, the tale surfaced once more. It seems back in 1917 a couple was traveling by wagon, headed to the little town of San Diego, west of Alice, to visit the man's elderly uncle. It was getting late and they had started looking for a good place to camp for the night. Way up ahead they spotted a light, which looked to be coming from a campfire. Not knowing the area too well, the man thought it might be good to camp near some other folks, and so he pointed his wagon in that direction and told his team of mules to "giddi-up."

The closer they came to the campfire, the dimmer it seemed to get. By the time they arrived, they saw they were on the banks of a lagoon, or pond, and the campfire, which was near a big oak tree, had died down to just a few embers. Disappointed that whoever had been there had left, the man started collecting some wood to build up the fire. Then he unloaded their supplies and bedrolls and spread them out under the big oak tree.

Just as the fire blazed up brightly, they heard horses' hooves, coming fast! Suddenly, right in front of them a huge gray horse materialized. He was running at break-neck speed, fast as the wind, and hanging onto his back was a rider, spurring the horse in its flanks as they rode by. But the rider didn't look quite right . . . because he had no head . . . .

The woman fainted. Her startled husband watched as the horse and his weird rider rode straight across the lagoon, as if it had been a paved highway. They disappeared on the other side of the body of water, and as they disappeared, the fire that had been burning also flickered and quickly went out, leaving them in darkness.

The man was very uneasy and when his wife came to, she was almost hysterical. Neither could explain the scene that had just taken place in front of their startled eyes. They decided they just couldn't stay the night in that strange place, and so they hitched up the mules and took off in the darkness. Before they left, the man tore some rags into strips which they tied to the branches of the oak tree to mark the spot . . . .

When they arrived at the man's uncle's ranch over at San Diego, they told him of the strange scene they had witnessed. Not at all surprised, the old man told them that he had heard lots of rumors about "Dead Man's Lagoon," which was, he was quite sure, where they had seen the headless horseman.

He told them the story of how four cattlemen who had big ranches in those parts had gotten together to see who had the best horse. They decided to have a race, and whoever won was to get everything the others had, their horses, land, ranches, and houses. All was to be bet on the outcome of the race.

One man, named Dickson, had a huge gray stallion named Hercules. When the race was run, Dickson and Hercules won with such ease, far outdistancing the others, that not only were they angry, they were humiliated as well. The three losers decided they wouldn't hold to their bargains. But they knew Dickson would tell everybody how they didn't honor their commitments, so they decided they would have to kill him. They did. They killed him with a machete, and then decapitated him.

Now, since then, many people are said to have seen old Hercules and his headless master running the race over and over again, just to prove how fast they were.

The couple and their uncle went back to find the spot where they had camped the night before. But there was no sign of a campfire ever having been there. The rags that had been placed in the oak tree were gone, and there were no tracks of the wagon and the mules in the soft mud along the banks of the lagoon. All was gone. Nothing was left but the indelible memory of the racing big gray horse and his headless rider.

The Strange Legend of Bouton Lake

The October 31, 1985 issue of the *Beaumont Enterprise* had an interesting article geared to ghosts in the area, as written by staff writer Julie Noble. The "Legend of Bouton Lake" tells a strange story about a farmer and his daughter. Transporting a wagon load of cotton they had grown, they were traveling on a dirt road about seven miles northeast of Zavalla in the dark and dense Angelina National Forest.

Lois Parker wrote in the *Texas Gulf Historical and Biographical Record* that "Suddenly they were swallowed in a large opening in the earth, and sank out of sight."

According to the story, at the spot where the man and his daughter, their wagon, and team vanished, a lake began to form. Ultimately it filled to its present size, one half by three quarters of a mile long, a lagoon blessed with "breath-taking beauty enhanced by countless moss-draped trees."

"But frequently," Parker writes, "the night air hovering above the water grows strangely silent and the nocturnal murmurs and the croaks of the frogs cease."

During the silence and stillness, a spectral form of a graceful young woman rises in the center of the lake. Wearing a filmy dress of gauze, she glides gently and rhythmically, almost as if she were ice-skating from the lake's center towards the moonlit banks.

Those who have seen her say she is the daughter of the cotton farmer.

(I'll buy that. But where's her daddy, and the wagon and mules?)

"Sara Jane...Oh, Sara Jane..."

There's an oft-told tale that circulates over in Port Neches. The story centers around the street that runs from the Texaco Neches Chemical Plant in Port Neches to FM 366 in Groves. There are several versions to the story, which has become quite a well-known legend. No matter which version is told, it always brings forth shivers.

One version, as noted by a *Port Arthur News* article (July 20, 1970) says the "old river holds the legend of Bloody Mary. She was a legendary woman pirate supposedly hung by the villagers for her transgressions. The old woman is said to still haunt the river road, calling out on foggy nights for her lost baby." The story goes that the child, named Sara Jane, drowned when thrown from a buckboard into the waters below the bridge which is now known as Sara Jane Bridge or Crybaby Bridge.

Another version, which was noted in the *Beaumont Enterprise,* October 31, 1985, claims that a pioneer woman supposedly drowned as she and her family were crossing the bayou, and true believers of the story say they've heard her plaintive cries for help coming from the bayou on moonlit nights ever since!

Still another twist to the story comes from the *Port Arthur News* October 31, 1992. The *News* story says that one night in the '50s, before the area did away with the pollution problems (as one longtime resident put it, "when it's cold, one can actually see the smoke or fog-like steam that comes off the refineries"), there was a woman who may have been named Sara Jane.

She was going from Lake Sabine to Port Neches in a wagon when she was accosted by a group of bandits. She had come to a canal where wastewater goes into the river. There was an old wooden bridge over the canal. For the safety of the infant, Sara Jane is said to have placed her in some weeds by the bayou and left her there, according to an old-time resident. "But when she came back, her baby was gone. The child had gotten into the canal or bayou somehow."

The legend has it that on some still and dark foggy nights, when someone goes to the bridge they can hear a voice calling, "Sara Jane ... oh, Sara Jane." No one knows for sure if "Sara Jane" is the name of the mother, or of the missing baby. Nobody wants to stick around long enough to find out.

Saratoga's Ghostly Light

Sometimes where the thicket is still and dark
Teens find the road there a good place to park;
The light comes from nowhere; it bobs down the trail
Where once ran the trains down the long silver rail.
It may be the ghost of a hunter, long dead;
Out searching the night for his still-missing head,
Or maybe the Spaniards out seeking their gold.
(There's treasure out there, so we've been told!)
We don't know what causes that eerie ghost light
That shines in the thicket, in the still of the night.

The southern fringe of East Texas' Big Thicket ends up around Saratoga, a little community 46 miles northwest of Beaumont, on the outer edge of that great wilderness of tall pines, dogwood trees, and thick underbrush. Within that vast area lies a story, or several stories, told and retold, embellished, and changed around, for nigh onto 100 years. The stories told are about the mysterious ghost light of the Big Thicket, and scores of people swear it's there, dancing and bobbing around on that long stretch of lonesome road that once served as the bed of the old railroad track that ran southwest from Bragg (now just a little ghost town) to Saratoga. For years the dancing light has defied all attempts at explanation, and so a multitude of legends have grown up centering around its reason for being.

The light, or lights, have been variously described, but most witnesses have said they've seen a single ball of light that just bobs up and down along that lonely road. The stories of why the light is there go way back, maybe even to the time before the Civil War, so we can rule out reflections from automobiles right away, because the light was reported long before there was such a thing as a horseless carriage.

Some of the more scientific-minded have said the light might be in the realm of jack-o'-lanterns, those strange luminations caused by gases from nearby swamplands, similar to the fox fires found near decaying logs or rotting forest vegetation.

There are almost as many stories explaining *why* the light is out there, as there have been sightings reported. These tales go way back to the early days when the loggers, oil field wildcatters, pioneers, and homesteaders first came to this wild country where alligators, panthers, and bears once roamed. That's why the story is a real legend in every sense of the word. Everyone agrees the light is there, but no one can pinpoint the real reason for its being.

One legend says a man got lost out there in the vast wilderness of tall trees and endless undergrowth and died before he could find his way out. Now his ghost is still trying to find a way out of the thicket. Another oft repeated tale talks about the railroad that went through there when the trains carried the big logs out of the forest. It seems one of the workers fell asleep near the tracks, with his head resting on the rails. He must have been a sound sleeper, because a train is said to have run over him, severing his head. Searchers couldn't find it anywhere, so his headless body was buried out there in the woods. The ghostly, headless figure is still there, swinging an old railroad lantern while searching for his missing head.

Another railroad-related legend says a brakeman was decapitated when a logging train derailed, and it's his spirit that's out there hunting for his missing head. A more poignant version says a railroad man's wife fell in love with one of the lumberjacks, and the two lovers ran off into the deep, dark woods and were never seen again! The unhappy husband died of a broken heart, and today his ghost is said to wander the woods as he holds his lantern high, searching for his faithless wife and the lover who stole her away.

We also have heard the tale of the light being held by a logger who lost one of his hands in an accident that could have been avoided, caused by the carelessness of a fellow logger. Now he's out searching for the responsible party in order to get his revenge. To back this legend up, it seems a couple of teenagers were out for a little "necking" on the dark road one night, when they saw a light. Soon they heard a strange metallic rapping sound at the rear of their car. They took off in a hurry! The next morning a metal hand-hook (the kind used to replace a lost hand) was found, caught on the rear bumper of the car! Wow!

Still another story says a man was out hunting (squirrels? 'coons? alligators?) in the forest, with his moonshine jug and his kerosene lantern to keep him company. Guess he over-imbibed because he fell asleep on the tracks. Familiar ending. Lost his head. He's still looking.

Then there's the story of the Mexican laborers who were hired to lay the railroad tracks. Rather than pay them for their labors, their employers paid them off in bullets. They are still out there, looking for the dirty-double-crossing villains who'd rather shoot them than pay them!

Then there are the stories of the Spanish explorers who buried their treasure chests deep within those woods. They never got back to claim their gold, so now their spirits are out searching, guided by, what else? The Saratoga light!

We must not forget the story that ran in the October 31, 1985 edition of the *Beaumont Enterprise*. It tells of a Confederate soldier who went A.W.O.L. from his regiment and was tracked down and shot as a deserter, there in the deep thicket. Somebody, maybe his wife or sweetheart, is still out there searching for his grave.

Now if all these tales were true, there would be a regular "gaggle" of lights bobbing up and down, like a multitude of overgrown lightning bugs! But one story must be true, because there have been so many reports of sightings of the light from all sorts of people from many walks of life for many, many years. There have been lots of articles printed, written by reporters who came out to the Thicket to check out the story. Many of them saw the light and reported back to their papers. Local residents of the southeast Texas area report a light, or lights, being seen, over and over again. Teenagers in old pickup trucks who use the road as a sort of "lover's lane" have seen the huge bobbing light. And, if you stop by the Big Thicket Museum in Saratoga, they'll tell you some more good stories.

There have been reports that the light chases cars, scorches hands, dances on top of cars, and chases people. The light has been described as white, as green, and as red in color. Some say just one great big light bobs around, moving laterally, very, very slowly. Others say the light comes straight at you, looking very much like the big light on the front of a locomotive.

Nobody really knows the source of the Saratoga light, or when, or where, it will show up next. Nobody knows what causes it to shine. All we do know, for "certain sure," is that it's still out there, illuminating the dark and mysterious woods of the Big Thicket, and giving a tingly, "goosebumpy" sort of thrill to those who see it shining in the night.

Epilogue

Even as this book goes to press, more ghost stories continue to pour in. Perhaps there will be a *Ghosts Along the Texas Coast, Volume Two* some day! Most of the stories contained in this collection are well documented and considered to be true. Others are legends, but because they are so well known, and "expected," they just had to be included!

I will leave you with this parting thought . . .

DID YOU EVER SEE A GHOST?

Is there anyone who'll boast
That they've ever seen a ghost?
Or heard a footstep on the stair?
Did you ever freeze with fright,
In the middle of the night,
Knowing, surely, "something" was out there?
Have you ever really seen
On the night of Halloween,
"Something" out among the costumed hosts,
That seemed out of place
Because it didn't have a face,
Well, my friend, I think you saw a ghost!

Happy hauntings!
Docia Schultz Williams

DID YOU EVER SIT AND THINK

Happy beginnings
Dede Scholz & Harris

Sources

Newspapers
Beaumont Enterprise
    Oct. 31, 1985
Brownsville Herald
    June 13, 1982; Oct. 31, 1993
Corpus Christi Caller Times
    Oct. 29, 1992; Oct. 31, 1993
Daily Express, San Antonio
    Aug. 26, 1879
Eagle Images, Galveston
    Oct. 1980
Galveston Daily News
    Oct. 31, 1989; Oct. 31, 1990
Houston Chronicle
    July 4, 1987; July 29, 1987; April 23, 1989; Oct. 31, 1991; Oct. 29, 1993
Houston Post
    Oct. 28, 1984; Aug. 3, 1986
Jasper News Boy
    Oct. 1993
La Voz Latino de Kuno (Laredo)
    April 1991
Port Arthur News
    July 29, 1970; Oct. 27, 1984; Oct. 28, 1984; Oct. 29, 1984; Oct. 28, 1992; Oct. 29, 1992; Oct. 31, 1992
Texas Express, Goliad
    Oct. 31, 1984
Victoria Advocate
    Nov. 8, 1992; Nov. 10, 1992

Magazines and Periodicals
Galveston County "In Between"
    Oct. 1978
Houston Chronicle Magazine Section
    Oct. 25, 1981
Houston City Magazine
    June 1985
Texas Highways
    Oct. 1983

Pamphlets
"Discover Historic Galveston Island," published by Galveston Historical
    Foundation
"Presidio La Bahia," Information Pamphlet, Goliad, Texas
"Ride the Texas Tropical Trail, " published by the State Department of
    Highways and Public Transportation
"Silver King Restaurant Newsletter," Aransas Pass, year unknown (article
    sent to me not dated)

Stories
"The Legend of Knox Crossing," Wilbur Butler
"Joe Lee Never Left Nederland," Anne Malinowsky Blackwell
"The Ghost of Turtle Bayou," Kevin Ladd
"The Cove Light," Kevin Ladd
"The Ghost of Christy Hardin," Kevin Ladd

Books
1001 Texas Place Names by Fred Tarpley, University of Texas Press,
    Austin, Texas, 1980
A Guide to Treasure in Texas by Thomas Penfield, published 1988 Carson
    Enterprises Inc., Deming, New Mexico
American People's Encyclopedia, Vol. 12, published 1956, Chicago, The
    Spencer Press, Inc.
Black Hope Horror, the True Story of a Haunting by Ben Williams, Jean
    Williams, John Bruce Shoemaker, published by Berkley Books, New
    York by arrangement with William Morrow and Company, Inc., 1993
Encyclopedia Americana, Vol. 16, 1940, published by Americana Corpora-
    tion, New York, Chicago
Ghosts Along the Brazos by Catherine Munson Foster, published by Texian
    Press, Waco, Texas, 1977
Ghost Stories of Old Texas by Zinita Parsons Fowler, Eakin Press, Austin,
    Texas, 1983

Historical Heritage of Goliad County, edited and written by Jakie L. Pruett, and Everett B. Cole, 1983, researched by Goliad County Historical Commission, Eakin Publications, Austin

The Jasper Journal by Nida A. Marshall, 1993, Nortex Press, Austin, Texas

Lafitte the Pirate by Lyle Saxon, Pelican Publishing Company, Gretna, Louisiana, 1989

The Legend of Chipita by Keith Guthrie, 1990, Eakin Press, Austin, Texas

Legendary Ladies of Texas, Publication of the Texas Folklore Society XLVII in cooperation with the Texas Foundation for Women's Resources, edited by Frances Edward Abernethy, 1981, E-Heart Press, Dallas, Texas

Off the Beaten Trail by Ed Syers, 1981, Texian Press, Waco, Texas

Readers Digest Illustrated Encyclopedic Dictionary, Vol. Two, L-Z, Readers Digest Association Inc., Pleasantville, New York, Montreal, 1987

Stories that Must Not Die by Dr. Juan Sauvageau, 1989, Pan American Publishing Co, Inc., Los Angeles, California

Studies in Brownsville History, edited by Milo Kearney, 1986, Pan American University Press, Brownsville, Texas

Texas Travel Handbook, published by Texas Department of Highways and Public Transportation, Austin, Texas, 1990

Time and Shadows by L.I. Adams Jr., 1971, Davis Bros. Publishing Company, Waco, Texas

Websters Ninth New Collegiate Dictionary, 1983 published by Merriam Webster, Inc.

Weekend Escapes, Southeast Texas Edition, edited by Mike Michaelson, Published by Rand McNally, 1986

Personal Interviews
I wish to especially thank the following individuals who shared information in the form of personal and telephone interviews and through correspondence:

Anne Malinowsky Blackwell, Nederland
Steve and Paula Bonillas, owners, Blackbeard's, Corpus Christi
Wilbur Butler, Beaumont
Donna Briones, Galveston
Julie Caraker, manager, Beulah's, Port Aransas
Tim Case, night manager, The Ale House, Houston
Sue Casterline, Estes Flats
Eleanor Catlow, Galveston
Patricia Chance, Jasper
Diane Clifton Cox, managing editor, *Jasper News Boy*, Jasper

Mary Lou Polley Featherston, librarian, Port Arthur
Clouis and Marilyn Fisher, Rockport
Charlie Faupel, Reeves Thicket
Dr. Joe Graham, Dept. of Sociology, Texas A&M, Kingsville
Yolanda Gonzalez, librarian, Arnulfo L. Oliviera Memorial Library, Univer-
    sity of Texas, Brownsville
David Goodbar, Galveston
Kathleen Fink, former director, Williams House Museum, Galveston
John Igo, professor, poet, author, San Antonio College, San Antonio
Ilona Langlinais, former employee, Wunsche Bros. Cafe and Saloon, Spring
Alma Lemm, former employee, Wunsche Bros. Cafe and Saloon, Spring
Brenda Greene Mitchell, owner, Wunsche Bros. Cafe and Saloon, Spring
Derek Neitzel, assistant to curator, resident graphic artist, U.S.S. *Lexington*
    Museum, Corpus Christi
Sam Nesmith, historian, psychic, San Antonio
Anita Northington, Egypt
Colonel Larry Platt, Pleasanton
Catherine Polk, La Marque
Nancy Polk, Houston
Susan Purcell, Reeves Thicket
Jerry Salazar, San Antonio
Debby and Jim Sandifer, Port Neches
Sherry Sinini, manager, Wunsche Bros. Cafe and Saloon, Spring
Newton Warzacha, museum director, La Bahia, Goliad
Mark Wilks, employee, "Beulah's," Port Aransas
Joseph Witwer, Galveston
Henry Wolff, columnist, *Victoria Advocate*, Victoria
Kevin Young, former director, La Bahia, Goliad

All photographs taken by Roy and Docia Williams, with exception of
Wunsche Bros. Cafe and Saloon, by Donna Brown, of the "Portrait Copying,"
Spring, Texas, and the photographs of the U.S.S. *Lexington*, which are official
U.S. Navy photographs, courtesy the National Archives.

Index